the Divorce

Moa Herngren is a journalist, former editor-in-chief of *Elle* Magazine and a highly sought-after manuscript writer. She is also the co-creator and writer of the Netflix hit-show *Bonus Family*.

Alice Menzies is a freelance translator based in London. Her translations include work by Jonas Hassen Khemiri, Fredrik Backman, Tove Alsterdal and Jens Liljestrand.

the Divorce

Moa Herngren

MANILLA
PRESS

First published in Swedish as *Skilsmässan* in 2022 by Norstedts
Published by agreement with Salomonsson Agency
First published in the UK in 2024 by
MANILLA PRESS
An imprint of Zaffre Publishing Group
A Bonnier Books UK Company
4th Floor, Victoria House, Bloomsbury Square, London, WC1B 4DA
Owned by Bonnier Books
Sveavägen 56, Stockholm, Sweden

A CIP catalogue record for this book is
available from the British Library.

Hardback ISBN: 978-1-78658-374-1
Trade paperback ISBN: 978-1-78658-375-8

Also available as an ebook and an audiobook

1 3 5 7 9 10 8 6 4 2

Typeset by IDSUK (Data Connection) Ltd
Printed and bound in Great Britain by Clays Ltd, Elcograf S.p.A.

Manilla Press is an imprint of Zaffre Publishing Group
A Bonnier Books UK company
www.bonnierbooks.co.uk

PART ONE

BEA

BANÉRGATAN, STOCKHOLM

June 2016

SHE TWISTS AND TURNS in bed, the duvet cover tangled around her legs. They had ditched the duvet itself a month ago, relegating it to the top shelf of the wardrobe on Niklas's side of the bed. The summer twilight sears through the closed curtains. She always has trouble getting used to the lack of real darkness at this time of year and spends the hot, bright nights in some sort of twitchy haze. Has she managed to get any sleep at all? It doesn't feel like it.

Bea reaches for her phone: 00:41. No messages. He's probably on his way home. They must be winding down, at the very least. Is Daphne's even open this late? She opens the message app and starts composing a conciliatory SMS. Maybe she was too hard on him earlier?

But mid-message, she stops typing. What does she have to apologise for? He's the one who should be saying sorry. Bea should be angry. She *is* angry. She wasn't the one who forgot to pay the Destination Gotland bill, meaning they're now stuck in town for another week because the ferry is fully booked until next Saturday. That's the first day with any space for cars – on the night ferry. Departure 01:10, arrival 04:25.

Another week trapped in a baking-hot apartment when they could be relaxing in the garden at Hogreps, cycling down to the dunes in Grynge whenever the heat gets too much. Enjoying the salty air rolling in from the sea, no more than a few steps from the cooling embrace of the water. But no, that isn't how it worked out, and now here she is: sweaty, sleepless and trapped in a vacuum.

Bea feels her heart rate pick up again. How the hell could he have forgotten to pay the bill? She'd reminded him several times.

So why didn't you just do it yourself? Wouldn't that have been easier? Rather than nagging me?

Because she did everything else. Because, as usual, it was Bea who planned the entire holiday: booking the tickets, leaving the spare key with the neighbours and arranging for them to water the plants, making sure they had everything they needed for the trip.

He had *one* job, and now he has the nerve to get annoyed? With her?

Bea's body tenses with irritation, and she rolls over again. *Stupid bloody man.* The windows are all wide open, but she is dripping with sweat. If she weren't so tired, she would get up and go through to the kitchen, wrap a towel around a couple of ice packs and put them on her stomach. But she's too tired to get up, too hot to stay in bed. Too annoyed to sleep.

A clicking sound from the hallway makes her jump: the key in the lock. He's back. Worse for wear after a few too many beers, no doubt. Probably still pissed off, too. Or maybe the booze has tipped him over into regret, and he'll crawl into bed behind her and whisper a breathless apology. As though that could make up for the fact that he's ruined their whole week. No, she isn't ready to forgive him yet.

Bea hears footsteps in the hallway, the bathroom door opening. She pricks her ears. The footsteps sound too light, bare feet tiptoeing over the creaking parquet. Nothing like Niklas's inconsiderate stomping as he noisily makes himself a snack or runs the tap like he usually does when he gets home late.

'Oh, sorry, did I wake you?' he always asks.

Thirty-two years together, and he still doesn't seem to realise that she's a light sleeper.

'But you love me all the same, right?' he says, cocking his head and giving her puppy-dog eyes. And no matter how annoyed she is, Bea always replies that of course she does.

There are times when she wonders just how much that irritation eats away at her love for him, but right now she really does hope it is Niklas. That he's just tiptoeing quietly for once, for her sake, considering what he has done. Or, more accurately, *not* done. But the footsteps fade away and disappear.

Curiosity forces her up, and she swings her legs over the edge of the bed and lowers her feet to the oak floor. There are no windows in the hallway, making it dark and full of shadows, and other than a low mumbling sound from Alexia's room, the apartment is quiet.

Bea carefully nudges Alexia's door open. The blackout curtains are drawn, and the light illuminating her daughter's semi-nude body is coming from the iPad on the desk, where an American YouTuber is delivering a shrill monologue.

Alexia grabs a pale blue wrap skirt, a hand-me-down from Bea, and quickly covers her breasts. '*God*, could you knock?'

'Sorry.'

'Seriously . . .'

Bea suddenly becomes painfully aware of her own naked body. The mortified look on her daughter's face makes her feel disgusting and ugly, the way she has increasingly come to see herself lately. Where once monthly cramps and bleeding took over her body, she has now been hit by the merciless onslaught of menopause. Secretions and dryness in all the wrong places. Dripping wet beneath her arms and like a desert between the legs. Thank you very much, Mother Nature.

'Did you just get home?' she asks, trying to hide her lower body, if nothing else, behind the door frame.

'Yeah . . . ? You said to be back by one,' Alexia mutters.

'Right. Where's Alma? Weren't you going to the same party?'

'What? No.' Her daughter shakes her head and turns away with a look of disgust. 'Seriously, Mum, can you . . .'

Mood-wise, mother and daughter are practically in sync. Both equally irritable, just at opposite ends of the fertility spectrum. Oddly enough, Alma doesn't seem to have been affected by the hormones raging through her; she is still as soft and sweet as ever.

Alexia and Alma, yin and yang. The twins who have never been alike – not even while they were in Bea's belly, or that was how it felt. Of course Alma is already asleep. Bea was too preoccupied to notice when her daughter went to bed, but she does have a vague memory of her saying goodnight.

She backs up and closes the door, making a quick detour into the hall to check Niklas's hook, though she already knows his linen jacket won't be hanging there. On the shoe rack below, Alma's riding boots and ballerina pumps are neatly lined up beside Alexia's hastily kicked-off trainers, Bea's Birkenstocks, Niklas's summer loafers and running trainers. A sea of coats and shoes, the family together yet scattered.

Bea heads back through to the bedroom, which now feels – if possible – even hotter than before. The balcony door is wide open, but there isn't a single breath of air. The ugly, eye-wateringly expensive column fan Niklas bought is on the floor by the door. She should have tried to find the remote control before she went to bed, but she was too tired.

Bea now sits down on his side of the bed and opens the drawer in the nightstand. Pared back and minimal, it contains just his e-reader and allergy pills. Not like her cluttered drawer, stuffed full of hand cream, books and other bits and pieces.

She eventually manages to find the remote on the windowsill and turns the fan up to the max. Accompanied by its low, monotonous whir, the air finally begins to move through the bedroom.

*

03:31. Bea must have dozed off, because she wakes with a start. Still on Niklas's side of the bed, and now almost chilly. She pulls the duvet cover over her and gropes for her phone on the other side. No messages and no missed calls. She is so annoyed that she is immediately wide awake.

> Where the hell are you?
> ??
> Hello!
> Answer me!

This is really starting to piss her off now. Why the radio silence? No forgive me's or apologies. Niklas has stayed out all night without a single word, like some sort of overgrown teenager, and that isn't OK. It's not OK at all.

Beneath the duvet cover, Bea is simmering with rage. Daphne's is definitely shut by now. She picks up her phone, puts it down. Pushes it away and then grabs it again. Waits. Not a peep. The room is much cooler now, but her cheeks are red hot.

*

04:48, and the bed sheets are a mess thanks to Bea's restless tossing and turning. Why hasn't Niklas been in touch? Yes, he can be scatty and annoying at times, but he would never make her worry on purpose. He always replies, even when he's travelling for work. The only exception was that day last autumn when Alexia had a meltdown at the film shoot and he was at a medical conference in Kenya, phone switched off.

Thanks to a variety of helpful people, she eventually managed to get hold of him, on a boat in the Indian Ocean, of all places – though he seemed to think his snorkelling trip was more important than his daughter and family. He called several times afterwards to apologise, once he realised just how out of line he'd been. But, right now, it's as though he is in some sort of dark zone.

Could something have happened to him? Bea's anger transforms into churning anxiety in the pit of her stomach. Is he hurt? Could he have staggered down to the Djurgården Bridge and fallen into the water? There have been a few occasions when he's had a bit much to drink lately, as though middle age has caught up with him and his tolerance has gone through the floor. Like a teenager who hasn't learned how to hold his drink yet, even though he is in his fifties.

Just take Calle and Charlotte Mörner's crayfish party, when he lost a shoe and Bea had to bundle him into the back of a cab. Or the last Christmas party he went to while he was still working at the hospital in Sollentuna. She had woken that night to noises she hadn't heard since high school.

9

Guttural retching and groans as gastric juices, gravadlax and lumps of chewed hot dog came spilling out. When she opened the bathroom door, Niklas was on his knees, crying in shame and gripping the toilet for dear life. Pathetic.

The fact that a middle-aged paediatrician could lose control like that wasn't OK. Bea had been embarrassed on his behalf, but she also felt angry. As luck would have it, the girls were already asleep, so they didn't have to see him in that state, but if he'd come home an hour earlier, they would have been wide awake, watching a film in the living room.

Thinking back now, Bea realises she has been angry with him quite a lot lately, and she hates that feeling. She doesn't want to be annoyed with Niklas. She loves him. It might not be with the same passion as the early days, but it's definitely deeper. They've built a life together, a fantastic family with two lovely daughters. OK, Alexia might not be at her most lovely right now, but the teenage years will pass. Once her frontal lobe has finished growing, or whatever it is.

Their apartment is more beautiful and homely than ever since they renovated the kitchen, and though the house on Gotland belongs to Niklas's family, it feels just as much hers. They've been through tough periods and phases like any other couple, but with each setback they have only grown stronger. Many other couples they've met along the way have come crashing down like a house of cards once the honeymoon period was over and their love was really put to the test.

Maybe things are different for Bea and Niklas because their life together began in tragedy, with Jacob's death. Because that, strangely enough, is what brought them together. Maybe that's why she knows they can handle anything: because they fell in love at rock bottom. She wouldn't have survived without Niklas, and given everything he did for her, she owes him a few drunken missteps. She just wishes he would reply to her damn texts.

Bea turns over again, swaying back and forth between anger and fear as one image takes over from another: Niklas in a bar or at an after-party at Freddie's place, interspersed with a search team dredging the water and an ambulance ride to hospital. She knows there is no way she will be able to get back to sleep, so she gets up and puts the kettle on instead.

The air in the kitchen is still stuffy, and she goes out onto the balcony, where the pale pink geraniums hanging over the black railing are covered in buds just waiting to bloom. It's ironic that they seem to do best when left to their own devices out here, as far from her green fingers as they can get.

She breathes in the scent of the pistachio-green leaves and slumps down onto the creaky wicker chair. Their balcony furniture is old and rotten, but the new set she has ordered from Paola Navone is delayed as a result of the heatwave in southern Europe.

The inner courtyards, which snake between the buildings on Karlavägen, Banérgatan, Wittstocksgatan and

Tysta gatan, connecting the entire block, feel oddly calm and quiet. Each is separated from its neighbours, some by low stone walls and others by tall wrought-iron fences. The dawn light rises up behind the building on the other side as Bea opens the book Lillis gave her, Hanya Yanagihara's *A Little Life*. Her mother-in-law waxed lyrical about it, and Bea really does want to like the novel everyone seems to be talking about, but she is finding it hard to concentrate.

After reading the same paragraph four times without taking any of it in, she closes the book and starts scrolling on her phone instead. She can't focus on anything other than Niklas right now. She debates calling Freddie or Calle to check whether either of them have heard from him, but instead she simply sits in the wicker chair, stiff and hollow-eyed, as the sun slowly climbs above the rooftops.

*

When he finally calls, he sounds perfectly calm. As though he has just finished a shift and wants to know whether she needs him to buy anything on the way home. Toilet paper, milk? Not at all like someone who has been ghosting his wife for the past ten hours.

'It's me,' he says.

'You're calling *now*?'

'Were you asleep?'

'What?'

'Did I wake you?'

'I haven't slept a wink all night, Niklas.' That isn't strictly true, but it definitely feels that way.

'OK.'

'No, it's *not* OK. Where are you?'

'Freddie's.'

'Couldn't you have called to tell me that?'

'I'm calling you now.'

'I've been worried to death for hours!'

His impassive tone is like fuel for Bea's anger. He doesn't sound the least bit remorseful. If anything, he is acting like this is all perfectly normal. He just vanished for a few hours, no big deal.

'We had a few beers, then we went back to his place and got talking.'

'OK, but why didn't you reply to any of my messages?' She can feel herself getting increasingly impatient. Raising her voice, as though this will make it easier to get through to him. 'Hello? Can you hear me?!'

'I can hear you, there's no need to shout.'

'So can you tell me why you didn't reply to any of my messages?'

A pause. 'I guess I didn't feel like it.'

His words cause Bea's brain to short-circuit. What on earth did he just say?

'You didn't feel like it?' she snaps. 'What the hell is wrong with you?'

Niklas doesn't speak.

'Surely you can understand why I was worried? I thought something might have happened to you!' He should say sorry now, should have said it a long time ago, but he doesn't. 'Are you still drunk?'

'No.'

'Answer me, then!'

'What do you want me to say?'

'I want an explanation, Niklas! An apology! First you mess up the Gotland tickets, and then you're gone all—'

The line goes dead.

She stares at the phone. Seriously? Did he just hang up on her? What is he playing at? He should be on his damn knees, begging for forgiveness. Promising to change, to make it up to her, the way he always does when he messes up. Yes, they both have their faults and shortcomings, but that's what living with someone is all about: loving the other person despite their less appealing sides. The key is to say sorry when you do something stupid, and they're both usually pretty good at doing that. But now? No remorse and no apology. Just like last night, when they'd argued about the ferry tickets. Rather than admitting his mistake and backing down, he'd pushed the blame onto her. Such bad form.

Bea immediately calls him back, but it goes straight to voicemail, to Niklas's soft voice.

You've reached Niklas Stjerne. Leave a message or send me a text.

She is completely taken aback. Has he switched off his phone? No, surely there's no way. The battery must have died. He's so scatterbrained he probably forgot the charger, like always. There's no way he would hang up on her like that.

14

She scrolls down to Freddie Scherrer in her contacts list and hits dial. It rings and rings, but he doesn't pick up.

As confused as she is frustrated, she sends Niklas a quick message.

Call me! What's going on here? I don't understand. What are you doing? Just tell me!

She then writes another, to Freddie:

Could you ask Niklas to call me? Now, please.

Bea sees three pulsing dots. Freddie is writing something, but he either can't or doesn't want to talk on the phone. She waits impatiently, but after a moment or two, the dots disappear and his reply never arrives.

*

She knows the recipe off by heart. Flour, salt and baking powder. Dice the butter and work it into the dry ingredients. Add the milk.

Bea frantically kneads the dough, which clings to her fingers in long, claggy clumps. It usually comes off after a while, transforming into a gloopy mass she can portion out onto the baking tray, but today the dough is sticking to her like glue, despite rubbing her hands like a woman possessed.

She fishes a wooden spoon out of the pot on the counter and tries to scrape the gunk off her fingers, but

15

that just seems to make her hands – and the handle of the spoon – even stickier.

'Bollocks!'

The word slips out just as she hears Alma's shuffling footsteps in the hallway, and when she turns around, she is met by a pair of inquisitive teenage eyes. It isn't just the swearing Bea is embarrassed by, it's the sense of having lost control. This isn't like her. She doesn't say that sort of thing. It must be her colleague Inger's influence, she thinks; the woman starts cursing the minute her computer starts playing up.

'Sorry, Alma. I'm trying to make scones, but I don't know . . . It's gone all sticky.'

'Yum . . .' Alma mumbles, taking a carton of Tropicana from the fridge. 'Let me know when they're done.' With that, she turns and shuffles back to her room with the juice in her hand.

Bea turns her attention to the baking tray in front of her, trying to get the claggy mixture to let go. She isn't entirely sure why, but she has a lump in her throat. Yes, she is disappointed and angry with Niklas, but that should make her want to break something or punch a hole in the wall, not start bawling. It's probably just her hormones again, she thinks, creeping up on her with their thick, confusing fog.

She has been feeling moody and low quite often lately, as though her life has suddenly hit a bum note. She knows her work with the Red Cross could make a difference in the world, but it is no longer anywhere near as invigorating as it used to be, and her self-confidence is slipping.

16

After everything with Jacob all those years ago, she needed to do something that mattered, something that felt real. Niklas said she could continue her studies if she wanted to, but he supported her when she applied for the job with the charity instead, agreeing that it was good, important work. Despite this, she continues to belittle her contribution – even though her work as a web editor has helped to increase traffic to the website. She feels oddly invisible and replaceable. Blue.

Is that why she has taken the whole Gotland thing so hard? She was really looking forward to a holiday, to finally heading over to Hogreps and spending some quality time with Lillis and Tore and the rest of the family. To being looked after herself for a while, which Niklas's parents are so good at.

Gotland might be the only place on earth where she can really relax, in the old limestone house, in their company. It's somewhere she has always felt safe and comfortable. Drinking wine in the medieval ruins in the evening, playing cards late into the night, cooking together and going for long walks. It's been that way ever since she became a member of the Stjerne family, since the summer after Jacob died, when she visited Hogreps for the first time, sleepless with grief.

Lillis had packed a thermos of coffee at dawn and directed Bea – kindly but firmly – onto Granny Betty's old Monark bicycle. They rode down the crunching gravel track to Grynge and took a dip in the sea. The water was icy cold, but it had helped to numb her grief. Afterwards, they warmed themselves up with coffee and watched the sunrise in silence. There had been no pressure for Bea to speak, and it felt healing just to sit quietly by Lillis's side. Lillis's hair was grey even then, thirty years ago, with the same bun on top of her head, and she was short in stature, like Little My from the Moomins, with puckered, tanned thighs. For the first few years after Jacob, those mornings on the beach did Bea more good than any therapy sessions ever could.

Bea's mother-in-law has always shown her a warmth and interest that her own mother sadly lacks. Over the years, she has come to realise that it isn't a case of being cruel, more an inability of her mother to see anyone else's suffering. Still, Lillis filled that void.

Their morning swim and coffee eventually became a habit, alongside many other traditions. Every summer brings new projects that help to fill their days with meaning. They have built something beautiful and enduring at Hogreps, something for future generations to enjoy. This year, Bea has promised to help Lillis sort and organise her studio, but that doesn't seem like an onerous task; it will be fun, satisfying, like when she helped Tore to repaint the veranda last year.

Niklas has never understood the point of 'slaving away' over the summer, as he puts it, but to Bea it brings her a sense of belonging. It irritates her sometimes that he takes his family for granted. His brother Henke and sister-in-law Sus are already at Hogreps, just back from yet another year in Brazil, and their children Olle and Hedda are eager

18

for Alma and Alexia to arrive – the way they always are when they haven't seen each other in so long. At times, the cousins seem more like siblings, despite living on opposite sides of the world.

The longing Bea feels for Hogreps is almost physical, like the longing for a loved one. And it isn't just the limestone house she misses, it's the whole community, Gammelgarn. She is desperate to walk along the beach in Grynge, through the nature reserve and the little fishing village in Sjauster. Stopping whenever she gets too hot, stripping off on the barren rocks, wading out and ducking down beneath the surface. Letting the waves rock her back and forth as the chill spreads through her body, happy hormones taking hold.

Thoughts of a summer on Gotland were a lifeline during the spring. Whenever things got too much at work, Hogreps was right there, dangling in front of her like a carrot. The knowledge that she would soon be able to escape their furnace of an apartment, the heat that seems to have settled over Stockholm like a cast-iron lid. Bea has been counting down the weeks, and the idea of adjusting their plans now, of holding out a little longer, feels almost impossible. Still, thanks to Niklas's stupid mistake, she has no choice.

Bea reaches for the bag of flour on the kitchen island. The beads of sweat come together as rivulets in the creases on her forehead, dripping onto the stone floor and forming a pattern of dark dots in place of the tears she refuses to shed. The oven has really cranked up the heat in the kitchen, and she feels like screaming – what a stupid idea to bake in this weather! She slides the tray of scones into the oven and slams the door.

On the marble worktop, her mobile phone pings and she snatches it up with doughy fingers. A message from Niklas. Has he managed to charge his phone? Or realised how weird it is to switch it off when his wife is trying to get hold of him?

She is expecting a serious *mea culpa*, but considering how disrespectful his behaviour has been, it'll be a while before her rage subsides. Exhausted from anger, her hands are shaking as she opens the message.

Not coming home.

Three short, simple words, but she still can't make sense of them. His message is utterly incomprehensible to her. *Not coming home?* Does he mean he isn't coming home now, as in *right* now, and that he'll be back later instead? In the evening? That whatever he is doing is taking longer than he thought?

If she wasn't quite so surprised, she would probably be angry – or *angrier* than she already is – but his cryptic message leaves her feeling more numb than anything. She needs to talk to him, now. About what happened yesterday and this morning. About him hanging up on her and then switching off his phone after a whole night of silence. About Gotland.

Should they try to get ferry tickets from Oskarshamn instead? It's a hell of a drive, no doubt about that, but surely even that would be better than being stuck in this tarmac jungle all week?

Bea quickly types a response.

What do you mean? When will you be back?

She waits, sees the three little pulsing dots, but his reply never arrives. She sends another two messages of her own.

Don't understand.
Call me!

He doesn't, of course, so Bea calls him. It rings and rings, but no one picks up. Instead, a message arrives.

Need to think.

Right then, she realises she can smell burning.

*

Bea feels dizzy, with a queasy weight in the pit of her stomach. Is it the heat, her faltering oestrogen levels? Her runaway husband? She has barely had anything to drink all morning and hasn't eaten since yesterday evening. Not even a single bite of scone, and Bea is someone who loves scones, ideally with butter and cheese melting into the hot crumb. Especially Lillis's scones, which taste even better at Hogreps. Was that why she decided to bake? Was she trying to conjure up Lillis and Tore in bread form, as some sort of consolation?

It's almost midday, but it could just as easily be midnight. Time seems to be moving at a crawl, but she still can't quite get a grip on it. She doesn't know it yet, but a new era has already begun. Today will reshape the rest of her life.

Bea picks up her phone again, staring at the screen as though she can coax Niklas into sending her another message. An explanation of why he is acting so oddly. An answer she can make sense of. But the only messages in their chat thread are Bea's own attempts to reach him. A long string of questions and exclamation marks. CAPS. Angry emojis. Furious red faces with slanting eyebrows and bubbling volcano heads. Demands for communication.

She can see that Niklas has received them all. Each one is marked read, with the time when he read it. He's active on Messenger like usual, but it's as though he has pulled down the shutters on her, blocking her like a teenager, the way Alexia might. The whole thing is exasperating.

Freddie is doing the same, ignoring her calls and messages. At least Calle Mörner phoned her back – not that he knew anything. He hadn't been at Daphne's and had no idea what could have happened.

Should she go over to Freddie's place and pound on the door? Demand to speak to Niklas? No, that probably isn't a good strategy. It'd be humiliating, too. She doesn't want to cause a scene. If he needs a few days to himself, he can have them. They'll just have to straighten everything out later, however unacceptable his behaviour is.

Bea goes through to the bathroom and runs a bath. Cold water surges down into the tub, thundering against the metal. She strips off and climbs in, watching the water level rise as her internal thermometer sinks. In her mind, Bea tries to escape from the damn tub, imagining she is in the sea in Grynge, but all the disappointment and confusion is making her eyes sting. Why did he have to start a big fight now, when they have a wonderful summer ahead of them? So unnecessary.

'Hello? Mum?'

She can barely hear Alexia's voice over the sound of the running water, and she turns down the tap to a trickle.

'I'm in the bath, do you need to come in?'

'Where's Dad?'

Bea hesitates, unsure how to answer. Should she cover for Niklas or tell her daughter the truth?

'He's at Freddie's.'

She decides she can tell the truth without sharing every detail. At least that way, she can't be accused of lying.

'He was meant to be taking me out to practise in the car.'

Bea fumbles for something to say.

'Oh . . . then I'm sure he'll be back soon, if that's what you agreed. Otherwise we can . . .' She trails off when she realises what she is saying. No, she can't do anything. Niklas is the only one with a driver's licence and a training permit. 'Why don't you give him a call to check? Or Freddie?'

She hears a murmur, followed by the sound of fading footsteps.

'Alexia?'

Bea listens for her daughter, but she is already gone. Alexia might not have said anything, but she could sense her disappointment through the door.

Alma has no interest whatsoever in learning to drive, but Alexia has enough enthusiasm for both of them, as though she can't become independent quickly enough. Bea had assumed it would be the other way around, given that Alma is the one who always needs a ride to the stables, but Alexia got a taste of grown-up life at the film shoot last autumn – despite being only sixteen.

Bea drags herself up out of the tub and reaches for her phone. It's one thing for Niklas to ignore her, but forgetting about his kids is not OK. Her hands are wet, which means the screen is less responsive than usual as she tries to write him a new message.

Where are you??? You'tre meant to be taking Alexia out in the cvar! She's really uposet Call me nopw!!!

He won't reply, she thinks, right as her phone pings with a message.

Just spoken to Alexia. It's cool.

Has he had time to speak to Alexia? Bea writes back.

Its not cool! She's reallyytyupset! When re you coming home?

Yet again, no answer.

Bea wraps a towel around herself and leaves a trail of wet footprints on the pale oak flooring as she hurries down the hallway to Alexia's room. She knocks quietly and opens the door slightly, too impatient to wait for an answer. Alexia is sprawled on her bed with her phone in her hand.

'Did Dad just call?'

'Mm.'

'What did he say?'

'That we can do it another day.'

'Did he say why?'

'Nah, just that we'll do it another day.'

'When is he coming back?'

'Dunno.'

Alexia's voice is languid. Drawn out, as though every word is an effort.

'Was he still at Freddie's place?'

'Nah, don't think so.'

'Why don't you think so?'

'Dunno . . .'

'Jesus Christ, he must've said something! Try to think. And speak up, so I can hear you. It's *don't know*, by the way.' Bea can hear just how harsh and critical she sounds. The whole *dunno* attitude Alexia has adopted lately is provocative, but this is probably the worst possible moment to lash out. 'Sorry, sweetie. Sorry, I was just wondering . . .'

But it's too late. Her daughter has already stormed out of the room, and Bea hears the front door slam behind her. In less than twenty-four hours, she has managed to push two members of her family away.

*

She roughly chops the pepper, followed by the onion and garlic, then tips everything into the blender and turns the dial. Gazpacho is perfect when it's too hot to eat. Or when the gnawing feeling in the pit of your stomach makes you so queasy you can't manage anything solid.

She sent a message to the family WhatsApp group earlier, telling them that Sunday dinner would be ready at seven. No one has replied, and though it's almost quarter-to, there is no sign of any of them. Alexia is probably still licking her wounds somewhere, hanging out with one of her new 'film friends'. Alma is at the stables, which could go on for hours once she starts fussing over the horses. If worst comes to worst, Bea can always eat on her own.

She tries to remind herself that every hour that passes is one hour closer to Niklas coming home, to the moment when they can finally sit down and talk through everything that has happened and put it all behind them.

Because surely it must be coming to an end, all this alone time he desperately needed? It's not that she begrudges him a bit of time to himself – there are days when she needs her own space too, and they're generally pretty good at giving that to each other – but the fact that he just disappeared on her makes her angry.

In truth, though, she doesn't have the energy to be angry any longer. Bea is exhausted, and all she wants is for this to be over, for everything to go back to the way it was. One day, they'll probably look back on all of it and laugh, a shared joke at a family barbecue on Gotland. They'll laugh at the summer they sweltered indoors because Niklas forgot to pay for the ferry tickets, and was so embarrassed about the whole thing that he didn't dare come home. Bea can just see herself animatedly telling the anecdote, Niklas filling in from time to time, affectionately taunting each other. She imagines Henke listening from over by the grill, turning the lamb burgers and shaking his head at his useless little brother. Lillis, Tore, Hampus and Sus would be drinking wine at the stone table, laughing at this crazy story that never seems to get old. Right now, it's hard to laugh, but in the future … Maybe even this evening, once they've managed to straighten everything out and forgive each other.

Bea turns the dial on the blender again. The sharp blades pulverise the vegetables, and she cranks it up to the max. The shredded tomatoes and onions pulse around at a furious pace, the whir of the motorised knives overpowering everything else. Right then, she thinks she hears a bang in the hallway, and she kills the power to the blender. Was that the door?

She hears keys landing in the silver bowl on the chest of drawers, and a moment later Alma appears in the doorway, still in her jodhpurs and with a canvas bag over one shoulder. Bea's budding hopes immediately fizzle into disappointment. Or maybe it's more a niggling sense of unease at the fact that she still doesn't know when Niklas will be home. She forces a smile onto her face.

'Perfect timing, honey, I just finished the gazpacho. Sit yourself down.'

Alma drops her bag to the floor and slumps onto a chair. She glances appreciatively over to the counter, where Bea is pouring the cold soup into a couple of Lillis's deep plates.

'Where's Dad?'

Bea thinks she can detect an undertone in her daughter's voice, though it could all be in her mind.

'I'm sure he'll be home any minute now.'

Alma reaches for a piece of garlic bread and starts nibbling at the crust.

'Did you have a good ride?' Bea asks.

'Issa had already gone out with Nico, so I just did the mucking out.'

'But Sundays and Wednesdays are your days, aren't they?'

'Yeah, but he's her horse.'

'And we pay so that you can ride him on certain days. Surely she could at least let you know if she wants to swap?'

'Emmy was there mucking out too, so it was fine.'

28

Alma rummages through her bag and pulls out a book, making it clear that she doesn't want to talk about it. Bea takes the hint.

'What are you reading?'

Alma holds up the book to show her the cover. Bodil Malmsten's *When the Chestnuts Bloom I'll Be Long Gone*.

'Very grown-up,' Bea says.

'I found it on the bookshelf. I like the picture.'

The cover features an image of Maurice, the protagonist, looking off to one side against a red background.

Alma pushes a finger between the pages and opens it at the end paper. Bea catches a glimpse of Niklas's hand-writing, and she leans in to get a better look over Alma's shoulder.

Christmas 1995.

To Beaver – my favourite person.

'Beaver?' Alma asks.

'That was Jacob's nickname for me when we were kids. Your dad started using it once we got together.'

'Why did he call you that?'

'Because I was always such an eager beaver to be by his side, doing whatever he was doing. And he let me, because he was such a sweet big brother.'

One of Bea's eyes starts to twitch, and Alma studies her anxiously.

'Are you sad?'

'No, no, it's a nice memory. I'm just hungry.' That is only half true, because she still feels like she might throw up. 'It's the heat, too.'

Bea has always tried to be honest with her daughters. She doesn't believe in hiding difficult things from them and thinks it is important to show that even adults can struggle sometimes, that they can be angry and sad. Despite all that, she can't bring herself to talk about Niklas, probably because she doesn't really understand it herself.

The front door slams again, and Bea feels her hopes rise, but they immediately come crashing down when she hears Alexia on the phone in the hallway. She forces another smile onto her face as her daughter comes through to the kitchen and peers around the room.

'What's for dinner?'

'Gazpacho.'

'That's not gonna fill us up.'

'There's garlic bread too.'

Bea holds out the plate, and Alexia takes a piece without a word. Her chestnut hair is loose, hanging in thick, damp strands.

'Have you been swimming?' Bea asks, resisting the urge to reach out and push her daughter's fringe back in order to make eye contact.

Alexia nods.

'Who with?'

'Tim and that lot.'

'Oh, fun. Which pool did you go to? Kampan?'

'Mm. But then some guy died.'

'What?'

Alma's spoon comes to a halt halfway to her mouth, and Bea flinches.

'My God, what happened?' she asks.

'He was just, like, floating there and everyone started screaming, then some people pulled him out and started doing that CPR thing.'

'Are you sure he died?'

'No, but he looked, like, pretty fucking dead when they pulled him out.'

'Don't swear, honey.'

Alexia stares at her. *Are you really doing this now? Seriously?*

'Sorry. Old habit.'

Bea tries to rescue the mood, serving another portion of the cold soup.

'So what did you do?' she asks.

'Not much. We stayed there for a bit, then we left.'

'How are you feeling?'

'Fine.'

'But you've just seen a dead person!' Alma blurts out, giving her twin a confused look as she munches on her garlic bread.

'I mean, what do you want me to do? Cry?'

Alma is upset by Alexia's tone, and she gets up.

'I'm going for a shower.'

'But you haven't finished your soup, honey,' Bea says.

'I'm full, it's too hot . . . It was really tasty though.' She carries her plate over to the dishwasher and loads it into the tray.

Alexia sits at the table, stirring her gazpacho with robotic movements. Her face is as white as a sheet, and Bea moves over and wraps her arms around her. She feels her daughter tense, making the hug awkward. It's been that way for a while now, ever since she got her first period. She doesn't like closeness anymore, unlike Alma, who still curls up in Bea's lap from time to time.

It's disappointing, the way things are with Alexia. Bea could see so much of herself in her when she was younger. They were so alike, and not just because they had the same thick mane of brown hair. They had the same nature, too. Alma's pale colouring and blonde hair are all Niklas, but Alexia was a tomboy, just like her.

Bea remembers the crazy games she used to play with Jacob, the way she wanted his old cast-offs rather than new clothes of her own. She had always thought things would be easy with Alexia, given how similar they were, but, if anything, the opposite has proved to be the case. It's as though they just keep rubbing each other up the wrong way. She has taken a step back, tried to give her daughter space and not be too pushy, but she needs to hug her now. Really hug her. So that she knows how loved she is.

Bea holds her tight until Alexia finally relaxes, until her gangly teenage body capitulates and gives in. Bea fills her lungs with Alexia's scent, so unique that she likes to think she would recognise it among millions of others. Her daughter sniffs and hooks an arm around her waist. So grown-up and yet so childlike, burrowing into Bea's soft belly.

Bea hugs her close, as though to protect her from the things she has already seen, that have already happened.

Perhaps she is also trying to protect herself from some unspecified danger, something as yet unknown, lurking at the edge of her field of vision.

They let go, almost embarrassed by the show of affection. Alexia abruptly gets up and takes her bowl through to her room, and as Bea watches her walk away, she wonders whether she really is OK. What happens to a person when they see someone drown? She needs to talk to Niklas. They both need to be here for Alexia now, to deal with this properly. Despite her swirling emotions, she writes as calm a message as she can.

Alexia saw a man drown today. Ambulance, etc. She's shocked and upset. Needs you. Please come home.

*

The plan was to stay up reading until Niklas came home, but she must have drifted off with Hanya Yanagihara's weighty tome on her chest, still open on the same page as that morning. It's two thirty in the morning, and Bea peers around the room in a daze. Niklas's side of the bed is still empty, and her initial surprise quickly transforms into a dull unease.

Not coming home.

Need to think.

What does that even mean? Is he planning on staying away for another night? What does he need to think about?

33

He hasn't replied to her text about Alexia and the accident at the pool. There isn't even a notification to say that her message was delivered.

She grabs her phone again and jabs at the screen. Another message or phone call is hardly going to make a difference, but should she maybe try WhatsApp?

She starts writing in the family chat group, only to stop herself. Doesn't want to worry the girls with her desperation.

Less than a day ago, the prospect of Niklas acting in this way would have been unthinkable. Ignoring her calls and texts, disappearing into thin air. She hesitates. Should she call Lillis to check whether she has heard from him? No, her in-laws will be asleep. Best not to disturb them. What about Charlotte? If Calle has heard anything, he might have told her, things he didn't want to share with Bea. Something makes her hold back. If she tells Charlotte about this, that will immediately make it real, whatever *this* is.

Bea wonders how many other couples like her and Niklas there are out there. Keeping each other's secrets, year after year, never sharing them with another soul – not even their closest friends. Both to protect each other and the image of their marriage. Less to maintain a facade than because that's just what you do for your best friend. You keep their secrets and you hold your tongue about their worst sides, part of a tacit agreement to tolerate each other, even in the ugliest moments. You protect and you endure, because you love the best parts of each other.

Bea has always been amazed whenever her friends and colleagues bad-mouth their partners. To her, sharing intimate details about her husband's less flattering sides is a form of betrayal, something she has never done to Niklas. She has admitted that they've gone through rough patches like anyone else, of course – it would be abnormal if they hadn't – and she has talked about the tough times with Charlotte. But she has never gone into any detail, and it has almost always been after the fact, once they've made it through to the other side. Always as part of some polished reconstruction in which their issues proved to be learning exercises, however hard they were.

It's not that Bea lies on purpose, but as with everything else in life, conflicts always seem slightly less painful with the passing of time. They can even seem funny, and all the bad stuff can be reshaped into an amusing story that doesn't risk revealing too much. Apart from anything else, it's Bea who does most of the listening in her friendship with Charlotte, because her friend's marriage always seems to be in a state of chronic yet stable crisis.

Her anxiety comes creeping back up on her, making her throat tighten. She needs to get out. Bea drags herself out of bed and grabs her tracksuit bottoms from the back of the chair, tiptoeing quickly through the living room and past the girls' rooms.

*

35

The cloudless sky is pale pink as she cycles along Karlavägen. Bea has the road almost to herself, and other than the odd late-night wanderer, staggering along the pavement on their way home from the pub, there is virtually no one else about. She quickly reaches the crossing of Birger Jarlsgatan and Odengatan, where Freddie lives – 'outer Östermalm', as he calls it in an attempt to sound fancy, though it's more like Vasastan. As Bea pulls up by the wooden door, a plump rat scurries along the edge of the building.

Freddie Scherrer is one of Niklas's oldest friends, part of the quartet of buddies with Jacob and Calle. They stuck together all the way through school and generally hung out at Niklas's place, because, unlike Bea and Jacob's parents, Lillis and Tore didn't mind him bringing his friends home.

Funnily enough, it was Freddie, not Niklas, who Bea had a slight crush on during her teens. If she is really honest, it wasn't *so* slight – not that she ever told him how she felt. Not even Niklas knows. Freddie has always had a special glimmer in his eye, something that Bea appreciates even now. He was the wildest member of the gang, the one who didn't stick to the template. While Niklas and Calle were in Uppsala, studying to become a doctor and a lawyer respectively, Freddie drifted about, went to New York and enrolled in film school. Everyone thought it was just another of his many whims, but he stuck at it and became a respected producer, working both in Sweden and abroad.

Bea has had a surprising amount of contact with Freddie over the past year, thanks to Alexia being cast in a minor part in his latest feature film – a fact that seems to have had a detrimental impact on both her grades and her personality.

But that isn't why she is here now. She is here to find her husband. It feels uncomfortable and embarrassing, but she is getting desperate.

Freddie looks like he has just woken up when he answers the door in his underpants and T-shirt. He clearly knows why Bea is there, but he doesn't seem especially guilty – not even for ignoring her calls. If anything, he is radiating some sort of pity from behind his Tom Ford glasses. The frames make him look like a younger version of himself, and he might have lost a little weight, too.

'Sorry, Freddie, but I need to talk to Niklas. He's not answering my calls.'

'I know, but he's not here.'

Bea stares at him in confusion.

'I've got Tilda this week,' Freddie explains, 'so I gave him the keys to the studio.'

Freddie's ten-year-old daughter stays with him every other week, and Bea can't work out what she has to do with Niklas.

'But you went out the night before last, didn't you?' she asks. 'To Daphne's?'

Freddie gives her a resigned shrug, as though he doesn't want to lie or betray his buddy.

'So you didn't go out?'

'Not exactly.'

'What does that mean?'

Freddie scratches the back of his head. He seems to be searching for an answer that will keep both Bea and Niklas happy.

'But you talked to him?' Bea presses him, growing increasingly impatient.

'Yeah, I guess you could say that. He came by to get the keys.'

Bea thinks back to Niklas's last message.

Not coming home.

'I really don't understand, Freddie.'

He looks like he is about to say something, though he quickly changes his mind.

'You should probably talk to him yourself.'

'Dad . . . !' Tilda shouts from somewhere behind him.

'Coming!' Freddie turns back to Bea. 'Sorry, I should . . .'

'Of course. I'm sorry I woke you, I just didn't know what else to do, he's acting so strangely.'

'If you want my advice, I think you should wait until morning. He'll probably be more receptive then.'

Bea moves slowly through the cool, dark stairwell. With each step, she tries to process what she has just learned. Niklas wasn't out drinking with Freddie after all, nor did he stay over there. He stayed at the studio, at Freddie's 'office' in Frihamnen, a charmless basement space where he does his editing. Full of tech, but also a bit of a man cave, with games consoles and a minibar. Freddie lived there for a while after he separated from Tilda's mother, and he has almost certainly taken a woman or two there over the years.

Bea has only ever been to the office once, when she and Niklas went to pick up a coffee table from the auction house next door. She remembers it as chaotic, though that was how that sort of place always looked. It makes no sense that Niklas would rather sleep there than at home, and for two nights in a row at that. She feels angry, upset and confused, deeply disappointed in her best friend.

By the time she comes out onto the street, all she can think is that she should cycle over there and confront him, but Freddie's advice about waiting until morning is still niggling away at her. Bea can usually always tell what Niklas is thinking and feeling, but right now she has no idea. What if he has been struggling more than she realised? Is this how burnout and depression begin? His job as a consultant on the new maternity ward is demanding, and he hasn't been sleeping well for a long time.

The idea was that this job would give him a new lease of life after *the incident* at Sollentuna Hospital that he'd been obsessing over – something that wasn't even his fault and happened to almost everyone in the profession. After years of service to the local authority outside of the city, he finally had an opportunity to shape a department himself, just a few blocks from home, with resources he could only have dreamed of back at Sollentuna – and to be paid well for his efforts. Bea has tried her best to pep him up and get him thinking positively, but rather than using his new position to delegate and take charge of his time, it's as though he has been consumed by the pressure and the responsibility, constantly trying to do too much.

What if the stresses of work have pushed him into some kind of breakdown? He did keep saying he was tired and run-down all spring, but Bea felt exactly the same, not least because she'd taken on the lion's share of the work at home – the kitchen renovations and everything to do with the girls' schooling and day-to-day activities, plus her full-time job. He undervalues her work and how tough it is, all because she earns less and has a less prestigious job title than him. Sometimes she wonders whether he thinks that doctors are the only people who know what human suffering is, even though she works for an aid organisation.

She comes face to face with the most awful things on a daily basis, both in the imagery she has to work with and in people's stories. Her job is about life and death too, on a global scale. But in Niklas's case, it seems to have had psychological consequences. She has been nagging him to work less and take more time off at the weekends. That's yet another reason why Bea has been looking forward to their holiday together. Niklas needs it. They need it as a family. And now this. Still, if Niklas is ill, then she has to be there for him.

The heat has finally broken, and the night air is like a cool caress on her bare arms and Birkenstock-clad feet, but cycling is still tough. It's like she has a lead weight strapped to her chest, and her tracksuit bottoms flap around her ankles, transformed into a couple of windsocks that slow her down even when she pedals as fast as she can. As though she needs to get there before it's too late.

She doesn't really believe that Niklas would do anything drastic, not after everything with Jacob, but she is scarred, and that fear sits deep. Her body remembers, and every single warning bell is ringing. The realisation that Niklas's state of mind is worse than she thought also makes her feel guilty. She should have taken the signs more seriously. Was that why he forgot something as simple as paying for the ferry tickets? Forgetfulness is one of the clearest signs of stress and exhaustion, as are volatility, anger and irritability.

Now that she thinks about it, Bea realises that Niklas's behaviour over the past few days ticks every box. And though she is worried, in some ways it also comes as a relief to finally have an explanation. She turns off from the roundabout at Gärdet, almost at her destination after what feels like a day-long marathon.

*

Freddie's office is in a large basement space by the loading docks in Frihamnen, the ones now surrounded by various production companies. Bea cycles past the building that once housed Sweden's first banana importer and a large parking area, empty save for a white van and a car with the logo of a gardening programme on one side.

She peers around anxiously in the gloom. On a summer's night like this, the area is eerily deserted, not another soul in sight, and when she pulls up outside Freddie's building, she doesn't bother to lock her bike; she simply leans it against a railing below the loading dock. Hopefully this won't take long. If she and Niklas take a cab home, she can always leave the bike in Freddie's office and come back to pick it up tomorrow.

Bea climbs the narrow staircase to the loading dock and walks over to the goods lift. She feels nervous, worried and angry, but she also knows she needs to keep her emotions in check. To be the strong one. All she wants is for Niklas to come home. That's the only thing that matters right now, so that they can prepare for their trip to Gotland next week and think up some fun things to do with the girls before they leave town.

They can still make the most of a few days in beautiful summery Stockholm, after all; this could be an opportunity for them to be tourists in their own town. Visiting the Kaknäs Tower, the Skansen open air museum, or going on one of the sightseeing boats, for example. They could even go swimming out in Ekerö or on the north shore of Lovön; you can have a whole bay to yourself out there if you know where to look. It could be a great week if they just put their minds to it. Either that or they could drive down to Oskarshamn and catch a ferry from there.

She steps into the lift and realises, as she presses the button, that her hand is shaking. The goods lift starts moving with a jolt, the creaking mechanical noise cutting through the silence. She has the sense of sinking deep underground, both physically and mentally, and when she glances up at the window in the lift door, she sees a pair of terrified eyes staring back at her.

Bea tries to convince herself that her fears are all in her mind. Irrational. But at the same time, this surreal situation is very much real and unpleasant. She suddenly wishes she had washed her face and brushed her teeth, or run a comb through her hair at the very least. Not to make herself look good for Niklas, but because she doesn't want to feel grubby. She smooths her hair and is in the process of trying to work out whether she can smell sweat beneath her arms when the lift stops with a soft thud.

LATERNA FILMS, she reads on the engraved sign by the heavy metal door. The light on the ceiling overhead is flickering, and Bea hesitates and takes a slight breath before she raps on the door just above the handle.

Her knock sounds irritated, which is precisely how she didn't want it to come across, but how exactly are you supposed to knock in a friendly, unobtrusive way? Just to be on the safe side, in case he hasn't heard her, she sends him a message.

She waits for a moment or two, exposed and alone in the eerie, creepy basement, even though Niklas is probably right there on the other side of the door. But there is no answer, either from his phone or the office.

Bea tries again, a little harder this time.

Could he be asleep? That wouldn't really be so strange, given it's the middle of the night, but Niklas has never been a deep sleeper – especially not when he's feeling down, and especially not on someone else's sofa. Maybe there just isn't much signal down here?

Bea glances at her phone and freezes. He has read her message. He's awake, and he knows that she is here. So why isn't he opening the door?

She waits another few minutes, but when he fails to answer she starts pounding on the door again. *Bang, bang, bang.*

Her heart is racing.

'Hello? Niklas! I know you're awake! Open the door!'

BANG. BANG. BANG.

'Open up, for God's sake! Otherwise I'll have to call the police!'

She isn't sure she means that, but one part of her definitely wants to. If he won't open the door, she'll force her way in. Enough of this madness. She is angry, but she is also terrified. Could he be suffering some sort of psychosis? Is he planning to hurt himself? What does she really know? We never know anyone as well as we think. She thought she knew Jacob.

BANG. BANG. BANG.

'Niklas! You're scaring me! Open the door so I know you're OK, please.'

She is desperate now, on the verge of tears. A note of panic in her voice.

Right then, just as she raises her fist, the door swings open with a scraping sound. And there he is, like an apparition suddenly transformed into flesh and blood. He looks just like his usual self, neither exhausted nor suicidal.

More troubled than anything, in fact, possibly even a little irritated.

Bea loses her nerve. The man standing in the doorway is her husband and best friend, but for some reason she feels like an uninvited guest.

'You're OK, then?'

Niklas nods. 'Just a bit tired. It's three in the morning.'

Yes, thanks, she knows what the time is, but it's his fault she is awake. Not that she says any of that.

Niklas is quiet, making no attempt to apologise or explain. If she wants answers, clearly she will have to ask the questions.

'What is this, Niklas?'

'Freddie's office . . .'

'No, I mean *this*. You.' Bea throws her hands up in resignation, peering into the room behind him. Freddie's office is a large, open-plan space with a pantry in one corner and a separate cutting room. She can see a poster for *Dreamcatcher*, the film Alexia has a part in, on one of the walls. In the foreground, a man and woman are staring blankly at the camera, and she is surprised to see that Alexia is included too – in the background, but still. Their daughter, on a film poster. So strange.

Through a door which has been left ajar, she can make out a number of cables and gadgets, all bathed in soft light. There is a leather sofa in the middle of the room, a caseless pillow at one end, plus a quilted blanket that probably hasn't seen a washing machine in years. So, this is where he would rather be than at home with her and the girls. In this musty dump of a place that smells like old coffee and bad breath.

It would be far easier to make sense of it all if he was showing any sign of instability, but other than a glimmer of defiance in his dark eyes, he seems remarkably calm.

'Why didn't you reply to my messages or calls?'

'I did.'

'You know what I mean.'

Niklas glances at his watch. 'It's late, Bea. I need to sleep.'

'OK, so let's go.'

Niklas shakes his head and moves to close the door. Bea reacts instinctively, pushing her foot into the gap.

'Stop being such an idiot and let's go home. Come on!'

She tugs at his sweater, but Niklas takes a step back and tries to push her away. Bea cries out as he attempts to prise her hand loose.

She is so shocked by his sudden aggression that she automatically lets go. Niklas loses his balance and is about to stumble back onto the sofa when he regains his footing. He no longer seems anywhere near as calm. His jaw is tense, and she can see a vein throbbing on his forehead.

'Please, Niklas, stop this. Let's just call a cab.'

'No.'

'What do you mean, no?'

'I told you, I need to think.'

'So when are you coming home? The girls want to know. *I* want to know.'

That stubborn glimmer is back again, the hint of defiance. If it wasn't for the stubble on his chin, she might almost mistake the look in his eye for Alexia's or Alma's.

'I can't do this anymore.'

It's as though he is speaking a foreign language, his lips forming noises instead of words. His voice is neutral, almost cold, like he is talking to a stranger and not his partner of thirty-two years. His Beaver.

'What do you mean?' She can barely get the words out.

'Us. You and me.'

His gaze is steady. Calm and determined.

Bea's eye starts twitching again, just like it did when she was talking to Alma earlier. It's as though he has just given her an electric shock, but she is also struggling to take him seriously. Not because she doesn't respect his feelings, but she can't bring herself to believe that he means what he just said.

It's clear that Niklas is not doing well, not doing well at all – even if he has managed to keep up the facade. Whatever this is about, she has no intention of allowing their 'us', Bea and Niklas, to fall apart. What they have isn't something you just give up in the middle of the night, in a dingy basement in Frihamnen. Like a late-night impulse buy you regret come morning. If he is unhappy about something, they can fix it.

The air is stuffy and hot, as though the walls have stored up the heat of the sun only to release it in the dark.

'We can talk about this tomorrow,' she says through gritted teeth, pulling her foot back. A retreating soldier withdrawing her sword.

Niklas doesn't say another word. If anything, he seems relieved to be rid of her as he slams the door, leaving Bea standing outside, staring at Freddie's sign. *LATERNA*. A light in the darkness, to help guide lost ships. That's what Freddie always says his production company should be, but Bea has never felt more lost than she does right now. Niklas has never been more lost.

I can't do this anymore. Us. You and me.

Dizzying words whose consequences she can't possibly comprehend – assuming he really means them.

Bea's bike is gone by the time she gets back to the loading dock. Of course it is. Someone in this ghost town has stolen the old ladies' bike Lillis gave her. The most rickety two-wheeler in all of Östermalm, but to Bea it was also the most valuable. Irreplaceable in terms of sentimental value. Tears spill down her cheeks as she walks away, then begins to run on autopilot. Legs moving in slow motion, eyes blurry.

Freddie was right. She should have waited.

*

The sun is on its way up over Stockholm by the time Bea gets back to the apartment on Banérgatan. The girls are still sound asleep, blissfully unaware of what just happened.

48

Her body is numb with shock. Too tired to be awake and too worked up to sleep. Bea tries to wash the night away with a cold shower, cleansing herself of everything that was said and done. She has a graze on one arm, she notices. When did that happen? In the struggle with Niklas? The expression on his face keeps coming back to her, the way he looked when he said *those words*. As though her husband had stepped outside of himself and become a version she doesn't know.

Bea scrubs her arms and legs, trying to think logically. Niklas is clearly in crisis, but crises can be solved. The fact that one of them is having a wobble after thirty-two years together isn't really so surprising, and she doesn't doubt they can get through this, just like they've got through everything else. Right?

Niggling doubts keep intruding on her thoughts, shattering them and exposing the unbearable. She can't imagine a life without Niklas, the love of her life, her best friend. The thought of losing everything they've created together is so absurd, she has to brush it aside. Scrub harder.

Once she gets out of the shower, she goes through to the kitchen and curls up on the daybed with a cup of coffee. She looks around the room. Her beautiful kitchen, which she lusted after for so long, finally became a reality after Niklas took the job at the Sophiahemmet hospital. Working alongside Nisse, the designer from Kvänum, Bea chose every last detail. The moss-green display cabinet that almost seems to hover like a painting, filled with all the beautiful objects they have collected over the years.

49

Carefully curated memories from their life together sitting alongside Lillis's handcrafted vases, carafes and bowls in various shapes and colours.

Bea had envisioned something simple yet interesting, taking inspiration from Lillis and Tore's snug, homely dining room at Hogreps. Gotland limestone mixed with warm Mediterranean colours. She wanted to create a welcoming space for the family to spend time together. Somewhere with different places to sit, with an inbuilt daybed, little nooks and crannies for pretty objects, and large entertaining spaces. The hand-painted tiles from Sicily that she and Niklas lugged home after their tenth anniversary trip there brighten up one of the walls like a sunny memory.

They celebrated the girls' sixteenth birthdays here just a few weeks ago. Bea gave a short speech during dinner, right here in the kitchen, telling them how it had felt when they had left Danderyd Hospital each carrying a baby. The surreal, mind-blowing fact that they were now parents, that the girls were theirs. The sheer terror and joy. The realisation that they were now a family who had begun a great and remarkable journey together.

It feels just as surreal and mind-blowing that Niklas claims to want to end that journey now. They were supposed to be in this together, but there is no joy left, nothing but fear.

She takes out her phone and writes him a message.

Sorry. I know I haven't paid enough attention to the way you've been feeling, but I'm glad you spoke up

and promise to do better going forward. Whatever it
is, we can fix it. Love you.

*

'When are you coming to see us, love? We're dying to see
you all.'

Lillis's voice is a little raspy, but it is still as warm as
ever. Bea struggles to hold back the tears she can feel
welling up, and, like always, her mother-in-law can hear
that something is wrong.

'What is it, sweetie? Are you OK?'

'Someone stole the bike you gave me. I'm so sorry, Lillis.'

'Goodness . . . Who on earth would steal that rusty old
thing?'

'I don't know, but . . .'

Bea clears her throat and tries to regain control of her
voice.

'It's just a bike, my dear,' says Lillis. 'It's not the end of
the world.'

Bea realises that her cheeks are wet. She has slowly but
surely lost her footing over the course of the past day, and
her otherwise steady world has taken a real knock. Lillis's
voice is a reminder of the sense of security she is missing
right now.

'Niklas is sleeping in Freddie's office. He says he can't
do this anymore.'

Bea has frequently confided in Lillis about all sorts of
things over the years, big and small. Worries about the

kids and her marriage when she and Niklas were struggling, particularly when the girls were younger and more
physically demanding. Everyday bickering about the traditional gender roles that many people find themselves
getting stuck in. Lillis is the only one she can really be
honest with, the only person who loves Niklas just as much
as she does.

There have been times when she has felt sick and tired
of being the project manager in their family, always planning and problem solving; sick of the fact that nothing
seems to happen without her. On the other hand, Niklas
has always been the one who brings in the most money.
Bea's job with the Red Cross covers only a fraction of their
monthly outgoings, which meant she was typically the one
who stayed home to look after the girls when they were
ill, who kept on top of things whenever Niklas was on
call or working late. Lillis often nags her about that, telling
her she should get herself an education, that their division
of labour is unequal and unhealthy, and Bea agrees –
though she does sometimes get tired of Lillis's preaching,
especially because she doesn't really feel the need to forge
a career or prove her worth by climbing the ranks. She
has always prioritised a life without the nine-to-five stress,
and Niklas's mother sometimes struggles to understand
that Bea is happy with that.

Not everyone has a mother-in-law who was once active
in a feminist organisation like Group 8 – even if it was a
long time ago. Lillis is a firm believer that equality can
only be achieved through absolute fairness, whether in

relation to the washing up, childcare, orgasms or work. A lovely idea, though, in reality, it doesn't work quite so well. Not unless you've got a small fortune to fall back on, like Lillis and Tore did.

Like many other boomers, they enjoyed low costs and plentiful opportunities, not least because Lillis's artistic endeavours were financed by inherited money. Niklas always moans about how detached his mother is from reality, but in moments like this, there really is no one better, calmly reassuring Bea that there is no need to worry.

'I'll never forget the time Tore was so angry with me that he ran off to Copenhagen. It was two days before I heard from him, and I thought he must have got in an accident. I spent hours calling around different hospitals, trying to speak my very best Danish.'

It's an anecdote Lillis has told countless times before, and it doesn't really compare to what Bea is going through right now, but it still serves as a reminder that it isn't necessarily so serious. The 'great crisis' between Lillis and Tore took place in the early sixties, before they had kids. They were living in Malmö at the time, with Lillis in art school and Tore studying to become a civil engineer. During a party that spring, Lillis had had a 'funny turn', as she likes to call it, and cheated on him with one of her classmates. When Tore found out, he simply disappeared, but they made up and got married in the town hall just a few weeks later. And the rest, as they say, is history.

'I'm mostly worried that Niklas doesn't seem to be doing so well,' Bea confesses. 'I don't recognise him.'

Her voice breaks, and Lillis takes over.

'It's that new job of his, sucking the life out of him. He probably just needs a bit of rest and some time to himself.'

'Do you really think so?'

'I know so, love. Why don't you and the girls come out here in the meantime? Niklas can join you once he's stopped his brooding. He promised me he'd sort out those roof tiles before it starts leaking, so he'll have to show up at some point.'

Lillis lets out a hoarse laugh, which makes Bea smile softly. Her mother-in-law is right. Niklas just needs to find his feet in town. A few days on his own and he'll be back to his usual self. It's a much better idea for her and the girls to head over to Gotland before him, and without a car it'll be easier to find tickets. It'll probably do him good to miss them a bit, too, to see just how fun it is to be stuck at home on his own when he doesn't have work to distract him.

In the meantime, she and the girls can stretch out on the sand in Grynge and fill their lungs with sea air. They can plough through books during the day and play table tennis in the attic at night.

'Good, then let's speak again tomorrow once you've booked the tickets,' Lillis says firmly.

The lump in Bea's throat immediately rears its head again, and she tries to force it back.

'What is it, sweetie?'

All she can manage is a pathetic croak.

'There's no need to get upset, Beamea . . .'

Bea swallows again.

'It's just . . . I really don't recognise him and I'm . . . I'm so afraid of losing him.'

Lillis is quiet for a moment, as though she is choosing her words carefully.

'These things happen when you've been together a long time, it's perfectly normal. All you can do is be patient. Don't let go, but give him space. I love that song, what's it called . . .'

She knows exactly which song Lillis means. 'If You Love Somebody Set Them Free' by Sting. Bea herself has never been a fan. Surely freedom also involves responsibility? Taking responsibility for those you love? She doesn't have a problem with giving other people space, but leaving your partner in the lurch? That's just cowardly. Really bloody low and cowardly. Although she can speak freely and criticise Niklas, Bea knows she can't go too far. There's always a limit, even for Lillis.

'Come and stay with us,' says her mother-in-law. 'We're dying to see you. Tore will pick you up in Visby.'

GARNISONEN, STOCKHOLM

THE TEMPERATURE HAS RISEN to thirty-three degrees in the shade. The entire city is baking hot, and it feels as though the soles of Bea's shoes might melt as she walks the short distance between Banérgatan and the office on Karlavägen.

The Garnisonen complex is usually bustling with business people, but, from a distance, it looks eerily deserted today, the red revolving doors at a standstill. Bea has worked there for years, but the same memory still rears its head every time she approaches the building: of Jacob, the day he tried to teach her how to skateboard. She can just see him, effortlessly zigzagging between the pillars, almost as though the board he'd bought with the money from his weekend supermarket job was an extension of his body.

Their parents had thought he should save the money instead, that skateboarding was a dangerous hobby, but the injuries he sustained were a small price to pay for the thrill it brought him. His eyes in that moment, so full of freedom and joy as he sped past her – that's what Bea remembers.

She takes the lift up to the Red Cross office on the seventh floor. The entire department is currently on holiday, and the stale air hits her like a brick wall. An aid organisation never really stops, of course, but most people not on leave prefer to work from home at this time of year. Bea finished her last updates to the home page the week before her holiday began, and if there are any issues, she can always resolve them remotely.

She is here today because Niklas has agreed to meet her before she and the girls leave for Gotland. It's absurd to think that he has to 'agree' to meet her, that the person she is closest to doesn't actually want to see her. He wants to be alone so he can think, whereas Bea needs the exact opposite. He doesn't want to come home, either, so meeting at her workplace was the compromise she had to make in order for them to talk in peace.

It's far too hot to be indoors, so she goes down to meet him by the entrance to number 108. They take the lift up to the fifteenth floor, standing quietly and awkwardly side by side. It feels so odd, because Niklas would usually put an arm around her or take her hand, but today they don't touch at all. They don't chat, either. His jaw seems tense, and the crease on his forehead is deeper than usual. Does he look older, or is it just her imagination that he has more grey hair than he did a few days ago?

'Wow, what a view.' Niklas's eyes scan the roof terrace.

'You can see the Djurgården Canal over there,' says Bea, making a vague gesture south.

Niklas nods, and she feels stupid for pointing out something so obvious. However strange and uncomfortable
their silence might be, that's nothing compared to how
odd it is to make small talk with her husband. Bea can't
remember them doing it before, can't remember ever even
thinking about how to talk to him. During all their years
together, they have always been in constant, fluent conversation, but now everything feels so artificial and unnatural.

And yet she has to try. That's why they're here.

'How are you?' she hesitantly begins.

'Yeah, I'm fine. You?'

'I'm really looking forward to getting away, though
obviously it's sad you're not coming with us.'

'I'm sorry about that.'

This is the first time Niklas has uttered anything close
to an apology, and that gives her a flicker of hope. She
had been planning to wait, but his words leave her feeling
so happy that it just slips out.

'I've actually booked you a ticket for next Thursday, so
you can have an entire week to yourself. We can tell the
girls you've got a bit more work to do here before you
join us.'

The look on his face changes. 'You've booked me a
ticket?'

'The ferry will sell out otherwise. I got you a flexi ticket,
so you can change it.'

He seems uncomfortable, clenching his jaw. How can
he be annoyed with her for helping him with his ticket?
If his plan was to book it last minute, there is no way he

would ever get one. The tickets always sell out in a flash. Bea doesn't understand the problem; he can always rebook for another day if he wants to. But Niklas seems so angry, just like he did at Freddie's office the other night.

Two women come out onto the terrace and sit down at one of the tables with their coffees. They look vaguely familiar, but there are hundreds of people working in the Garnisonen complex, and Bea knows next to none of them.

She and Niklas move over to the other side of the rooftop in silence, taking a seat on a bench so that they can talk in peace, now with views out towards the Kaknäs Tower. She knows she needs to focus on finding a solution, and she makes a real effort not to sound angry or annoyed.

'Can't you tell me what's going on? I'd really like to help if I can.'

Niklas wrings his hands, twisting his wedding ring. 'I'm not really sure myself.'

'No?'

'No, sometimes you just don't know. Weird, huh?'

Bea didn't mean her question to sound critical; she mostly just wanted to reassure herself that she had understood the situation correctly.

'I appreciate that,' she says, 'but I'm just wondering what you're thinking.'

Niklas crosses his legs the other way, twisting his wedding band again. His face seems to soften briefly, like a door being cracked open for a moment.

'I'm thinking that I'm not OK and that I need to work out why.'

Bea nods. She agrees with him there. He isn't OK and clearly needs help.

'Should we book an appointment?' she asks. 'With Robert?'

'No, I'll sort it.'

'With another psychologist?'

'I said I'll sort it.'

'But if you're struggling, you really should speak to someone. Especially if you're not going to talk to me.'

Bea's voice becomes shrill, and it's as though the door in Niklas slams shut. His face hardens. She will have to make a real effort to stop the conversation from spiralling out of control now, becoming as futile as their last one – despite the fact that it feels crazy that she's trying to fix a problem that he caused.

'OK . . . but what's your plan?'

'To try to feel good again.'

'That's great, because I've been saying all spring that you work too much, that—'

Niklas raises a hand to stop her. 'This has nothing to do with work.'

'Oh?'

'Or not just work, anyway.'

'Not just?'

'Like I said the other day, this is about us.'

The fear is like a red-hot poker in the pit of her stomach.

'But we're OK, aren't we?' she asks. 'In the grand scheme of things . . .'

Her voice sounds weak and pathetic, pleading. It's pretty obvious that they aren't doing particularly well right now, not even in the grand scheme of things, and Niklas confirms that with what sounds like a snort.

'I just don't understand,' she continues. 'Can't you . . . explain?'

'That's the problem: you don't understand.'

'But how am I . . . Please, Niklas, give me a chance here.'

Bea hates the sound of her own voice, hates everything about herself. Without a single scrap of dignity or logic, she is desperately trying to find a lifeboat to cling on to, ready to do whatever it takes to avoid drowning.

'If there's anything I can do, I'll work on it, you just have to tell me what it is . . . I'm really sorry if I've . . . you know, contributed to you feeling . . . like this. I just want you to be happy, honey . . .' Her voice breaks and she trails off, the urge to cry making her throat ache.

'Please, Bea . . .'

Niklas puts his hand on hers. The first touch in what seems like an eternity, which only makes it harder to keep it together.

'Sorry,' he whispers. 'I don't want you to be upset.'

There is no stopping the tears now, and in the end, she gives in. She leans towards Niklas, who puts an arm around her shoulders.

'Hey . . . It's going to be OK, Bea. It's all going to be OK.'

That is what she needs to hear: that it's all going to be OK. That the old Niklas is still in there somewhere, behind this strange, stiff version of him who turned up without warning. The one who comforts and loves her, who takes care of her and is always there for her. He's in there somewhere, the world's kindest man, and he still loves her.

Going out to Gotland with the girls feels OK now, like the right decision. Bea is relieved, and Niklas seems to feel the same way; he even promises to give them a ride to the ferry terminal.

BANÉRGATAN, STOCKHOLM

NIKLAS SEEMS TO BE in a good mood when he comes to pick them up the next day. He hugs Alma, then Alexia, and tells them both how much he loves and misses them.

Bea stands off to one side, waiting her turn like an awkward child. Waiting for him to embrace her and say that he loves and misses her too. But instead he just nods, says a quick hello, loads their luggage into the boot and then walks around to the other side of the car. She gives him a confused look, but he avoids her eye as he chats with the girls.

'Are you excited? It's going to be great, isn't it? You'll have to take a dip for me once you get there.'

They fasten their seat belts, pull out onto Valhallavägen and head south, towards the ferry terminal in Nynäshamn. Niklas turns on the radio, something he never normally does. In the rear-view mirror, Bea sees the girls gazing out through the windows, each with their headphones on. She leans forward and turns down the music. Niklas doesn't seem to notice.

'Are you OK?' she asks cautiously.

'Yup.'

He drums the wheel while he waits for the lights to change.

'Have you spoken to Lillis?' she asks.

'About?'

'This,' says Bea, gesturing to them both. 'About why you aren't coming.'

'No, but I'm guessing you have.'

Niklas turns the volume up again, and they spend the rest of the drive in silence.

Yes, she has spoken to Lillis. But it's still a little strange, she thinks, that he hasn't called to explain.

When they reach Nynäshamn, he hugs the girls again.

'See you soon,' he says, without specifying when.

Alexia looks up at him with a certain envy in her eyes. 'God, it'll be awesome to have the whole place to yourself.'

'Boring without you, though.'

'True.'

Niklas clears his throat. 'Plus I have to work, so maybe you should be feeling sorry for me.'

He just lied without batting an eyelid, Bea thinks, though she quickly realises the white lie was her suggestion.

The girls head off towards the waiting area with their bags, leaving Bea and Niklas behind.

'I wish you could come too . . .' she says.

Niklas tries to smile, though his mouth is so stiff, it looks more like a grimace.

'Yeah.'

She can hear that he doesn't mean it, that he is saying it just to get rid of her, the way a parent might lie to a small child to prevent any tears at nursery.

'Are you going to come out and join us next week?' she asks lamely.

'I don't know.'

'Because otherwise you'll need to rebook . . .'

'OK.'

'OK? So if not, when?'

'I don't know, Bea!'

She flinches as he raises his voice. A family walking past with their luggage and an old Labrador glance in their direction. They have become *that* couple, the one that argues in public. With that, the lump in Bea's throat is back with a vengeance.

'Please . . . not this again,' Niklas mutters, half to himself.

Bea gasps for air. What does he think, that her getting upset is some sort of desperate attempt to gain sympathy?

His eyes no longer seem anywhere near as kind as they did yesterday, when he said sorry, tried to comfort her and tell her that everything would be OK. The look on his face now suggests something else entirely. *Are you seriously playing this game? Again?*

'I just want to know roughly when you might be coming,' she says, keeping her voice as calm as she can. 'The girls do too.'

But Niklas doesn't seem to be listening. He just shifts impatiently from one foot to the other and glances back over his shoulder to the car.

'Listen,' he says, 'I have to go, speak later.'

He gives her a quick, awkward hug, mostly to calm her down and send her on her way instead of causing a scene.

Bea stays where she is, watching as he pulls out of the parking space and drives away without so much as a second glance in her direction.

*

She isn't quite sure how they boarded the ferry, but somehow they end up sitting in the front lounge, among the tourists and young families. Three seats together, in blue and orange synthetic fabric. Bea stares out at the waves as though paralysed. Neither of the girls says anything, but she is sure they must be able to sense what is happening. She should say something, she thinks, try to reassure them or explain, but she can't bring herself to tear her eyes away from the breakers outside.

A light touch on the arm makes her jump.

'Do you want anything, Mum?' Alma asks. She and her sister are going to the cafeteria to buy sweets and sandwiches.

Bea shakes her head; she isn't hungry or thirsty.

She remains where she is in the ugly blue recliner, staring up at the ceiling-mounted TV screen, where an old rom-com starring Ethan Hawke is playing. There is no sound, but it's still marginally better than the waves outside. She lets herself get caught up in the drama, trying to breathe deeply to help ease her anxiety.

Ethan is just about to knock on Greta Gerwig's door when Alma's blonde head appears, blocking the screen. She holds out a tray.

'I got you a tea. You usually like that.'

'That's sweet of you. Thanks, honey.' Bea gets up to give her daughter the middle seat. 'Where's Alexia?'

'She wanted to have a look around.'

'OK. I'll be right back, I'm just going to the toilet.'

Bea walks past row upon row of seats, all full. She can no longer see the mainland, which means there is now a whole sea separating her from Niklas. She makes her way through to the toilets and hurries into an empty cubicle, feeling queasy again. What little she has in her stomach immediately comes spilling out, spattering the toilet seat, and Bea whimpers, then flushes and blows her nose.

When she opens the door to the cubicle, she meets Alexia's eye in the mirror above the sinks. She tries to come up with an explanation for the sounds she just made, but her daughter turns and walks away before she has time to open her mouth.

Bea stares at herself in the mirror, looking back over her shoulder to the empty cubicle behind her. The low rumbling of the engine reverberates through her body, wrapping her up in a quivering cocoon. A familiar sound on a familiar journey – only this time nothing is the same. She and the girls have made this journey without Niklas before – he often stays in town to work – but the difference now is that he hasn't stayed because he has to; this time, he doesn't *want* to be with his family. He doesn't want to be with *her*.

GOTLAND

LILLIS SENDS A MESSAGE to say that Tore's back is playing up and that she has a studio full of tourists, so Hampus will be picking them up from the terminal in Visby instead. The minute Bea spots him waving in the arrivals hall, everything suddenly seems a little easier. Niklas's little brother is tanned and happy, with curly brown hair and a kind smile, the same gap between his front teeth as Tore.

'Hello, who are these strangers?' he shouts. 'And where are the two little girls who came to stay last summer?'

The mood immediately lightens. Alma and Alexia seem to soften as Hampus hugs them, and the difficult, tense atmosphere from the mainland is forgotten. Hampus has always been the twins' favourite, possibly because he is the most playful and carefree of their uncles.

Niklas was fifteen and Henrik – or Henke as he is known to family – seventeen when he was born. Lillis was well into her forties at the time, and he wasn't planned. A surprise baby, with a serious age gap. He grew up virtually an only child, without any real bond with his siblings. Lillis and Tore were older and wiser, and he was often left to his own devices. For anyone less secure in themselves, that probably would have been damaging, but Hampus has always been a free spirit, with a calmness and an inner grounding that makes him a pleasure to be around.

In some ways, it feels like he is as much Bea's little brother as Niklas's; he was only five when they first got together, after all. He is a grown man now, but, unlike his older brothers, he has neither started a family nor gone to university. He spent most of his childhood in Lillis's studio, running barefoot through the clay dust and playing with her broken ceramics. It isn't surprising that he decided to follow in her footsteps, experimenting with the potter's wheel himself.

*

Bea can smell the barbecue the minute they pull up on the gravel outside the house. Henke waves to her from the ruins as they get out, and Sus is in the sunroom, with the drinks table ready and waiting. Something yapping and wet brushes up against Bea's legs, and she bends down to stroke Otis, only managing to graze the Jack Russell's rough fur before he darts off again.

A couple of tourists emerge from the studio with their purchases wrapped in paper. Lillis follows them out, and her face breaks into a smile when she spots Bea and the twins.

'My girls!'

Bea knows that Lillis is talking as much about her as she is the twins. Her mother-in-law's arms are open to all three of them, and when Lillis says that she has missed them, she really means it. What a difference to their goodbye back in Nynäshamn. Like a child, Bea runs towards her mother-in-law's embrace.

'Everything will work out just fine, my dear. Everything will be just fine.'

The cousins come out, and there is more hugging. Hedda is a year older than Alma and Alexia, Olle one year younger, but they have always been close – despite the fact that they only see one another during the summer holidays, when the family comes back to visit from Brazil.

Another car pulls up in the yard. Bea squints over to it, and though she knows it can't possibly be Niklas, she still feels a flicker of hope. Imagine if it's him after all. He could have changed his mind and decided to surprise her. But no, it's just another group of tourists, here to buy some of Lillis's sought-after ceramics.

'Let me just see to them, then I'll shut up shop for the day.'

Lillis hurries over to the studio, and Bea watches as the four cousins disappear into the house together, heading upstairs to their domain. She can hear Hedda and Olle chattering away, wanting to know everything about Alexia's film role, Alma asking whether Hedda can teach her how to make the bracelets she sells online. They are no longer children; they're teenagers. The house might be the same as ever, but the gangly bodies stumbling inside, their long limbs like fast-growing shoots, are a reminder that time marches on. That everything changes.

'Do you really expect me to drink all this on my own?'

Sus drifts down from the sunroom with a smile and a carafe of rosé wine. She is wearing a simple, brightly coloured sarong, an expensive silver necklace accentuating her tanned collarbone. Yet another set of arms for Bea to land in.

'We were thinking of having an early dinner, given you've been travelling? Lamb entrecote and couscous salad.'

Bea nods appreciatively, though, in truth, she still doesn't have much of an appetite.

'Sounds perfect. Is Tore doing any better?'

'Still flat out in his room. He's been completely floored for the past few days.'

'Poor thing. I'll pop up to say hello later.'

'He's not in the best of moods.' Sus pulls a slight face and rolls her eyes.

Unlike Bea, she often finds her parents-in-law a little irritating, possibly because she likes everything to be structured and neat, whereas Tore and Lillis prefer a more bohemian lifestyle. The irritation is actually mutual sometimes. 'The old folks' never come out and say it, but between the lines, Bea knows that they are critical of the life their eldest son and his wife have chosen. Living in the most exclusive part of Rio de Janeiro, their home in such stark contrast to the slums nearby. Henke's well-paid job as MD of an American shipping company, with all the bonuses and tax breaks that entails. Sus's role as the housewife, with staff working for a pittance. The kids' private schools.

Fifteen years ago, when the girls were only small, Bea and Niklas went to visit them there. It was a fantastic, if eye-opening trip. It had been hard to ignore the vast gulf between the widespread poverty and the family's home in a gated community, and they never quite managed to get used to the driver who took them everywhere, nor the staff who waited on them hand and foot. The trip proved a kind of turning point for Bea, who realised that she needed to do something meaningful once she got home. Not just any old job; one that made a difference. The position with the Red Cross turned up not long later, and her life finally gained purpose again – after Jacob.

In some ways, she has Henke and Sus to thank for that.

'How are you?' Sus asks, filling Bea's glass and giving her a sympathetic glance.

'Yeah, I . . . I'm OK . . . Niklas has had a pretty tough spring, so he, uh, isn't quite his usual self, and I don't know . . . Maybe he just needs to find his feet . . .'

'Henke went through something similar a few years back.'

Her words pique Bea's interest. This is the first she has ever heard about this.

'Came home one day and said he wanted a divorce,' Sus continues, taking a large sip of her wine. 'Some sort of midlife crisis. Nothing was right – me, his job, the country.'

'So what did you do?'

'I said no.'

Sus is deadly serious as she says it, making it sound so self-evident, the way only she can.

Bea glances over to the ruins, where Henke is struggling with the meat in the haze from the barbecue.

'No?' Bea repeats.

'Yup. I refused, and then it all blew over. He just needed to get it out of his system. Honestly, so many people end up getting divorced for no reason.'

Bea feels like she needs to clarify, to stop her sister-in-law from getting the wrong end of the stick.

'I think he's just burnt out. We're not getting divorced or anything like that.'

Sus looks up at Bea and smiles. 'Of course not.'

*

Bea sleeps restlessly that night. Every time she wakes, she reaches for her phone to check whether Niklas has been in touch, but the display is as empty as his side of the bed.

When the girls were younger, they had a couple of child-sized beds in this room, but as they got older, Tore transformed the spacious attic into a room for the cousins. Somewhere for 'sleep and play, but mostly play', as he put it. There is space for everything up there, from beds to ping-pong tables, pinball machines and sofas, perfect for teenage lounging and horror film marathons.

The cousins' closeness. Henke and Sus. Lillis and Tore's life's work, the limestone house and the studio. Hampus, who always manages to make everyone happy. Bea tries to take comfort from the fact that she is surrounded by family, a safety net that will catch her if she falls – no matter what.

She gets out of bed and walks over to the window. Pushes back the blackout curtain. It's five in the morning, and beyond the old windmill on the other side of the meadow, the burning dawn has painted the sky pink. All she can hear are a couple of cows lowing to each other over in the neighbour's farm. The cousins' giggling and chatter died down a few hours ago, not long after the wine-fuelled babbling from the ruins.

Bea stayed up with the others for a while, but after an hour or two, she excused herself and went to bed. Not that it hadn't been enjoyable – even Tore came out to join them, despite his back pain. She was just so exhausted from all the worrying and insomnia of the past few days, and here, in the room she and Niklas share, she could finally lie down and relax a little.

When Henke and Sus built their own house on the property, Bea and Niklas ended up with an entire floor to themselves, a space they could do up as they liked. It was another display of generosity from Tore and Lillis, but there was also an ulterior motive to it. As Tore explained: 'It's purely selfish, because this way you'll want to come and stay with us.'

What a contrast to Bea's own parents, who never do anything but whine. Either she and the girls don't visit their place in the country often enough, or it's all too noisy and difficult when they do. Their lives centre around dissatisfaction, whatever it might be about. Even when Jacob was still alive, her parents had always felt hard done by for one reason or another, her mother in particular.

Bea is usually grateful to have so much space to herself at Hogreps, but it feels almost overwhelming this morning – even though Tore, Lillis and Hampus are just below her, the kids in the attic above her head. Even Henke and Sus are only a short walk away, right beside the barn. Everyone is here. Everyone but Niklas.

Bea pulls on his old dressing gown and pushes her feet into a pair of wooden clogs, things that have been waiting for her since last summer and the summer before that. Her Gotland clothes, the items that never leave. Always ready to remind her of summer and of holidays. The scent of the fabric, having hung unused all winter, impregnated with summer meadows and old limestone. Clothes that are never used anywhere but here, and which carry the memory of brightness and relaxation. Of the sleep-deprived early years and quiet lovemaking on warm July nights.

She pulls the dressing gown tight around her waist and allows the memories to come flooding back. Of yearly trips to Hoburgen, the sea stacks and lunch at the creperie in Hablingbo. Of car rides to Hemse to buy food and alcohol, a moment to themselves while Tore and Lillis watched the girls. Even the most boring, day-to-day activities were fun so long as she and Niklas did them together. She still believes that, even if it's just going to the tip to get rid of junk.

When she opens the front door, Otis bolts outside before Bea has time to stop him. She leaves the door ajar, like she would for a cat. That way, he can head back inside whenever he gets sick of chasing rabbits.

The old Monark bicycle is leaning against the barn wall, and Bea climbs on and sets off down the gravel track towards Grynge. The air is mild, despite the early hour. She leaves the bike by the barrier at the edge of the nature reserve and walks down to the beach. The gravel track transforms into a woodland trail, needles giving way to fine sand, the sea nothing but a soft whisper beyond the trees at first, becoming a jubilant roar as the glade opens out.

She kicks off her clogs and feels her feet sink into the cool sand. It won't be long before the sun starts to warm it, and by afternoon, the beach will be so hot it burns. Bea can make out the sea and the horizon through the reeds, the little hollow where they usually sit just off to one side.

Right then, she spots Otis racing along the beach towards her, his fur sopping wet. He must have followed her without her noticing, and before she has time to take cover, he hurls himself into the hollow and rolls himself dry in her arms. Niklas's dressing gown is quickly soaked and sandy.

Bea hears the reeds shake, and catches a glimpse of a grey plait behind a clump of grass in the distance. Lillis emerges with her thermos and basket hanging from her arm, and Bea feels an immediate sense of calm.

*

Everything is almost like normal at Hogreps. The days pass, filled with one familiar activity after another: relaxing on the sand, swimming, eating, planning meals, shopping, barbecues in the ruins, a bit more relaxing on the sand. Bea tries to keep herself busy in an attempt to avoid thinking about all the things she can't control, but it proves tricky, her mind constantly creeping back there, unable to stop herself from peering over the edge of the abyss.

As promised, she clears out the old smithy to make more room for Lillis's ceramics. The little stone building is full of leaky air mattresses and rusty barbecues, punctured footballs and empty bottles. Bea hauls everything out onto the grass to sort it into three piles – repair, toss and save – and anything destined for the tip ends up in the back of Lillis's pickup.

On the other side of the lawn, Tore is busy scraping flaking paint from the wall of the house, slightly stooped over and with a hand pressed to his back. It's clear he is in pain – his lumbago hasn't eased, despite the fact that almost a week has passed – but he refuses to accept any help.

'I'm fine, I'm just working at my own pace.'

In one corner of the smithy, Bea finds some toys and a pair of roller skates the girls have grown out of. Should she take them back to town and donate them to the Red Cross? Do kids still skate during war? In refugee camps? Or would it be better to—

Her phone starts ringing, interrupting that thought. Unknown number. Probably a cold caller, she thinks, though she answers anyway.

'DHL here, we're outside your door at Banérgatan 37. Stjerne, fifth floor. Delivery from Paola Navone. Rimini deckchair, according to the packing slip.'

The new furniture for the balcony. Bea got a text from the delivery company a few days ago, and she sent a message to Niklas to let him know when to be at home.

'We've been knocking for a while, but it doesn't seem like there's anyone in.'

She checks her watch. Afternoon. It probably isn't because he overslept, in any case.

'OK, let me check. Could you just leave them outside the door?'

'Not without a signature. We'll have to take them back to the depot.'

'OK, just give me a minute.' She ends the call with the delivery man and scrolls down to Niklas's name on her phone.

Shit. Where is he? As the phone rings, she writes a quick message.

DHL are outside! You're meant to be there, where are you? You'll have to go and collect the parcel from some depot on the outskirts otherwise! Hello??

But Niklas neither replies nor picks up, and Bea has to call the DHL driver back. She repeats her request for the chairs to be left by their door, but that is apparently out of the question.

'It has to say so in the order notes, and it doesn't. Sorry. The depot's in Västberga. We'll keep your items for thirteen days, then they'll be returned to sender.'

'Could you wait another five minutes? I just need to get hold of my husband.'

'I've already waited fifteen.'

Bea hangs up on the driver and tries Niklas again. Still no answer. Unbelievable. She even sent him a reminder that the delivery was delayed. It was supposed to arrive in early June, and that was one of the few benefits of him staying in town for a few more days: that he could be there to receive it. Yet now he has to go all the way out to the damn DHL depot to collect it.

Call me as soon as you can. About DHL. IMPORTANT!

*

Lillis has her latest creations lined up on wooden planks to dry in the sun behind the barn. She will eventually transfer them to the kiln for firing, and then she'll glaze them and fire them again. The whole process requires a huge amount of patience, and Bea never ceases to be amazed by the transformation her mother-in-law's ceramics go through. Not even Lillis knows exactly how they will look once finished.

Sometimes the failures or mistakes turn out to be the most successful pieces – a bit like life itself, according to Lillis. Events that might seem catastrophic at first glance can actually lead to something good. Her favourite example of this is her unexpected pregnancy with Hampus, of course, something she often brings up. Lillis was too old, the risks too great, and they decided to abort, only to find out she was too far along. Lillis likes to joke that her 'failed abortion' became her favourite child, and though she is only kidding, everyone knows it is true. Hampus has, as Sus likes to tease, the kind of 'biblical calm only possible in someone loved by God'. He also shares his mother's passion for clay.

Just inside the open barn doors, Lillis is crouching down, working on a lump of clay. Her greyish-white hair is tied up in a messy, pretty bun on top of her head.

'Am I bothering you?' Bea asks.

'Never, my dear.' Lillis holds out another lump of clay. 'Here, take this. The best stress ball on earth. Knead!'

Bea does as she is told, and she quickly discovers that her mother-in-law is right; it really is soothing.

'How are you doing?' Lillis asks.

'Just a bit annoyed with Niklas.'

'What's he done now?'

'He was supposed to be at home when our new outdoor furniture was delivered, but he's not answering the phone and now they've taken it back to the depot. It's all just so stupid!' She bites her lip. 'Sorry, it feels like all I do is moan about your son at the minute.'

'Moan away, otherwise it'll just take up precious space in your head.'

'It's like he refuses to communicate. I don't even know if he's coming tomorrow, whether he changed his ticket.'

Lillis listens, but she doesn't speak.

'I don't want to put pressure on him,' Bea continues. 'But I want to be able to tell the girls what's happening . . . I have no idea how he's doing, because he won't talk to me.' She kneads harder, her thumbs leaving grooved prints in the grey clay.

Lillis stops working and looks up at Bea, her face serious.

'I think you should go home,' she says.

Bea tenses, and the ball of clay gains a twin in the pit of her stomach, a dead weight. Lillis is usually the cool, calm one, the person who thinks you should try to avoid rocking the boat, but she seems anxious.

'With the girls?' Bea asks.

'No, on your own. The two of you need to work this out, I can feel it.'

Lillis wipes a bead of sweat from her forehead. The heat is unbearable, even in the shade, breaking all sorts of records across Sweden.

'I'm sure there's no reason to worry,' Lillis adds, 'but disappearing like this doesn't sound like Niklas. Maybe it would be a good idea for you to check in on him?'

Her words cause the lump in Bea's gut to grow. Over the past few days at Hogreps, she has managed to pretend that everything is more or less the same as ever. Bea has dismissed her anxiety and fears, telling herself that it's all just in her head because everyone else seems so convinced

81

that Niklas is simply burnt out. But if Niklas's own mother is worried . . . then Bea is terrified.

Lillis seems to read her thoughts.

'I just mean that sometimes it's good to be left alone, and sometimes it isn't. Not for too long, anyway. He's all alone in this awful heat, walking around with his thoughts. Maybe that isn't so good for him? Sometimes we can think too much, when what we really need is to talk. I can give you Agneta's number, if you like? It might do you both good to see her?'

Bea nods. She knows that Lillis's conversational therapist is good at her job.

'If I can convince Niklas, that is. He didn't seem too keen on the idea . . .'

Lillis pats her on the cheek.

'Then you let me know, and I'll have a word with him.'

Bea suddenly realises that her mother-in-law is right. Of course she should go home and straighten things out with Niklas.

'I'll message him now.'

Lillis shakes her head. 'No, just go. Don't give him a chance to complicate things.'

The lump in her stomach grows again. Bea felt calm a moment ago, or at least sure that she wanted to stay on Gotland until Niklas was ready. To avoid putting pressure on him. But right now it feels urgent – vital, even – that she sees him as soon as possible.

*

The ferry docks in Nynäshamn just after eight o'clock that evening. It feels strange not to say anything, but Bea knows that Lillis is right and that there is a risk Niklas will just try to stop her if she gives him advance warning. He claims not to want any help, after all. The only way she can force him to get to grips with the situation is to go home and confront him, in some sort of solo intervention. When it really comes down to it, that's all an intervention is: an attempt to force the person you love to face up to the truth, without any warning; taking them by surprise in a moment of awakening.

Niklas has cut her off to an even greater degree since they left the city, avoiding all her calls and messages. As Lillis said: it can't be good for him to be left alone with his thoughts. It's far better that they work through the problem together, whatever it is. Bea has already been in touch with Lillis's therapist Agneta and made an appointment. She won't let him get away this time.

It feels odd to get off the ferry and not have Niklas waiting for her outside. Instead, she catches a cab back to Stockholm. It costs her a small fortune, but she can't face the idea of getting on the commuter train right now.

Bea gazes out through the car window, watching the countryside race by. Her mind is racing too. She is both excited and afraid, misses Niklas so much that it hurts. It's the first time she has admitted that to herself, so fully and openly. Until now, her focus has been on just trying to keep it together, but it feels like an eternity since she was last close to him, since he last held her the way he does. Since he last said that he loves her.

It isn't so much the length of time as the distance between them. The lack of dialogue. Niklas shut down, like some sort of border force, with no warning whatsoever. And Bea simply adapted, accepting his odd behaviour and trying her best to be understanding. She *wants* to understand him, but it's like Lillis said: coming to someone's aid when they're incapable of understanding their own needs is also a form of love.

The taxi turns off onto Centralbron. Other than a few tourists strolling along the waterfront, the city centre seems empty. Bea has the sudden sense that she is doing something forbidden, though she has every right in the world to go home to her apartment if she wants to. To talk to her husband.

Niklas has taken liberties she would never even dream of, leaving his family in the lurch. Deep down, it feels like he has abandoned her and the girls. It takes a real effort to keep her anger in check, though she also has a niggling feeling that she is making a mistake by coming back. An odd sense of guilt.

BANÉRGATAN, STOCKHOLM

THE JULY AIR IS like a heavy blanket over Banérgatan as Bea gets out of the taxi with her little suitcase, no cool evening breeze rolling in from the sea to bring any respite.

She glances down at her watch. Almost quarter to ten. What if he's already in bed? What will she do then? Leave him to sleep and crawl in beside him? Wrap her arms around him? Or should she wake him up and demand to talk right away?

She feels the anxiety come creeping up on her again. Is she doing the right thing? What if he gets angry? She hesitates by the door, as though at a crossroads. As though the next step is crucial. That's when it arrives: a text from Niklas.

Hope the three of you are having a good time. Thinking of you.

A rush of happiness pulses through her. Niklas still cares about her and wants to know how she is, for the first time in weeks. There is such a stark contrast between her anxiety earlier and the relief she feels now that he has shown this tiny grain of consideration. It's a sign. Could she have blown this whole thing out of proportion? Made everything much worse than it really is?

She briefly considers calling for a cab and heading back to the ferry terminal, giving Niklas all the time he needs. Maybe it really is as simple as that, though, on the other hand, now that she's here, it would be absurd not to go inside and take the lift up to their apartment. All she wants is to see him.

Bea smiles to herself as she pulls her case up the steps and enters the door code. So stupid, all of this. It isn't the first time she has let her imagination run wild, and she does have a tendency to overthink things. She and Niklas have discussed it over the years, the idea that everything with Jacob could have contributed. The fact that the worst happened right when she least suspected it, suddenly and without warning. Her fear of disaster has been lurking in the background ever since, a backdrop that has followed her through life, causing her to imagine all sorts of nightmare scenarios at the slightest hint of trouble. Perhaps this whole thing has simply grown into a monster in her head, for no reason whatsoever. After so many years together, it isn't so strange to think that one of them might need a bit of time alone.

Now much calmer, Bea opens the heavy oak door and takes the lift to their floor. Maybe they could drink the expensive bottle of Chablis that Calle and Charlotte brought over last time they came for dinner? Sit out on the balcony and enjoy the soft evening breeze caressing their skin. They don't even need to talk. They could just sit opposite each other in their creaky wicker chairs. Niklas could put on one of Tore's old LPs, and they could sip the velvety wine to the tones of Mungo Jerry, like they have so many times before.

In the summertime, when the weather is high …

Bea pushes her key into the lock and turns it slowly. The door opens with a click, and she steps over the pile of junk mail Niklas has left on the hallway mat. The card from DHL is there too, announcing that no one was in when they called and that the depot is in Västberga.

Strange, it isn't like Niklas not to have picked up the mail.

The apartment is quiet, and through the gap between the sliding doors, she can see the living room bathed in golden evening light. Bea drops her key into the silver bowl and notices that Niklas's isn't there, though he does often keep it in his pocket. The air is hot and stale, and she tiptoes across the parquet floor to avoid waking him if he is asleep.

On the coffee table in the living room, there is a bowl of cereal and rancid milk. Alexia's breakfast from the morning they left for Gotland. Bea is surprised that Niklas hasn't cleared it away, and she picks up the bowl and carries it through to the kitchen.

Only then does she realise that something is wrong. Everything is exactly how she left it, and the air is heavy with the sour, musty odour from the dishwasher she forgot to close. Why hasn't he set it running? Why does it feel like no one has set foot in here since she and the girls left?

Bea leaves the bowl on the counter and marches through to the bedroom. Their bed looks untouched, the covers neatly tucked beneath the mattress. The green bedspread is still folded at the foot of the bed, and the note she left for Niklas is still on his pillow.

Come soon. We love you <3
Bea

As she reads the words, her stomach turns. Niklas hasn't been home since she left.

*

Freddie seems surprised when he opens the door to Laterna Films in Frihamnen.

'Aren't you meant to be on Gotland?'

Bea doesn't have the energy to pretend, she wants answers, and she barges straight past Freddie into his office. A young man with slicked-back hair and horn-rimmed glasses peers up at her from behind a large screen. Freddie hurries in after her.

'Please, Bea, he's not here.'

'Where is he, then?'

Freddie gives her a look of pity, hesitating for a moment as though he is debating with himself, before eventually giving in.

'I think he said he was going to Maria's . . .'

'Maria?'

Freddie nods, but Bea doesn't understand a thing.

'Who's Maria?'

'Some neighbour.'

'Maria Axelsson?!' Bea snorts in a warped laugh. 'Are you kidding?'

'No, but I could be wrong . . .' He shrugs apologetically, his gaze wandering.

Maria Axelsson, married to Jonas. Her daughter, Emmy, has been in the same class as the twins for years, and she rides at the same stables as Alma. They have taken it in turns giving the girls lifts to various competitions – or rather, Jonas and Maria have done most of the driving, since Niklas is constantly at work and Bea doesn't have a driving licence.

She and Niklas have always thought there is something slightly overwrought and fake about the Axelssons. They often joke about it when they pass Maria's interiors shop on Skeppargatan, packed to the rafters with boho chic tat and a horrific collection of animal-print cushions and gaudy candlesticks.

Maria and Jonas invited them to a New Year's party at their place on Wittstocksgatan last winter. Their apartment is bigger than Banérgatan, and they almost certainly have a guest bedroom, but why on earth would Niklas want to stay there when he could have their own beautiful apartment all to himself?

Freddie seems distressed, like he has done something wrong purely by virtue of being Niklas's friend and having broken the news.

'Sorry,' he mumbles.

'It's not your fault,' Bea replies, though when he awkwardly tries to give her a comforting hug, she turns and walks away.

She feels almost feverish with confusion as she makes her way back out onto the loading dock. None of this makes any sense. Maria and Jonas Axelsson? They're not even friends. Just acquaintances they occasionally bump into through the girls and the stables.

Bea takes out her phone and scrolls down to Maria's number. It takes her a while – she has her listed under 'Emmy's mum' – and after hesitating for a moment, she hits the green button. The phone rings twice, then goes to voicemail, and she instantly has the sense that Maria is avoiding her.

'You've reached Axelsson Gallery & Design. I can't take your call right now, but please leave a message. You can also email me at axelssondesign@gmail.com. Have a great day!'

Maria's bright voice. Should she leave a message to ask what the hell is going on? Bea is just about to hang up when her phone starts buzzing with another call. Niklas.

Is it a coincidence that he is ringing her right now, or has Maria just been in touch to let him know that Bea is looking for him? Why does it feel like that matters? Surely the important thing is that he is calling?

He sounds a little short of breath as she answers, or is that all in her mind too? As though he has just run up a flight of steps. As though he is nervous. Bea thinks

90

she can hear a slight hint of uncertainty in his voice, too, like he is making an effort to sound the same as ever.

'Sorry about the whole DHL thing, I'll sort it out. Are you having a good time at Hogreps?'

'I'm actually back in Stockholm.'

Niklas doesn't speak.

'Who got to you first?' Bea hears herself ask. 'Freddie or Maria?'

Niklas clears his throat. 'I just saw that you'd called . . .'

She has a thousand and one questions for him, but she can't quite work out how to continue. Can't bring herself to confront him, even though this is her chance and she knows she should. As though, afraid of how he might answer, she wants to cling to her hope.

Instead, it is Niklas who takes the baton.

'It's not what you think.'

Bea swallows. 'I don't think anything. I don't understand any of this.'

She tries her hardest to force the air out of her lungs, but her voice is nothing but a flat, hoarse whisper.

'Maria and Jonas have a little rental place they're letting me use.'

'But why?' Bea can hardly hear herself.

'This seems like a bad line,' says Niklas. 'Can we do this tomorrow? It's late, I'm already in bed.'

She takes a deep breath.

'Why, Niklas . . . ? Please, just explain.'

Silence.

She tries again. More force this time. Petrified of what might be about to come, she pushes on. 'Our apartment is empty. What are you doing at the Axelssons' place?'

'I don't know.'

'You don't know?'

'I just need to be somewhere else right now.'

'Come home, love . . .'

'I don't think—'

'If you don't come home, I'll come to you.'

Another moment of silence.

'OK, see you there in twenty,' Niklas says.

Bea agrees and hangs up before she has time to change her mind. For the first time since all of this started, she is the one making demands. It doesn't feel good, but it's definitely better than being left at the mercy of his unwillingness.

*

Bea can feel his presence the moment she opens the door to the apartment after a lonely bus ride back from Frihamnen. He must have raced over. Niklas is sitting on the sofa in the living room, and he leaps up when she comes in. She pauses in the doorway, and they stare at each other in silence.

Her body starts moving, taking her around the edge of the sofa without so much as touching him, over to the armchair opposite. Niklas seems nervous, which somehow makes her calmer. As though she suddenly has the slight upper hand, at least for the moment.

'Are you sleeping with her?'

Niklas looks up at her as though the question is absurd. 'Come off it.'

'It's not really so strange that I'd wonder, especially since you're apparently living there now . . .'

'That's just temporary, while we—'

'Stop!'

Bea doesn't want to hear the end of his sentence, not under any circumstances, but there is nothing she can do to stop him. Whatever advantage she might have had is gone, and her fears come surging back. It's Niklas who is in charge now, his words that will determine how the rest of her life pans out. He has a new-found power over her, and he ignores her outburst.

'. . . I think we should separate, Bea.'

Her reply comes out automatically: 'No.'

'No?'

He seems confused, like he doesn't understand.

'No, as in no. I refuse.'

This was what Sus did when Henke wanted a divorce. She simply said no.

Niklas composes himself for a moment. When he next speaks, he sounds far more authoritative, as though he were talking to a child.

'I really think it would be for the best.'

'How could that possibly be true?'

'Because we'll be happier. You, me. The whole family.'

Yet another lame explanation that doesn't mean a thing. However painful a straight answer might be, it would be far better than this evasiveness.

'It's *you* who isn't happy,' she says. 'You need help.'

Niklas shakes his head like she has just said something unreasonable. Down on the street, the number four bus pulls up by Östermalmsskolan, the primary school where she, Niklas, Jacob and the twins have all been pupils. The automatic doors open and close with a hiss.

'These things happen,' he says. 'People go their separate ways.'

'We're not *people*! If you would just tell me what the problem is, we could fix it.'

'You're not listening to me.'

Her heart starts racing with both anger and panic. Where does he get the nerve? All she has done these past few weeks is try to make sense of someone who refuses to communicate.

'I've made an appointment with Agneta,' she says.

'Not Agneta.'

'You owe me this, Niklas. You owe it to the girls.'

'Fine, but not Mum's therapist.'

'What about Robert Lindgren, then? The one you spoke to last time.'

He resolutely shakes his head.

The last time Niklas spoke to a professional was after *the incident*, the thing they weren't allowed to talk about at home. A couple whose daughter died of leukaemia filed a complaint against him, despite the fact that it was Niklas who spotted the cancer and made the referral. No matter how much Bea and everyone else told him that he'd done all he could, he was consumed by guilt. He said he really had missed a test a few months earlier, when the parents first brought their daughter to hospital, concerned about a number of strange marks on her body. Niklas dismissed them as bruises, but when they brought the girl back with even worse discolourations, he realised something wasn't right and sent her for further tests. The girl's parents claimed that the reason her leukaemia proved fatal was because it had been allowed to gain a head start. They were convinced that their daughter's life could have been saved if her illness had been discovered sooner.

Niklas's therapy sessions went nowhere, and in the end, it was Bea who encouraged him to find another job, to make the move from Sollentuna Hospital to Sophiahemmet. Things finally seemed to take a turn for the better there, enabling him to focus on his new position, but clearly he has been struggling far more than she or anyone else realised.

For the first time in all their years together, she can't get through to him. Niklas has always been the one to seek solutions whenever they argue or run into problems, but right now he seems to have switched off entirely.

'Are you on something?' she asks, her tone suspicious.

Niklas laughs.

'I have to ask. It feels like you are.'

'Aspirin and caffeine. Real heavy stuff,' he says, laughing again.

Ordinarily, she would laugh with him. They would find their way back to each other, joke about the bizarre situation and say that this was all just a load of nonsense that didn't mean a thing. But Bea can't bring herself to laugh today, because none of this is funny. And Niklas's laugh isn't warm. If anything, it sounds mocking.

'Are you enjoying this?' she asks.

His face turns serious again.

'I'm not doing this because I want to, Bea. I'm doing it because I have to.'

'Have to? It's completely bloody absurd that you've suddenly decided you need to live with our weird neighbours . . .'

'Because I feel like I can't breathe here!'

He throws his arms up in a dramatic gesture, like he deliberately wants to hurt her with this outburst. It hits her square in the gut, knocking the air out of her. Bea isn't Sus, and she has no idea what to say or do. Niklas is her everything. More her family than her own parents have ever been. He was the one who saved her from death. Literally.

'I love you,' she manages to whisper.

Niklas doesn't speak. It looks as though he is crying.

AUGUST 2016

TORE LOOKS LIKE A crooked cheese puff in the front seat of the Jeep, his gnarled hands gripping the wheel. Lillis is beside him, with Otis in her lap. She glances anxiously at her husband from time to time, asking whether he wants to stop for a 'pee and drink break' – despite the fact that they are only driving the forty kilometres from Nynäshamn to Stockholm.

'I can drive for a bit if your back is hurting, Grandpa,' Alexia offers from the back seat, where she is squashed in between Bea and Alma.

'I'm fine,' he says with a strained smile, shifting to fifth gear as they pull out onto the motorway. It's obvious he is anything but, and he rummages through his pocket for a painkiller, popping it into his mouth and chewing as Lillis struggles to take the lid off a bottle of water.

'Are you sure you don't want Niklas to take a look at your back while we're dropping off Bea and the girls?' she asks.

Tore shakes his head and mumbles that it is what it is.

On a normal day, Bea would insist that he came up to the apartment with them, that of course Niklas should take a look, but nothing is normal right now.

She sent Niklas a message to let him know that they were on their way home after an entire summer without him. She has given the girls a variety of hazy explanations about him having to work, but, oddly enough, they don't seem particularly interested. Bea asked him whether he would be at home when they arrived, but he hasn't replied. She doesn't know what she is most scared of: Niklas being there or not.

When they reach their building on Banérgatan, Lillis gets out to help them with their luggage.

'Call us if you need anything,' she whispers into Bea's ear, giving her an extra hug. 'I'll be just round the corner all week.'

'Same to you, Lillis,' says Bea, nodding to Tore in the driver's seat. He waves, weary and pained.

*

There is yet another reminder about the new chairs lying on the mat in the hallway. They have now been returned to sender, and all because Niklas didn't bother to collect them, despite having had the whole summer to do it. Bea is sick to death of always having to be the one who makes sure things get done.

The apartment is like a sauna, and Bea drops their luggage to the floor and starts opening every window in an attempt to create a through breeze. Her eyes scan each room as she moves across them, searching for signs of Niklas, but everything looks the same as it did when she left a month ago.

She finds the note she left him – *Come soon. We love you* – on the floor in the bedroom. It must have fallen down there when she tore back the covers last time she was here. She snatches it up, crumples it into a ball and shoves it into her pocket, then sits down on the edge of the bed and closes her eyes.

A door slams, followed by another; both girls have gone straight to their rooms, and Robert Smith's voice soon starts drifting out from Alexia's. Bea recognises the song – 'In Between Days' by The Cure – with its strangely upbeat tempo contrasting with lyrics that speak of getting old and feeling like dying.

Bea hears someone flush the toilet and start the shower. She opens her suitcase, takes out anything clean and carries it over to the pretty chest of drawers they bought from Nordiska Galleriet last autumn. As she opens the drawer, she stops dead. Niklas has been here, at the very least. All of his socks and underwear are gone, ditto his clothes from the wardrobe. A few empty hangers are all that is left on his side, rattling like lonely skeletons on the rail.

Bea's hands shake as she reaches up and touches them. It's like she has just been punched in the face. Why has this come as such a shock? He told her he wanted to separate; that's why he is renting the Axelssons' place. He wants to be straight with her, that was what he said when she came back to Stockholm to confront him. And yet, safe in the comforting embrace of Hogreps, the whole thing felt more like some sort of abstract, hypothetical future. *We'll see how it goes once summer is over.*

Well, summer is over now, and Niklas has cleared out all his clothes and left. That is a fact. This is really happening, and she needs to try to put a stop to it. She needs to make him understand what he is doing, to see that he is tearing their family apart. He has totally lost control – like some sort of madman.

'Mum!' Alma shouts from the bathroom. 'There's no toilet roll! Mum!'

Bea tries to open the bottom drawer to check whether he has taken his passport and the cufflinks Tore gave him.

'Mum! Loo roll!'

The drawer opens a few centimetres, but then it sticks. Bea can't get it to budge. Her heart rate seems to get faster each time she tugs on the handles, Alma's shouting increasingly shrill.

'Hello! Can someone please get me some loo roll? Mum! Alexia!'

'Alexia! Get your sister some toilet roll!' Bea roars as she yanks the handles.

She pulls so hard that the entire chest of drawers shakes, channelling all her frustration, rage, fear and disappointment into the oiled Danish teak. Then the draw suddenly comes unstuck. Bea shrieks and finds herself flying back into the bedframe.

*

Ten minutes later, she is out on the balcony with a glass of wine in one hand and a bag of frozen meatballs against the back of her head. Everything went dark for a few seconds when she fell, and she is pretty sure she passed out – not that she has mentioned that to the girls. They're already worried enough as it is and have been trying to convince her to call Niklas. Bea insisted it was just a bump, though it feels like her head might burst.

One good thing about being in pain is that it forces her to think about something other than how strange and empty the apartment is without Niklas. It's odd how a person's absence can feel so physical, as though the lack of Niklas is staring at her from the walls. Then again, maybe that isn't so strange after three decades together.

On the wall in the kitchen, there is a picture from the trip they took to Costa Rica when Niklas turned forty. The girls were only six at the time, and Bea can't quite believe how quickly the time has passed. The photographs in their bedroom are from just after Alma and Alexia were born. Freddie came to visit them in hospital and took a series of beautiful black and white snapshots of the new family. Bea's face is raw from childbirth, puffy from exhaustion and water retention. Eyes glossy after twenty-four hours of pain, but also full of happy hormones. Niklas looks almost hungover, with three-day stubble and dark stains on his T-shirt, probably blood or vernix.

Almost everything in their home tells a story. The big turn-of-the-century cabinet from India is a piece they won at auction before they became parents. It was blowing a gale when they drove it back from Malmö, and the ties almost came loose, forcing them to spend the night at Bea's parents' place in the country near Mjölby. She has fond memories of the trip, despite how chaotic it was.

The olive tree Niklas gave Bea for her birthday a few years back is on the balcony beside her. They often joke that the little tree is moodier than their teenage daughters, and every winter he has to drive it over to Charlotte and Calle's 'plant hotel' – aka their glazed balcony, which is the perfect temperature for Mediterranean plants. Niklas has developed a sweet fondness for the tree, so much so that he even goes over to visit it from time to time. Right now, he probably loves that olive tree more than he loves her.

Bea gazes out at the courtyards, and her eyes come to rest on the Axelssons' building peeping out from behind the tall oak. During the summer, the crown of the tree is so lush and thick that you can barely see it, but in winter, once the branches are bare, they have a clear line of sight to the latte-coloured facade. When they were younger, Alma and Emmy used to wave to each other from their respective balconies.

Bea's phone starts buzzing, and she stares down at the display. *My love.* Not so long ago, that title seemed natural and obvious, but now it is almost absurd.

'Hi, it's me. It's Niklas.'

As though he needs to introduce himself.

Despite everything, Bea feels a small flicker of hope – he has called her, after all.

'I heard you had a fall? Are you OK?'

Of course, one of the girls must have snitched. Not that she can blame them.

'I'm fine. Just a bump.'

'Alma sounded worried. Maybe you should go to A&E and get it checked out?'

That hurts, him suggesting she go to hospital rather than offering to help her himself. Just a few weeks ago, she was someone else to him.

Bea takes a sip of wine. Tries to swallow.

He seems to be able to sense it too, how wrong that sounded.

'Or I can always come over and have a look . . .'

'No, there's no need.'

'OK, but just say the word. Or if you want me to talk to someone who—'

'Where are you?' Bea interrupts him.

Silence.

'What am I supposed to tell the girls?'

'They know I'm staying with a friend.'

'A friend? Are the Axelssons your friends now?'

'I just wanted to check you were OK, but you seem fine, so . . .'

Her pain transforms into anger. At the fact that he isn't here, that he has told the girls he is no longer living at home, without talking to her first. That he isn't taking any responsibility, offloading everything onto her instead.

'Why didn't you pick up the chairs for the balcony?'

'What?' He doesn't seem to have kept up with the change of subject.

'You were supposed to pick them up from Västberga after you missed the delivery driver. I've already paid for them, but they've sent them back to Italy now!'

The other end of the line is suddenly oddly quiet.

'Hello? Niklas?!'

Has he hung up on her without even bothering to say goodbye?

Call time 2 minutes 23 seconds, she reads on the screen, the searing pain on the back of her head shifting to her heart.

*

The cold air from the chiller in the fruit and vegetable aisle is pleasantly cool on Bea's face, and she gives the avocado an extra squeeze in order to linger a little longer. The heatwave is showing no sign of breaking any time soon, and the apartment feels more oppressive than ever. She is also dog-tired. The bump on the back of her head is still tender, preventing her from sleeping on her back like usual.

'Hello, stranger! I thought you were on holiday?'

Her colleague, Inger, appears out of nowhere with a boxed salad in one hand.

Bea hesitates, unsure how to explain the fact that she – a woman who always stays on Gotland for as long as she possibly can – is already back in town.

'We decided to come home a bit earlier than planned so we could get a few jobs done around the apartment.'

Inger suddenly seems concerned. 'I'm here if you ever want to chat, you know,' she says.

Bea isn't sure how to respond.

'I heard about Niklas,' Inger continues. 'It must be tough on everyone.'

Bea finds herself squeezing the avocado again. Has Niklas been talking to people about this? Even though they still haven't decided what's what? She hasn't been part of any decision-making, that's for sure. Is there some sort of rumour mill or something centred around Karlaplan?

'Niklas has been really burnt out at work,' she says, absent-mindedly returning her natural stress ball to the shelf. 'That's all, so I ...'

Inger's eyebrows rise slightly. 'Oh, sorry! I thought it had all gone to shit. Marianne from Finance said she'd seen him holding hands with his new squeeze ...'

'What ... ?'

'Yeah, in that sweet little interiors shop on Skeppargatan. But you know Marianne – she's blind as a bat. A bit senile, too. Either way, it's good to see you. You're very welcome to come back to the office earlier than planned. The whole home page needs redoing for the latest campaign, and they're being as optimistic about the timeframe as usual ...'

But Bea has stopped listening. It feels like the bump on the back of her head has suddenly started growing inwards, putting pressure on her brain like some sort of aggressive tumour. The pain is unbearable.

The interiors shop on Skeppargatan. Isn't that Emmy's mum's shop? Holding hands? Who with? And why? The nausea hits her without warning, with such force that she has to leave. Somewhere behind her, she hears Inger asking whether she wants to join her for lunch.

*

It's as though someone else is in charge as Bea's feet carry her along Karlavägen, past the turning to Banérgatan. The girls have a teacher-training day today, so she can't go home. Not in this state. The robot inside her takes her past Gustav Adolfsparken and the Garnisonen complex. She glances up at the Red Cross office on the seventh floor. Going back to work isn't an option either.

Bea feels a rush of anxiety as it dawns on her that everyone in the office already knows what is happening – or everyone who is back after the summer, anyway. Not just Inger and Marianne from Finance, but Bea's boss, Martin, the project leaders, Caroline and Ulrika, all the others. She pictures their pitying faces and lowers her head in shame. She doesn't want anyone to see her. Her holiday will be over in a few days, and she will have to face them all.

Moving quickly, she walks all the way to Oxenstierns-gatan, past the entrance to the Sveriges Radio building and up the slope to Nobel Park, where she and Jacob used to ride snow racers as children. They crashed into a tree one winter, leaving her with a scar beneath her eyebrow, almost like a boxing injury.

She looks all around, double-checking that no one has seen her, that she is alone, before taking out her phone.

Her hands are shaking so much that she struggles to push her AirPods into her ears. This isn't something she wants to do, but she also knows she has no choice. There is no other way. She hits dial, and the voice on the other end answers much faster than she expected.

'Hi, Bea. I was actually thinking I should give you a call.'

What an ominous coincidence, she thinks as Jonas Axelsson starts talking, not pausing to ask what she wanted.

'The girls have a chance to move up a level in their riding, but that means two evenings a week, plus more competitions and everything that entails,' he says.

For a split second, Bea is relieved. Emmy's father sounds the same as ever as he calmly talks about the logistics of ferrying their daughters around. Marianne from Finance must have seen someone else. Not Niklas. And certainly not Maria.

'I'm sure we can work something out,' she stutters.

'OK, yeah, because it's looking like a pretty chaotic autumn with all the moving and everything.'

'Moving?'

'Yeah, now that Maria and I have separated, it's a bit trickier to work things out, though I guess it's the same for you? Or are you staying in the apartment on Banérgatan? The market's so sluggish right now . . .'

Bea feels like the wind has been knocked out of her, like she can't quite fill her lungs. She slumps to the ground like some sort of shrivelled husk, trying to speak, but nothing will come out. Not that she needs to say anything; Jonas has enough to say for both of them.

He and Maria are going their separate ways as best friends, and he wants Bea to know that he doesn't have a problem with Niklas. In some ways, it's good to know that his ex is dating a good guy. Getting divorced isn't a bed of roses, of course, but it's better than clinging on to something that wasn't working, you know? Emmy's father keeps talking as Bea desperately tries to process the news that Niklas has been cheating on her. So this is why he has been acting so strangely; she has her explanation at last. But it's also utterly incomprehensible.

Bea hadn't noticed any signs before that evening when he failed to come home. Yes, he did a lot of overtime in spring, but that wasn't exactly surprising, given his new job. He was tired and stressed, but otherwise he seemed the same as ever.

She is utterly numb, like she has just been run over, too badly injured to feel a thing. A parallel universe forces itself onto her, one that has nothing to do with her life. Maria Axelsson? That can't be right. She and Niklas have spent years poking fun at Emmy's parents, at how try-hard they are, which always seems so fake and over the top.

'We can meet to do some planning, if you like?' says Jonas. 'Or if you want me to arrange everything with Niklas, I—'

Bea tears out her AirPods and hangs up. She gazes out at the trees, which have been there for an eternity, and whose leaves will soon start to turn yellow. The familiar slope, which is always covered in wood anemone in spring, leaves in autumn, where children still go sledging every winter. She can see down to the street through the greenery. Everything is just like normal, and yet everything has changed.

BRÄNNKYRKAGATAN, STOCKHOLM

THEY SAY A BRIEF hello when they meet outside the building, like a couple of strangers, then stand quietly in the stairwell while they wait for the ancient lift, which seems to be moving at a snail's pace. As they step inside and Niklas reaches to press the button, Bea catches a glimpse of something beneath his long-sleeved T-shirt. She flinches, struggling to believe what she has just seen.

'Did you . . . get a tattoo?'

Niklas gives her a defiant look, and she almost bursts out laughing.

'You can't be serious?'

His jaw tenses.

'Maybe we should just forget about this,' he says, glancing irritably back out into the stairwell.

'No, sorry, I'm just . . . a bit surprised. Please, let's do this.'

The cramped lift struggles slowly upwards, floor after floor. Niklas clears his throat, clearly uncomfortable, and Bea can't help but steal glimpses at his arm, where what looks like a small black twig is peeping out. She is still trying to process the full extent of his midlife crisis. All he needs now is a motorcycle.

'What's it of?'

'Why, so you can make fun of it?'

She tries to restrain herself, to hold back the sarcasm. 'I'm just curious.'

Niklas shakes his head and demonstratively tugs at his sleeve as the lift jolts to a halt.

*

Mona Falk's office is on the top floor of the building on Brännkyrkagatan, just a stone's throw from Maria Magdalena Church. The room seems to be part of her private residence, and the hallway smells like cooking. Bea guesses she must have a tray of root vegetables in the oven.

The therapist invites them both to sit down, then takes a seat in the chair opposite. Mona Falk is in her sixties, her face neutral and a few wisps of pale, staticky hair hovering above her knitted cardigan.

She doesn't speak. Is that her strategy? Part of their couple's therapy? The atmosphere is as awkward and tense as it can be when two people who have lost all faith in each other are supposed to lay their souls bare in front of a complete stranger.

After what feels like an eternity, Mona finally breaks the silence. 'Would you like to tell me why you're here?'

Niklas seems to have developed a new-found interest in his nails, stubbornly avoiding Bea's eye. Bea, in turn, is trying not to stare at his forearm and whatever it is that keeps poking out from beneath his sleeve. He is like a different person. The Niklas she knows and loves would never even think about getting a tattoo. She focuses on Mona instead. The lump in her throat grows, and she steels herself to say at least some of the many things she has been trying to express since she first found out about Niklas's affair.

Though she understands, on an intellectual level, that these things happen, she simply cannot believe it is happening to her. To them. It isn't some one-time thing, either. According to Jonas, the affair with Maria Axelsson has been going on since the spring.

Bea feels disgusted and dirty, for some reason, even though he is the one who has been unfaithful, who should be ashamed. Niklas said sorry when she called to confront him, but it sounded more dutiful than genuine. Like a child who knows he has done something wrong and now needs to apologise because that's what his parents want. Bea herself would hardly be able to live with the shame of having been with someone else; the guilt would eat her alive. Even the *thought* of cheating would overload her with anxiety.

She knows that because it happened to her a few years back, when they brought in a temp to cover for Inger after a knee operation. Mattias was funny, and they laughed a lot. He was at Inger's desk, which meant he was directly opposite Bea, so it was natural for them to talk, for him to turn to her for help and advice. Slowly but surely, Bea began to feel something other than collegial friendship for him, an indistinct tingling sensation whenever she left for work in the morning.

She started making more of an effort with her appearance, something Niklas noticed. That in itself made her feel bad. She had no idea whether Mattias felt the same way, but the simple fact that she was attracted to him – possibly even on the verge of falling for him – was all it took for her to be wracked with guilt.

It was a relief when Inger eventually came back to work and Mattias left, though, of course, she missed him. Bea was also proud of herself for never acting on her feelings. The whole thing passed without incident, and she never doubted her love for Niklas. Anyone could develop a crush, but that didn't mean they would also be unfaithful.

'I just want us to get through this somehow,' she eventually manages to say. 'I haven't forgiven you, but I want to.'

Mona nods slowly and then turns to Niklas.

'What do you make of that, Niklas? Bea saying she wants to find a way to forgive you.'

He continues to study his nails. 'Well, obviously I want her to forgive me, but . . .'

Bea holds her breath. It feels like her entire life hinges on what he says next.

'. . . I still want us to get a divorce.'

'A divorce?' Bea blurts out, her voice shrill. 'We've never talked about that?'

'I told you I wanted a separation, that's basically the same thing.'

'No, because we're here to try to . . . fix things. You just disappeared, I know next to nothing.'

But Niklas just shakes his head and stares down at his damn nails.

'You're shaking your head, Niklas. What does that mean?' Mona asks. Her eyes are fixed on him, but her face remains inscrutable.

'There's no point.'

'What do you mean?' Mona presses him.

'I've already tried.'

'When did you try? When?!' Bea shouts, causing Niklas to glance up at the therapist with a look that says *See, I told you.*

'Could you elaborate, Niklas?' Mona asks.

'I just want a different kind of life . . . but it's like there's no room for that. Everything is always about Bea and what she wants.'

Bea slams her fist into the armrest on her chair. 'So say that! Instead of sleeping with our neighbour for six months and then lying about staying in their rental flat, when in actual fact you were with her the whole time. I know all about it, I've spoken to Jonas. My God, seriously . . .' Her voice breaks. She is insulted. Sad, furious.

'It wasn't like—' Niklas begins, but Bea interrupts him before he has time to go on.

'No? So what was it like, then?'

Mona holds up a hand to tell Bea to let him finish. The calm but firm gesture makes her reluctantly lean back in her chair, arms folded in silent protest.

Niklas lets out a deep sigh and seems to be searching for the right words.

'We were friends at first . . . then I stayed with her on and off over the summer . . . OK, it might not have been *quite* how I said, but I was in the middle of . . . I didn't know how I felt or how I could explain it to you. I was drowning, that's how it felt, and . . .'

Bea snorts and Niklas immediately stops speaking, staring down at his knees with a dark look in his eyes. Shutting himself off.

Bea turns to Mona Falk, seething. 'You see, this is exactly what I mean. It's always like this. How are we supposed to fix anything?'

Mona calmly meets Bea's eye.

'I like to tell the people who come here that both sides need to be willing to work on themselves. But that doesn't necessarily mean they need to have worked out what they want.'

Niklas tears his eyes from his nails and looks up at Mona.

'Fine, but I can't change the way I feel.'

'Anything is possible if you really want it!' Bea now sounds more despairing than angry.

'Feelings come and go in a long relationship,' Mona points out.

'You need to give me a chance, at the very least . . .' Bea begs. 'You owe me that much. Me and the girls, our family . . .'

With that, she breaks down in tears. Niklas looks up at her with sad, guilt-laden eyes.

'I'm sorry. I still care about you, but not like . . . *that.*'

Bea's sobbing becomes silent, now that Niklas has finally opened up.

'Everything I should feel for you, I feel for someone else. And that's not something I can change, even if I wanted to. I'm myself for the first time in years, and a lot of that is down to Maria.'

With that, he twists the knife right where it hurts most. This is way worse than sex. A union of minds. Niklas has a new best friend.

GARNISONEN, STOCKHOLM

September 2016

SHE HAS NO CHOICE but to get used to the unacceptable, forcing herself to go to work, even though getting out of bed feels impossible. Every waking second is painful. It's like being dead inside, a zombie staggering around in slow motion.

All her senses seem off, somehow. She keeps losing her balance, jumping at sudden or loud noises. Sleep is non-existent at the moment, and nothing has any taste. Bea has been struggling to eat and is constantly queasy. Her job brings some semblance of normality at the very least, a sense of being needed and a welcome reminder that there are people out there who have it much worse than her. People who are starving or dying of illness and undernourishment, people stuck in war zones.

Bea might not physically save any lives through her work, but she is still a cog in the machine – even if she does just stare at a screen all day. Letters and layouts merge together, and though the deadline for the new home page is fast approaching, she can't think straight, can't work on it at the pace she needs to.

When the boss asks if she wants to join the others for after-work drinks at Oscar's on Narvavägen, in the building next door to her parents' place, she politely declines, telling him she has to get home to her family. That's half true, because the girls are there. Or rather, Alma is; Alexia is out with friends. Bea is relieved to have an excuse to escape her colleagues' curious questions. Besides, she hopes she might finally be able to focus and get a bit of work done before she heads home to make dinner.

Right then, she hears someone clear their throat from the doorway.

'Did you really think I'd leave you on your own in this state?'

It's Inger. Bea tries to smile, but all she really wants is to be left alone.

Her colleague slumps down into the chair opposite with a satisfied smile, as though she has just done Bea a huge favour.

'We should spruce things up in here,' she says, twisting on her chair and peering around the room. 'Make it a bit more homely, less office-y, don't you think?'

Bea nods.

'Just because we work for a charity doesn't mean we have to ignore our own needs. A few plants, some nice posters?'

'Great idea, Inger. I can bring some cuttings from my geraniums.'

'Perfect.'

There is a moment of silence. Bea knows that Inger has been wondering what is going on ever since their conversation in the supermarket, since the day she mentioned that Niklas had been spotted with someone else, but her colleague hasn't dared bring it up.

'How are you?' she asks now.

'I'm OK.'

'I just wanted to say that if you need some time off, I can arrange that. Caroline can step in and take over, or I'll just work a bit more.'

'That's so sweet of you, but the deadline for the home page is coming up in a few weeks, so that's probably a bit much.'

'Maybe that's precisely why it would do you good?'

Bea bites her lip. 'It's a super kind offer, it really is, but I'm totally focused on work right now. I need it.'

That isn't a lie. Her job is currently all she has, the only thing keeping her head above water. Deep down, she is also afraid that the others will realise they can get by just fine without her. Bea knows that the finances are tight. The global recession means that people are less willing to donate money to charity than before, and there have already been staffing cuts and efficiency drives at several Red Cross offices around the world.

'You know,' says Inger, 'I went through a horrible divorce once, but looking back now, I'm glad it happened. I've never been happier.'

She doesn't look particularly happy, never has. Bea has to admit that she is surprised, though; she has never thought of her colleague as the marrying type. It must have been before she started working for the Red Cross.

Bea tries to force a smile onto her face, hoping to convince Inger that her little pep talk has cheered her up. In actual fact, it hasn't made the least bit of difference, but she doesn't want to upset her colleague. If anything, it actually feels worse, as though Bea has lost a relative and is being told that one day, once enough time has passed, she'll rejoice in that loss.

There are moments when she really does wish that Niklas had just died. In some ways, that kind of grief would be far easier to handle. As it is, she is grieving someone who is still very much alive, still living in the same neighbourhood. Östermalm has transformed into a kind of war zone in which every step might lead her to coming face to face with the enemy, and she deliberately takes detours sometimes, hoping to minimise the risk of running into Niklas and Maria.

Inger leans in and gives her an awkward pat on the arm.

'It'll be OK. Have you signed up for Tinder yet? I can help you, if you want.'

Bea has a lump in the pit of her stomach, and she excuses herself and hurries towards the door, on the verge of tears. She doesn't want to join Tinder. She doesn't want anyone but Niklas.

GOTLAND

As the plane's wheels hit the tarmac at Visby airport, it feels like she can finally breathe again. Right now, this is probably the only place on earth where she can. Bea's safe harbour. She is glad that the girls are with her, too. And she hopes, deep down, that it means they are on her side, though they haven't come out and said so.

Tore's cancer diagnosis has probably played its part too. 'The Rot', as he calls it – something they initially dismissed as nothing but a bad back – is in his bones. A 'real bugger', according to Lillis. He plans to fight it, though they all know it will be a tough battle and that the outcome is far from certain. Still, it's good to come to Gotland and focus on something other than her own pain. Bea guesses that Tore must feel the same way, and that having her and the girls around will allow him to think about something other than The Rot.

*

The apple trees outside Hogreps are all laden with ripe fruit, their leaves starting to turn autumnal shades of rusty orange and red. Lillis has the cider press set up in the old smithy, and there are countless bottles of juice lined up in the kitchen.

'Want some?' she asks, pouring a few glasses without waiting for an answer. 'Dinner will be a while yet. There's also some Hogreps chardonnay if you'd rather have something a bit stronger, Bea.'

Bea happily accepts a glass of wine and takes her bag up to her room as Lillis and Tore grill the girls on everything that has happened since their last visit. She drops her weekend bag to the old floorboards and then slumps down onto her and Niklas's bed, gazing out through the window. Dusk has already started to fall, but if she closes her eyes, she can just picture the view outside. The ruins down below, the mill, the drystone walls snaking across the barren land, all the way over to the neighbouring farm. She takes one deep breath after another. The room smells good. Reassuring, comforting. But there is something else there too.

The crease on Bea's forehead deepens as she rummages through her memories, trying to sort the scent into the right compartment. Is it jasmine? Lavender? No, spicier than that.

She opens her eyes and peers over to one side. On the nightstand beside her is a Voluspa candle in a gold frosted glass.

Clove Spice and Amber Autumn Squash.

Her feet are like blocks of ice, and her stomach turns. Lillis would never buy a Voluspa candle, never mind put it in Bea and Niklas's room; at most, she might leave a vase of flowers from the garden to welcome them to Hogreps. It can't be Niklas's, either. He has always said that scented candles smell artificial, that they make him queasy.

That means it must have been *her*. Maria. She has been to Hogreps. Slept in Bea and Niklas's bed.

Bea leaps up and staggers through to the bathroom, but she immediately spots more objects she doesn't recognise. A hand towel. Lavender soap. A bottle of shampoo.

*

'Oh, sweetie, you're as white as a sheet. Are you coming down with something?'

Lillis is busy cooking in the kitchen. Alma and Alexia are both listening to music through their headphones on the window seat, but Bea walks straight over to the hob and lowers her voice so that they won't hear.

'Was she here?'

Lillis looks deeply unhappy.

'Sorry, love. I didn't want to upset you. They were here last weekend, when we were in town . . .'

Bea swallows. Can't allow herself to start crying.

'We thought it would just be Niklas, but then we real-ised he'd brought her . . . We can't exactly say anything, he's a grown man and . . . But it does feel odd.'

Bea nods, still trying to hold herself together.

'. . . This place is just as much yours,' her mother-in-law continues. 'No matter what happens. Always will be . . .'

Lillis gives her a pleading look and a shrug, as though she desperately wants what she just said to be true, though they both know it isn't. Hogreps isn't as much Bea's at all, however much it has always felt that way. And now Maria has invaded her safe space. Slept in her and Niklas's bed. Her hands have been everywhere: among Bea's clothes, in her bathroom, on the stair rail. Using her conditioner and hairdryer. Everything is soiled. Including Bea herself. The floor seems to sway beneath her.

'Why don't you sit down, love?'

Lillis leads her over to the table. Alma glances up from her phone and gives her a confused look, but she doesn't say anything.

'I'm sorry,' Lillis whispers.

Bea wants to say that it isn't her fault, but the words catch in her throat.

*

The girls head up to the attic after dinner, and Bea wraps herself in a blanket in front of the fire. Tore and Lillis are on the sofa, and Lillis pours three cups of tea as she tries to make sense of what is happening between Bea and Niklas.

'Have you discussed what you're going to do about . . . everything? Has he said anything else?'

'I'm still hoping we'll be able to . . . work things out somehow. That he'll come to his senses.'

Tore shakes his head. 'I just don't know what he's playing at. Absurd, the whole thing.'

'And the tattoo,' Lillis adds. 'Awful.'

'Have you seen it?' Tore asks, turning to Bea.

'No, he wouldn't show me, but she has one too. Several, actually.'

Lillis has a theory: 'I think he's depressed and this is some sort of protest. It all started when that poor girl died, he hasn't been himself since.'

Tore digs a pill box out of his pocket and starts fiddling with it, and Lillis continues her questioning.

'How did it go with the therapist, Monika?'

'Mona,' Bea corrects her.

'Wasn't she any good?'

'I thought so, but Niklas didn't like her.'

'No? Why not?'

'She thinks we should keep trying, that we can save our marriage. But that assumes both of us want it.'

Tore clears his throat. 'Can't you just try to talk to each other, rather than getting all these strangers involved? That just makes things harder, if you ask me.'

'Don't you think that's what Bea has been doing?' says Lillis, giving her husband an irritable but loving shove, the way she often does.

Tore cries out in pain, and Lillis looks horrified. She always forgets how fragile the cancer has left him, how much pain he is in. How serious his illness is.

'Oh, love, I'm so sorry.'

Tore attempts to put on a brave face. It's clear that Lillis wants to comfort and hold him, but every touch just makes it worse.

125

They are lost in their shared agony, with Bea watching them like some sort of spectator. She sees Lillis's despair, her fear of losing her partner, and she tactfully retreats to her room in order to give them some space. Otis follows her up the stairs, as though he too wants to give his owners a little time to themselves. As Bea slumps onto the bed, he jumps up beside her. She never usually lets him do that, but it's nice to have company.

She knows she is self-obsessed, which also stirs up her guilt; her problems are so petty in comparison. And yet it's painful to see Lillis and Tore together. They have always been role models for her and Niklas. Being like them, growing old together, that was the dream. Here, at Hogreps, surrounded by their children and grandchildren. Family. Bea's family, which she gained through Niklas. Now, in more ways than one, it is all falling apart.

DJURGÅRDEN, STOCKHOLM

October 2016

'YOU REALLY SHOULD SPEAK to someone,' Charlotte says as they pass the Maritime Museum.

'I know, but it feels weird. This is Niklas we're talking about.'

'Yes, and he's no longer on your side. He's on the Interior Designer's side. Do you understand that? You need to get your house in order.'

Bea understands; she isn't stupid. It's just that, despite everything, she still wants to work things out with Niklas. And, deep down, she is hoping that he will realise his mistake during the six-month cooling-off period after he submits the divorce papers.

'OK, let's say he changes his mind,' Charlotte continues. 'Do you really think you'd be able to forgive him? The man went behind your back for half a year.'

All Bea knows is that she wants her old life back, the way it was before all this started. It wasn't perfect, and there were times when she grumbled about Niklas – about how slow he was to pull his finger out, how she always had to be the driving force, taking the initiative and coming up with ideas – but he really was great at other things.

Like supporting her, encouraging her, being there for her. He always picked her up when she needed it. They complemented each other, and she misses him. They were a team, they had plans. They were supposed to grow old together.

Bea just wants them to start talking again, the way they always had. None of this strange warfare, the hostility – things she suspects Maria has had a hand in from the sidelines, pushing Niklas right where she wants him.

'I just think it would be weird to consult someone I don't know, that's all,' says Bea. 'Can't you help me instead?'

'I want to, of course I do,' says Charlotte. 'But Calle and I have talked about this. It's not right that we get involved; it would be better for you to get advice from someone you aren't friends with.'

Bea nods. She understands what Charlotte is saying, but she would much rather not have to air her dirty laundry and talk about her wreck of a marriage with someone she doesn't even know. Besides, lawyers cost a fortune. And as Tore so brilliantly and simply put it: why drag a complete stranger into it when they could just talk to each other?

'You're very kind, sweetheart, but you're also incredibly naive,' Charlotte continues.

'Better naive than cynical,' Bea snaps, though she immediately regrets it. 'Sorry. I'm not saying you're cynical.'

'I'm a lawyer, it's my job to be cynical,' replies Charlotte, roaring with laughter – so loud that a passing power walker glances back over his shoulder. 'He'll spend the rest of the day wondering if I was laughing at him,' she says, which makes Bea laugh too.

It's strange, but the weight on her chest seems to have lifted a little. Bea is slightly surprised she is even capable of happiness anymore. It reminds her of Jacob, of Niklas. Of the way he had made her laugh and helped her realise that that was OK, even though she was grieving.

BANÉRGATAN, STOCKHOLM

WHEN BEA OPENS THE door, it feels like she is welcoming a guest, only that guest is Niklas. If she wasn't quite so tense, she would probably say 'welcome home' to lighten the mood, but she doesn't have the energy for jokes. There is nothing funny about any of this. Each time they meet seems more painful than the last. Besides, he is late, and she only has an hour before Martin will start wondering where she is. Bea has asked Inger to cover for her in case she is late from her 'lunch meeting' at home, where she and Niklas have arranged to meet while the girls are at school.

The first thing she notices is his denim jacket. A new wardrobe: a classic sign of change. Pretty pathetic, but hardly unexpected. Especially not after the tattoo. She isn't sure she has seen Niklas in a denim jacket since they were both teenagers, if even then. He has always been a blazer man.

There is something about the look in his eyes, too; it seems different to the last time they met. Softer, more like it used to be, with none of the hostility she has had to force herself to get used to.

That surprises her, because the whole purpose of this meeting is to come to some sort of agreement about the future. Or rather: for her to hear Niklas's plan, what he has decided and what she will have to accept. Because the truth is that although Bea still doesn't want to get divorced, she knows she will have to reconcile herself to the fact that Niklas has ditched her. That he's with the Interior Designer now. For some reason, calling her that is easier than using her name, as though it makes her less real somehow.

Niklas sits down on the sofa with a calm look on his face. It almost feels like at any moment he might turn on the TV and ask what she fancies for dinner.

'How're things at work?' he asks instead, the way he might if he were making small talk with a vague acquaintance.

Bea plays along, answering in the same way.

'We're getting ready to launch the new home page soon, in conjunction with a new monthly donation campaign, so things are a bit stressful . . .'

Niklas nods. 'But you're the best at home pages, I'm sure you'll ace it.'

Bea smiles. It's odd to hear him compliment her, to hear him say anything kind at all. As though the old Niklas is suddenly sitting opposite her. Even his kind voice is back. The man who was always on her side, eyes so full of warmth.

In some ways, this version of him is even harder to deal with. A heartbreaking illusion that he is back, with her, as though nothing has happened. She wants to curl up in his arms and hear his calm voice tell her that he's changed his mind, that everything will be OK.

'Do you want anything to drink?' she asks, more to feel slightly less vulnerable than anything.

'A glass of water, maybe? I can go and get it.'

'No, no, I'll go.'

She hurries through to the kitchen. Takes a couple of deep breaths. She knows she can't allow herself to get too excited, to hope for too much, and yet she also can't help it. What if he really has changed his mind?

When Bea returns with two glasses, he is busy texting someone, a slight smile playing at the corner of his mouth.

'Is that her?' The question comes out as though by reflex, before she has time to stop herself, and Niklas's face hardens. Bea wishes she could cut off her own tongue.

'No, it's not her.'

'Sorry.'

The relaxed atmosphere is gone, and he takes a sip of water.

Bea feels stupid, like she needs to walk on eggshells to avoid annoying him again. Deep down, she tries to cling to his soft side, to that tiny glimmer of hope.

'OK, so where do we start?' she hears herself ask in an attempt to extend an olive branch.

'I guess it's pretty simple really. We follow the law.'

Bea swallows. Any hopes she might have had have just been crushed. Niklas doesn't want her back; he wants to follow the law. Fifty-fifty. She returns to the strategy she came up with before their meeting: trying to convince him to let her stay in the apartment for as long as possible. That way, they won't end up selling it unnecessarily in case he does eventually change his mind. With all the work they've done on Banérgatan over the years, they have slowly but surely transformed it into their dream apartment, a safe space for the girls, their childhood home. Giving that up and losing it forever would be madness. Bea steels herself.

'I'd like to keep living here, at least until the girls finish school. We can always sell it later . . .'

Niklas takes another sip of water and Bea goes on.

'I thought that might be best since it seems like you already have somewhere to live . . . and because, well, maybe it's a good idea to wait a while and see how everything . . . feels. There's the reconsideration period, too.'

'I hadn't really thought about selling,' says Niklas.

Bea's hopes rise again.

'Not at the moment, anyway,' he clarifies. 'The market's terrible right now, we'd just end up losing money. The easiest thing is probably for me to buy you out.'

'Buy me out?'

Niklas starts picking at his nails again, the way he always does when he gets nervous.

'Yeah, or you could buy me out, but that might be tricky, considering your . . . finances.'

'What? But half of it is mine?'

'Exactly. Half the apartment and half the mortgage, too. Considering how much we borrowed, the monthly repayments are pretty big.'

Bea's mouth is like sandpaper. She should have listened to Charlotte. Everything he is saying sounds so simple and self-evident, but she doesn't understand what he means. Why is he doing this? He has already taken everything from her.

When she next speaks, her voice is high-pitched and weak.

'But this is my home too, you can't just take the apartment. I've done all this . . .' She gestures to the pretty turn-of-the-century stucco she found when she removed the plasterboard that someone had nailed over the top during the sixties. She has carved out their beautiful home, inch by inch, centimetre by centimetre. Every lamp and picture, every single object and the position of it, the colour of the walls: all of it was her doing. But she can't convey everything she wants to say, can't get through to Niklas. All she knows is that she needs to stay at Banérgatan. In her home. The girls' home. Their fortress.

'It was just a suggestion,' he says drily. 'But if you'd rather buy me out, that's fine by me.'

Fine? None of this is *fine*! Niklas always promised he would take care of her no matter what. That they would take care of each other. He supported her when she applied for the job at the Red Cross, even though it wasn't especially well paid. Said there was no need to worry, that they were a family. But he is now acting like her finances are nothing to do with him, as though the problem is hers and hers alone, despite the fact that it was always her who stayed home with the girls. She took maternity leave, cared for them when they were ill, spent all summer on Gotland while he worked. Did the heavy lifting at home whenever he'd had a hard day.

He knows all that because it was a decision they made together, for the good of their family. Bea obviously doesn't have enough money to buy him out of Banérgatan, but he knows that too. Her hand shakes as she raises her glass to her lips.

'We've been together thirty-two years,' she eventually stutters.

Niklas nods.

'I'm not the one who wants any of this, so you need to do the right thing,' she continues. 'For me and the girls. Was it Maria's idea for you to buy me out?'

'Don't drag her into this.'

'That's kind of hard when she wrecked our marriage.'

'Our divorce has nothing to do with Maria. I'm going to get some more water, do you want any?'

This time, Bea is incapable of getting up, so she lets him go. As she hears his familiar footsteps in the kitchen, she has the sense that she is about to lose everything, that the apartment will slip between her fingers.

'What's the rush?' she asks once he comes back. 'Can't I at least stay here a year?'

'I've been living out of a rucksack since the summer.'

'But that was your choice! I've wanted you to come home the whole time.'

Silence, as though he can't hear her.

'Please, Niklas. We're a family, how can you do this to us?'

Niklas puts down his glass and gets to his feet, stiff as a robot.

'Think about it. I'll formalise everything on paper so we're both on the same page. I guess you should make a list of anything you want to keep, and we'll divvy everything up.'

PART TWO

NIKLAS

SOPHIAHEMMET HOSPITAL, STOCKHOLM

June 2016

THE BABY'S WET HAIR is thick with vernix, and his wrinkled red skin seems much too big for his little body as Niklas hands him to the new mother. She clutches her son to her chest and gazes down at him in wonder. The pain of childbirth is now nothing but a memory; the miracle of life is here, a brand new birthday to celebrate for the very first time. But Niklas is struggling to muster much happiness, because he knows he is about to cause her more agony.

By this stage in his career, he has seen so many babies with Down's syndrome that a quick glance is all it takes for him to be sure – even if they have become increasingly rare as a result of advances in antenatal testing. He also knows that things are often much better than the parents are able to believe in the beginning. Still, the initial shock is merciless, and for this particular mother things will likely only get harder. She is alone, with no one by her side to share her current joy. That will only make it harder to process her grief for the future she must have imagined, which will now play out in a very different direction.

'Niklas! Room five, now!'

Katta is an experienced midwife, and the panicked look in her eye tells him it must be serious. The rush of adrenaline blunts his exhaustion after the long double shift, and he runs through to the delivery suite a few doors down.

Katta is right behind him, and she gives him a quick briefing. The first-time mother-to-be came in half an hour ago in real pain. The baby's stats were all fine, but the mother has just started vomiting and gone into cardiac arrest.

They hear the expectant father's cries on the other side of the door. 'Do something! Do something, for God's sake!'

Niklas feels another rush of adrenaline, heightening his senses even further. He spent part of his training in the critical care unit at the Karolinska Hospital, and in situations like this, his autopilot kicks in. Emergency caesarean section. Cardiopulmonary resuscitation. Additional life-saving interventions and intensive care.

*

As he leaves the sterile, air-conditioned hospital building a few hours later, the scent of the lilacs growing in lush purple clusters outside hits him like a brick wall. Niklas walks along Valhallavägen in the warm evening air, eventually turning off towards Karlavägen via Jungfrugatan. There is a relaxed, summery sense of expectation around the people he passes. Groups of colleagues and friends have gathered outside Broms, drinking white wine and eating green olives, and by the fountain in Karlaplan, he sees a mother trying to bribe her toddler not to jump into the water with promises of ice cream.

After so many years in the medical profession, he is used to having to switch between worlds. Niklas knows that light and life can transform into catastrophe and death in the blink of an eye – and the other way round, too. Or maybe he isn't really used to it at all. Maybe that was why he worked as a paediatric doctor for so long, to avoid the kind of chaos that reigned over the past few hours. They couldn't save the baby, and the mother is still in a critical condition.

The adrenaline has begun to ebb away, and what comes next is always the worst part. In the heat of the moment, there is no time for thinking; he simply does. Acts. Any thoughts and feelings come later. Maybe taking this job was a mistake after all. He hadn't realised it would be quite so hands-on, but the severe shortage of staff has an impact everywhere, even in the private sector.

The salary and the title were a step up, but he is also paying a higher price. Niklas hesitated right up until the last minute, but in order to be able to afford Bea's new kitchen and the loans they had to take out to pay for it, he had virtually no choice. Sometimes he wishes he could go back to the plodding, comfortable atmosphere of the children's ward in Sollentuna – though it hadn't really been all that comfortable towards the end, as Bea likes to remind him whenever he starts doubting his decision.

Everything got so much harder after *the incident*, even though he was cleared of all wrongdoing and had the backing of his colleagues, reassuring him that he did nothing wrong. The problem is that he *knows* he did. Making mistakes is human, even for doctors, but when the consequences are a child's death, there are simply no excuses.

Niklas lingers by the fountain, walking in one slow loop around it, then another. He is utterly drained, but he tries to muster up some sort of energy – not that he knows what for. He probably just needs a holiday like everyone else, but for some reason, it doesn't feel like five weeks on Gotland will be enough. Has it ever been enough?

He is often even more exhausted after the summer, rather than rejuvenated, as though he is on tenterhooks for the whole trip, trying to keep up the facade that they're the best five weeks of the year. He has spent years trying to lobby for them to do something else, for a different kind of holiday. For him, Bea and the girls to jump in the car and head off to Europe, no real idea where they might end up, checking in to a charming little hotel somewhere and laughing at the disappointments, letting each day determine where they go next. But he has given up trying to convince her now; he already knows what the answer will be.

Bea always tells him that his idea is a naive fantasy that would be nowhere near as fun in reality, that it'd be stressful and draining to drive around in a hot car, looking for somewhere to spend the night. She claims it's much calmer and more enjoyable to spend the summer at Hogreps. Besides, it's what the girls want, it's what they're used to, the only time they ever get to see their cousins. And in some ways, he knows she is right.

A loud shriek makes him jump. The toddler is back, now with an ice cream in one hand, using the other to drag his mother towards the fountain. It's time to go home.

*

Niklas can sense it the minute he opens the door. Sometimes it is almost as though he can sniff out her mood without even being in the same room as her, as though it leaves a scent in the air. Maybe that's just what happens after so many years together.

Bea is busy emptying the dishwasher in the kitchen, but she stops as he comes in. The look on her face is demanding, but he can also see a hint of sadness there, as though he has hurt her somehow. Her jaw seems tense, and he can see her chest rising and falling rapidly beneath her blouse. She is disappointed. No, disappointed probably isn't the right word. She's angry. Furious.

How the hell could you forget to pay the bill? This means we can't go to Gotland tomorrow, the tickets are all sold out!

What he has done is unforgivable, verging on punishable. What was he thinking? They'll be stuck here in this awful heat all week now, rather than having a nice time on the beach in Grynge.

Niklas feels like shouting back at her, telling her there are worse things. Like being a single mother who has just found out that her newborn son has Down's syndrome, for example. Or being the man on the ICU ward, watching over his wife as his stillborn daughter is taken down to a cold storage unit two floors below. He feels like roaring that his head is so full there isn't room for the damn ferry tickets and all the terrible, exhausting planning she has apparently had to do.

Niklas wants to shout, but instead he turns and walks away while she is mid-sentence. He can hear Bea's agitated voice behind him, but to his surprise, he just keeps on walking, down five flights of stairs and back out onto Banérgatan. The feeling is so sudden and powerful: he needs to get away.

How could you forget something like this? Seriously, how stupid can you be? You had one job – I did everything else.

It doesn't matter where he ends up, he just needs to get away. Each step is a relief.

A moment of clarity and confusion. What is going on here? He normally feels sad whenever Bea is sad, anxious when she is angry. Unhappy when she is down. Why doesn't he just stop and apologise like he usually does? Say sorry? He should tell her that he messed up big time and that it's entirely his fault. Take responsibility for the situation and try to solve the problem. But there isn't a single part of him that wants to do any of that. He feels empty inside, like a jug of water that has had the very last drop shaken out of it. He doesn't have anything left to give.

Niklas has had far worse days at work, but the conversation with the new mother didn't go the way he had hoped. He felt oddly switched off and came across much too cold and clinical, not sympathetic enough, overcome by the same sense of emptiness as now. Unable to give what he usually can. His signature, if you like: the fact that he always has such a good rapport with his patients. Flowers and thank you cards, grateful parents who stay in touch for years afterwards.

It was the same with the woman who went into cardiac arrest, whose child died. None of it was his fault, he knows that. She had blood clots on the lungs, congenital heart disease, waited too long to come in. Not that it was her fault either – they didn't realise she was ill. But Niklas didn't take the same amount of time with the father that he usually would. Explaining, listening, sympathising. Answering questions. Answering even more questions, though he had already answered everything. Providing comfort. The kind of thing he is usually so good at. But not today.

*

He crosses Narvavägen and pauses outside the Swedish History Museum. A sudden impulse makes him round the corner of the big yellow building onto Linnégatan, and cut up the grassy slope to the playground where he used to smoke with Calle, Jacob and Freddie in the evenings.

It looks different these days. Rather than a play area, there is a restaurant and a neat garden. Light and bright, fully visible from the street. Nothing at all like it was back then, when you could indulge in various illegal substances and other dubious activities in peace.

Niklas has generally avoided coming here ever since Jacob died. Has it really been that long since his last visit? Over three decades? Was this where it all started and ended? The thing that cost Jacob his life and shaped his own. If what happened had never happened, would he and Bea have still got together?

They had no real reason to start spending time together, but she had sought him out, and it felt as natural for him to take care of her as it did for the rest of his family to welcome her with open arms. In some ways, it was healing for him, too. They needed each other. They fell in love. Celebrated that love. As Jacob would have wanted, they said in their wedding speeches. A glimmer of light amid the tragedy. But, deep down, he knows it wasn't true.

SOLLENTUNA HOSPITAL

One Year Earlier – May 2015

HE DRIVES TO AND from work on autopilot. Along Valhallavägen to Roslagstull, then north on the E4 for most of the rest of the way. It takes less than half an hour, door-to-door – providing there aren't any tailbacks, of course, which there often are. If the traffic is moving at a crawl, it can take anywhere up to an hour.

The commute doesn't really bother him, nor does the fact that there isn't much prestige in working on the paediatric ward at Sollentuna Hospital. The few classmates he still sees from time to time have all gone on to do more impressive things. Nils Almqvist, for example, is now chief thoracic surgeon at the Karolinska University Hospital, and Karin Lage has made an international name for herself in the field of biotechnology. There are times when Niklas is ashamed that he lacks the same drive as his old peers, but it isn't like he is completely lacking in ambition – he managed to complete his studies and find a job in a clinical setting, after all. Is it a matter of fear? Is he afraid of failure? Or is he simply satisfied with what he does and where he does it?

He turns off into the car park outside the hospital. It isn't the most handsome of buildings, but, oddly enough, it evokes a warm feeling in him, something verging on love. A safe little universe where he knows his place. He and Per Alvén, who has become something of a friend, share the workload on the paediatric ward. They used to cover the maternity ward too, but it was shut down a few years back as part of a political cost-cutting initiative. The number of babies being born hasn't gone down – on the contrary – but the politicians don't seem to care about that.

Niklas sits quietly for a moment before unfastening his belt and getting out of the Volvo. The air is chilly for mid-May, giving him goosebumps on his bare legs. Rather than making his way over to the main entrance, he turns in the opposite direction and jogs down towards Edsviken, a green oasis right by the hospital.

It isn't even six o'clock yet, and his first patient of the day isn't due in until eight, but he still woke around four. Lay awake for a while, listening to Bea's calm breathing. If there is one thing he envies her, it's her ability to sleep.

Niklas follows the trail along the shore. The cushioning in his Hoka running shoes is soft and springy, but he can still feel every step in his knees. There is nothing wrong with his fitness levels, in any case; if it weren't for his bad joints, he would probably be able to run a marathon.

Today's run doesn't bring him the sense of respite he was hoping for. His legs are as heavy as lead, and the thoughts he has been trying to drive away refuse to leave him in peace. A tidal wave of fears and problems of varying degrees and scopes races through his mind at such speed that he doesn't have time to come up with any solutions. What if they find against him, if the Health and Social Care Inspectorate is critical and decides to investigate further? If Lovisa's parents talk to the press?

No, why is he torturing himself like this? He knows he wasn't negligent. But he also knows that he could have done certain things differently, that he fell short. Maybe Bea is right, and he should take the job at Sophiahemmet. The fact that he has been offered a management position at such a prestigious hospital proves that no one is taking the parents' claims seriously. It would be closer to home. Better paid. More responsibility, of course, but also more opportunities.

So why the hesitation? Is he just being a coward, as Bea says? Afraid of failing? This is a chance for him, for the whole family. She is right about that. It would mean new opportunities. They could take out that loan, renovate the kitchen. Take the girls to Vietnam over the summer, like he has always wanted to.

The loan. They are right at the upper limit of what they can afford. But with a higher wage, they could pay back more, they could manage it – assuming the interest rate doesn't go up too much, of course. But why would it? No one expects a repeat of the crazy rates of the nineties. But still, what if? Asking Henke for help again is out of the question. Fuck.

He doesn't want to think. Just run. Niklas turns off from the trail, onto a path with more uneven terrain. He ignores the stabbing pain in his knees, forcing his thighs to carry him forward. There, now he can't think about anything other than pushing his fifty-year-old dad bod to the absolute limit, up the hill and over the rocks by the water.

Without warning, the sole of one of his trainers gets caught on a root. He seems to float through the air for a moment, and before he has time to work out what is happening, he is lying in a bilberry bush with his ankle at a horrible, unnatural angle. Niklas cries out in agony.

It takes him a few minutes to compose himself enough to shuffle down to the shore, where he pulls off his trainer and lowers his ankle into the cool water. His foot is throbbing. Will he even be able to make it back to the hospital? It isn't broken, but it's definitely a nasty sprain. Possibly even a fracture. The chill numbs the pain slightly.

Niklas gazes out across Edsviken, where a thin veil of mist is swirling over the calm surface of the water. A few metres away, several crested grebes swim by in search of food. One of the younger birds drops behind, paddling frantically but failing to keep up. By the end of the summer, the little bird family will no longer be intact. One or more of the babies will probably be dead, either because they fall victim to predators or because they simply aren't strong enough. Survival of the fittest.

Do animals grieve? In the same way Lovisa Grenberg's parents are grieving? Or is it just part of the circle of life?

*

He manages to hop back to the hospital building and through to his office, where he slumps down onto his desk chair and studies his ankle. It looks much more swollen now, with a slightly purplish hue. He really doesn't have time for this. Not only does he have patients all day, he is also due to hear the Inspectorate's verdict. An unpleasant yet unavoidable meeting.

Niklas pops a couple of painkillers and limps into the shower in his office bathroom, grateful for the handrails by the toilet for the first time.

It is quarter to eight, and he has just finished bandaging his foot when he hears a soft knock at the door. Bibbi pops her head into the room.

'Good morning ... or ... ?' She glances down at the chaos on the floor with a look of surprise. A scrap of gauze bandage, surgical tape and a pack of painkillers on top of the socks he was wearing during his run.

'Bit of a misstep on the trail, that's all. Nothing serious.'

'Exercise is dangerous, especially for middle-aged men.'

Niklas attempts a smile, but his mouth quickly curls back into a pained grimace.

'Dante Källén is in the waiting room with his parents, but I can reschedule the appointment if you—'

'No, no, it's fine, I'll be right out.'

The idea of cancelling appointments, giving him even more time to worry about what the Inspectorate might say, seems far worse than being busy with patients all day.

'I did a bit of baking, by the way,' says Bibbi. 'Since it's a certain someone's name day today.'

'Oh, congratulations. I'll try to stay alive until this afternoon's coffee break, then.'

'Not me. It's your big day, Niklas *Tore*.'

Bibbi grins and closes the door, and Niklas feels such a powerful warmth in his chest that his eyes almost start to well up. On any other day, he probably would have laughed at the fact that she not only knows his middle name and when its name day is celebrated, but also went to the effort of baking. He might even have poked fun at her, teasing her a little. But Niklas is oddly fragile today, hit by the sudden realisation that it's people like Bibbi that make Sollentuna Hospital such a special place to work. It has nothing to do with the ugly building or the beautiful surroundings.

The whole name day thing is just an excuse, of course. She knows he has a tough shift ahead of him, that today is judgement day. Bibbi understands him, and she also understands just how unpleasant he has found the whole thing. And though freshly baked buns and kind smiles won't solve his problems, they're exactly what he needs right now.

Bibbi is almost sixty-three, and she was already working as a secretary on the ward when Niklas first joined the hospital eighteen years ago. He must have seemed like just another young whippersnapper to her, yet she welcomed him with open arms – despite the extra work he brought with him. Cutbacks were a fact of life even then, meaning that a position had been axed. He and Per were forced to share a secretary as a result, but Niklas has never heard Bibbi complain. If anything, she is the beating heart of the paediatric ward, where the staff have become a little bonus family to him. Niklas, Per, Bibbi, Lena the ward sister, Tove and Joar the nurse.

He looks down at his swollen ankle. God, it hurts. He should probably congratulate his dad on his name day too, he realises.

*

Niklas knows he should be relieved, but instead he feels oddly down and empty as he gets into the car at the end of the day. He has a bad taste in his mouth after too many cardamom buns and just as many painkillers.

The meeting felt more like a health and wellbeing check-in than anything. Christian asked how he was and whether there was anything, in his capacity as manager, that he could do to help. He also emphasised that he, the management team and the rest of the unit were all on Niklas's side before pushing the Inspectorate's decision across the table with a slight smile. They had found no fault in Niklas's handling of the incident, he said. If you pored over every word of the report, it did conclude that the girl's treatment could have started sooner if the cancer had been detected earlier, though, on the other hand, Niklas hadn't been directly negligent. His decisions regarding the patient fell within the margin of error. Human error.

And yet the fact remains that Lovisa Grenberg is dead. Niklas knows she had only a slight chance of survival, but he can't stop thinking that if he hadn't messed up she may still be alive today.

He starts the engine and gives the accelerator a soft tap, causing the pain in his ankle to immediately rear its head. He won't be able to drive home like this. He reaches into his inner pocket for the pack of stronger painkillers, the ones containing codeine, though he hesitates for a moment. It probably isn't the best idea to drive after taking such strong stuff, but as long as he takes it easy and remains alert, it should be fine. It's certainly better than driving home with an ankle so painful it makes his vision go black.

Just to be on the safe side, he takes only half a tablet, though he quickly changes his mind and pops the second half, too. As he swallows, it strikes him just how desperately he needs pain relief. And not just for his foot.

*

Bea has a bottle of champagne ready and waiting in the kitchen, and she welcomes him with a smile.

'You're the best, honey! Congratulations!'

Niklas lets her hug him, but he is having trouble sharing her joy.

'I've booked a table at Daphne's,' she chirps. 'I knew everything would be fine.'

'Can't we just eat here?'

'No, we need to celebrate. You can finally put all this behind you and take the job at Sophiahemmet. God, what a relief!'

'I'm not sure I actually want that job.'

Bea pauses and takes a step back. 'Why not?'

'I'm happy where I am.'

'But you've said it yourself: there's no future for you in Sollentuna.'

'Of course there is. I was talking about the cutbacks more than anything.'

'You've been complaining about your job there for years, and this is your chance. It's an amazing opportunity. You'd get to shape the maternity ward, choose your own team, get paid more, escape the commute. And they want you, despite . . .'

She trails off when she notices the sharp look in his eye, though she continues again almost immediately.

'I just mean that it could've been tough if the press had started writing about what happened, if they'd found against you for . . . you know . . . But it's all fine now.'

Niklas slumps onto a chair at the kitchen table, trying to find a position that doesn't make his foot ache.

Bea stares at him with a confused look on her face. 'What's wrong? You've been exonerated!'

'She's still dead, Bea.'

'Yes, and that's not your fault. I really think it would do you good to move to a different hospital; you'll never be able to let it go if you stay there.'

Niklas bites his lip. Why isn't she listening to him?

'I missed the tests.'

'And clearly the Inspectorate doesn't think it was your fault, otherwise they wouldn't have cleared you.'

'OK, but no one knows what might have happened if I'd been quicker.'

'Exactly, no one knows.'

'*I* know it would have given Lovisa more time. Her parents, too.'

Bea doesn't speak, just sips her champagne. She pushes a brochure across the kitchen table.

'This came today.'

Niklas looks up at her. What is she talking about?

'The kitchen Nisse and I have been working on.'

'Nisse?'

'Nils Hedberg, the kitchen designer from Kvänum.'

'Right . . .'

'It's all made from natural, organic materials, to minimise the environmental impact. The entire kitchen would be built in situ. Just look at this, it's incredible . . .'

She flicks back and forth between different designs.

'The company started in this tiny village out east, and now they fit kitchens around the world, it's so impressive. They're even suppliers to the royals, not that that really matters, but it's still pretty cool.'

Why does she always do this? The minute he is going through anything difficult, anything painful, she immediately wants to change the subject. Always has. Whether the problem is to do with work or something he wants to get off his chest about Lillis or Tore, it's as though she is incapable of dealing with it. Is it because she can't be bothered to listen to him? Or has he just spent so many years listening to her and her problems that neither of them remembers how to switch roles?

'So, what do you think?' Bea gives him an eager glance. 'It's solid ash, guaranteed for twenty years.'

'What's wrong with the kitchen we've got?'

'Is that really how you want to live? With things that are just fine? I don't want Ikea furniture or a semi-functional kitchen . . .'

'Ikea furniture? We haven't bought anything from there for years.'

'No, but we still have plenty of it knocking about. My point is that we're old enough to be able to treat ourselves to a bit of quality. It's the same with work – it shouldn't just be OK; it should be fulfilling, shouldn't it? I really think it would be a mistake to turn down the Sophiahemmet offer. You can handle much more than you think, love. We'd be able to do all sorts of things here, too. We could afford a new kitchen, to travel more. It's win-win . . .'

Niklas closes his eyes. A torrent of words. An intense pain. The throbbing in his ankle has climbed up his leg, all the way to his head, like a red-hot wire about to burrow into his brain.

'For God's sake, Bea. Can't we talk about this some other time?'

'Relax! I was just trying to help you think about something other than the Inspectorate.'

'OK, but I don't have the energy to think about anything right now. Not about that and not about a new job or a fancy kitchen.'

Bea seems insulted, her face tense. 'We need to leave now if we're going to make it to Daphne's to celebrate,' she says.

'Seriously! There's nothing to celebrate, for God's sake!'

She looks like she is on the verge of tears, steeling herself to say something, but Niklas can't bear to hear another word. He can't bear to hear that it isn't his fault or that a new kitchen or sofa would make their lives so much fucking better, that he should take a job he doesn't even want just so she can live the way she wants to.

He limps out of the kitchen without waiting to hear what she has to say. He just needs to get away, needs fresh air. Now. Otherwise he'll suffocate. He makes his way down to the street, and if it wasn't for the red-hot poker in his ankle he would probably have broken into a run. Instead, he hops down to the garage on one leg, jumps into the Volvo and drives away. Accelerating is still painful, but as soon as he gets out onto the motorway, he can let the cruise control take over.

Out of sheer habit, he heads north. He is so worked up that he has driven almost ten kilometres before he realises that he has both powerful painkillers and a healthy swig of champagne in his system.

When he reaches Järva krog, he pulls off into a parking area and tries to slow his breathing by counting to himself. He learned the technique during a CBT course he took to overcome his fear of needles when he first enrolled in medical school. *Breathe in, two, three, four, and out, two, three, four* . . . As a sense of calm settles over him, he starts to cry.

For Lovisa. For himself, both out of relief at having been cleared, and because of the pain and hopelessness clawing at him.

He is shaking, his nose dripping onto the wheel, when a message comes through from Bea, followed by a sad emoji.

Where are you?

Shame wells up inside him. What happened earlier? The pressure must have combined with the pain in his ankle to make him blow his top. Shouting at poor Bea, who was only trying to be nice. Yes, it was incredibly bad timing for her to start talking about new kitchens and jobs, but she meant well. She was only trying to help distract him, like she said.

How could she have known that he'd hurt himself on his run that morning? He never got a chance to tell her. He didn't give Bea a chance to understand just how shitty he feels, either. Why does he do this kind of thing? Vanishing on her without a word. It's pathetic. He wants to run away from his emotions, from his anger, but that isn't OK. It's not fair on her. He writes back.

Sorry. Tough day. Sorry.

A series of anxious and worried emojis arrive almost immediately.

At Daphne's with the girls. Worried. Upset. But I love
you.

Niklas wipes his snot and tears from the wheel and clears
his throat. What is he doing here, in a super bleak car
park in Järva krog? Why did he have to ruin the evening
for Bea and the girls when all she wanted was to celebrate
the fact that everything is going to be OK? How is she
supposed to know how he feels? She isn't a mind reader.
Bea is clearly just trying to cheer him up, the way he did
with her after Jacob died. *It wasn't your fault. No one
could have known.* That helped her back then, and now
she is trying to help him in the same way.

His phone buzzes. Yet another sad, anxious emoji from
Bea.

He writes a quick reply.

Love you too. Sorry. On my way <3

He starts the engine, feeling utterly drained. Because of
his day, his ankle, his outburst. What he really wants is to
go home and sleep, but he needs to apologise properly as
quickly as he can. Bea is the last person he wants to hurt.

THE GOTLAND FERRY

June 2015

'DO YOU WANT ANYTHING from the cafeteria?'

Alexia has hung back by Niklas's seat while her sister goes off ahead.

'No, I'm fine, thanks,' Niklas replies. 'I thought we could get something to eat at Strykjärnet once we arrive. It's been ages since we last went.'

Alexia's face lights up. 'Crêpes!'

Bea looks up from her interiors magazine. 'I promised Lillis we'd eat with them. She wanted to wait for us to have dinner.'

'But that'll be so late!' Alexia moans.

Niklas agrees. 'We won't be at Hogreps until nine at the very earliest.'

'Yes, well, we'll just have to be a bit Mediterranean for a change,' says Bea. 'Have a sandwich to tide yourself over. They're excited to see us.'

Alexia slopes off towards the cafeteria, and Bea turns to Niklas with a confused look on her face.

'I don't see the issue,' she says. 'They're your family, and it's been nearly a year since we last saw Henke and Sus.'

'I know, but we'll be with them all summer and I'm exhausted. I was looking forward to something a bit more relaxed this evening, just the four of us; it's always so chaotic with everyone else around.'

Right then, Bea's eyes light up. 'Look, that's our kitchen! The same colour and everything, moss green.'

She holds out the magazine and points excitedly at the page.

'It comes with a twenty-year guarantee. It'll last us the rest of our lives, as they say at Kvänum.'

'Very nice,' says Niklas. 'But why does it cost so much? It looks pretty basic.'

'It's timeless, and you're paying for the quality.'

Bea turns her attention back to the magazine, reading the article as Niklas glances at the images. She has shown them to him before – he approved all the plans and sketches – and it does look good, simple and elegant, but it is also costing them nearly half a million kronor. Money that will come from his new job at Sophiahemmet. The familiar niggling doubt rears its head again. Is it really worth it?

HOGREPS, GOTLAND

NIKLAS IS BUSY LACING up his running shoes on the porch when he spots a dressing gown-clad Bea cycling towards him on the Monark. Lillis is right behind her, on Tore's old military bicycle, a basket hanging from one handlebar. Strictly speaking, he hears them before he sees them. Lillis's deep, hoarse voice and Bea's lighter tones. Odd fragments of sentences, laughter.

'Up already, Niklas?'

Lillis feigns shock, though it can hardly be much of a surprise that he gets up early.

'Feels like just yesterday that we had the fire alarm right by your bed, but not even that could get you up. We always found a quick spray of water more effective.'

Bea laughs at the anecdote Lillis likes to tell at regular intervals.

Niklas smiles politely, too tired to mention that it was almost forty years ago. Instead, he presses his hands to his thighs and gets up.

'I'm going for a run.'

'Is that really wise, with your knees?' Bea asks. 'Your ankle can hardly have healed yet, either.' She gives his foot a concerned nod, and Lillis quickly agrees.

'Bea is right, it's a terrible idea for you to go out jogging on those knees.'

His wife and mother exchange a glance, united in their belief that he is about to do something stupid. They seem to agree on most things, especially when it comes to him.

'I appreciate the concern, but I'll be fine as long as I take it easy. I am a doctor, after all.'

Their eyes meet again.

'Don't you remember what happened last summer?' Bea gives him a pleading look.

Niklas remembers. He wore himself out after just a few weeks by running so much that he gave himself shin splints, which proved pretty debilitating – at least when it came to long walks and driving. It prevented them from getting out and about.

He also remembers why he likes to go running every day during the first few weeks of the holiday. Early summer is always worst, when Lillis has promised his services to half the parish and the little sunroom is busier than his waiting room at the hospital ever gets. As her friends and acquaintances have got older, they have begun visiting him more and more often, and with every year that passes, the doctor's bag he has to bring with him gets heavier and heavier.

He does feel guilty that he resents having to help the locals check their blood pressure, patch up minor wounds and listen to their accounts of various aches and pains. Being a doctor is a calling and a duty, as his mother likes to remind him. *Is there a doctor in the house? On this plane?* He wants to help if he can, of course he does, but he also needs to take off the white coat and simply be himself from time to time. If Lillis would at least check with him first . . . but she just takes it for granted that her son will be there for her friends and acquaintances.

'I'll go and get breakfast ready,' says Lillis. 'But you should listen to your wife; she's a smart woman. Anki Thorgren is coming over this morning, too. She's been having a bit of pain in her breast.'

Niklas glances down at his watch. It'll be tight. Maybe it would be better to get a proper run in this afternoon instead.

'I guess I'll go after lunch, then.'

Bea looks up at him, eyes pleading. 'Please, Niklas. You're wrecking your body.'

'I need to run, otherwise I'll go crazy.'

'You need to find some other way to take out your frustration. Actually, we're going over to the blue lagoon to swim with Henke and Sus later, so you probably won't have time anyway.'

'But we went to Hoburgen with them yesterday.'

'The girls want to spend time with their cousins. They only get to see them once a year.'

'Once a year, for three months. How would you like it if I wanted to spend all my time with your family?'

Bea has no answer to that, and she looks away. Niklas immediately feels guilty; he knows this is a sensitive subject. It came out wrong, especially as Bea's family is so dysfunctional. Jacob was always the most important to her, but he is gone, and her parents are so self-obsessed that they rarely show any interest in either Bea or the girls.

'Sorry, I just mean . . . Doing everything together gets a bit much sometimes, and I'm . . . trying to recharge ahead of starting the new job.'

Bea is quiet for a moment, taking in everything he just said. Her face softens, and when she next speaks, her voice is much warmer.

'I understand that . . . I'm just trying to make sure everyone has a good time. And Lillis and Tore really like having us all here together.'

'I like it too, it just gets a bit intense. It's so easy to fall into old habits, and that can be . . . tough.'

Bea pauses, as though she is considering her words.

'Don't take this the wrong way,' she says, 'but Lillis finds it a bit tricky that you seem to regress when you come out here, that you get so passive.'

Niklas can hardly believe his ears.

'I take one person's blood pressure after another, fix things around the house, while Henke just takes it easy on day trips and Hampus messes about in the studio. If anyone has regressed, surely it's them?'

'OK, but you never do anything voluntarily,' Bea continues. 'She and Tore constantly have to ask you, rather than you taking the initiative.'

Niklas tries to process what she is saying, and Bea goes on, more confident now.

'Besides, Henke comes up with fun things to do, and Hampus isn't just messing about in the studio – he's working.'

'So the fact that I removed a hornets' nest from above the smithy, putting my own life on the line – and also cleared the drainpipe while I was at it – doesn't count, just because they asked me to do it?'

'I'm only telling you what Lillis said. It's more your general attitude. You don't have to take it so personally; maybe you could just think about it?'

Niklas tries to stop himself from getting worked up. He doesn't want an argument, but this really does feel like a personal attack. He could count the number of times he has taken a moment to himself, lying back in the hammock and trying to start his book, on one hand; he does jobs around the house every single summer, things that seem to have been saved specifically for him over the course of the year. Then there's the shift he puts in as the visiting doctor, not just here but in town, for his parents' friends and their children – even their grandchildren. And that isn't including Bea's friends and colleagues, plus their children, who apparently count as his on-call patients too. He has treated ear infections, given tick-borne encephalitis vaccines, prescribed more penicillin and written more referrals than he can remember. And now Bea and Lillis are ganging up on him, treating him like a child.

'You could help with the meal planning and food shopping, for example,' Bea says in an encouraging tone that just infuriates him even more.

'Whenever I try, there's already another plan. I can't even go to the supermarket to buy milk without doing something wrong.'

'You bought three litres of milk and a huge block of cheddar without bothering to check whether anyone else had already been shopping. It's not really so surprising that Lillis might be annoyed, is it? I mean, the fridge is full as it is, and the food will go bad if the door won't close.'

Niklas notices his face growing hot.

'Clearly I can't do anything right.'

'God, you're being so childish.'

'Go without me, then. You'll have a much better time.'

'We can't all fit in one car, so if you don't come, the girls and I will have to stay here too. Though obviously I don't want to force you . . .'

The look on Bea's face . . . She is right: he's being childish and selfish, and he is ashamed of that. And yet Niklas does toy with the idea of staying home at Hogreps. The girls will be annoyed at missing out on a chance to swim in the blue lagoon at the old quarry. He'll go straight into their bad books, Bea's too. Lillis and Tore will probably offer to drive them instead, even though they don't really have the energy.

The price of a few hours' peace and quiet is just too high – especially if you add his own guilty conscience into the mix. Besides, he feels sorry for Bea. She's only trying to be nice and keep everyone happy.

*

'Hey, great news about the film. Was it Freddie's idea?' Henke asks, nodding to Alexia, who is standing on the other side of the lagoon with her sister and cousins.

'No, she actually saw the casting call and applied herself,' says Niklas. 'Freddie didn't have any idea until he saw her name on the list of people who'd made it through to the screen test.'

'Oh, cool. So do they shoot this autumn?'

Niklas nods.

'Bit risky though, isn't it?' Henke asks, studying his nails.

Niklas shudders. His brother's mannerisms are so like his own. Bea always complains that he starts fiddling with his nails the minute he says anything critical, as soon as there is even the slightest hint of tension in the air, and she is right: it looks so nonchalant. He makes a mental note to break the habit.

'Risky how?' he asks, squinting in the sun as he tries to find Alexia on the other side, but the teenagers seem to have jumped in the water again.

'Well, considering she's been struggling at school.'

'Mmm, it was more that she was sick of it than anything. The plan is for the kids to keep studying during the shoot. They're actually being given their own tutor, so I think it could be good for her. It'll give her a new sense of motivation.'

'I won't stick my nose in.'

But that is precisely what he is doing: Henke's annual inspection of his little brother's life. Assessing and appraising all his failures and missteps. No doubt there'll be a follow-up next year. Why does Niklas still feel like Henrik has the upper hand, even though they are both grown men? The power balance between them has always been warped somehow.

'Hey, relax. You're on holiday,' Henke tells him, as though he can read his mind.

'Kind of tricky when there are so many people here and you don't know what could happen.'

The lagoon is busy, with teenagers and children leaping into the water. It looks so idyllic, though there are probably rocks and other leftovers from the quarrying days lurking just beneath the surface. Any minute now, their joyful shrieks could turn into panicked cries from the people watching from the shore, and the thought makes him tense.

'There are doctors on Gotland, you know,' Henke continues. 'It's not like you have to save the world every second of every day – even if you and Mum seem to think you do.'

Niklas decides not to get into that particular discussion. He has reached the point in life where he accepts that he and his brother will probably never see eye to eye. They're just too different. Henke has spent almost his entire adult life abroad, working in the luxury cruise liner industry, whereas Niklas's job is about life and death – though Henke does like to claim that their professions ultimately come down to the same thing: keeping the customer happy. However absurd it might seem, he probably has a point.

In Lovisa's case, however, it isn't just a case of unhappy – despairing – parents and the sense that he failed her. She also reminded him of Alexia as a child. Cocky, comfortable in her own skin, with an innate sense of confidence. Convinced that Niklas would be able to make her better. She told him he was her superhero.

The last time they met was on the paediatric oncology ward at the Karolinska Hospital. She was like a different person, her self-confidence replaced by an acute awareness of how serious illness and long-term pain felt. The kind of suffering many adults would struggle to manage. Her eyes were empty, resigned, disappointed, full of the knowledge that death was looming. Looking back, Niklas saw Jacob in them.

'I would've been furious if you hadn't taken that job. If you're going to insist on being so stressed all the time, you might as well get paid for it, you know?'

Yet again, Niklas has the sense that Henke has seen right through him.

'Maybe.'

Henke chuckles. 'I think it'll do you good to step out of your comfort zone and get a new perspective.'

Quite the statement for someone who lives in a gated community in one of the wealthiest areas of Rio de Janeiro, Niklas thinks, though he lets it pass. His brother wouldn't understand.

'Doesn't hurt to earn enough to make ends meet, either,' Henke continues.

'I'll pay you back. Soon.'

'That's not what I meant, no rush at all. I just mean that it might be nice not to have a knife to your throat all the time, you know?'

Niklas doesn't know what to say. The money he borrowed from Henke all those years ago – a down payment to be able to buy Banérgatan – has been like a millstone around his neck ever since. He still hasn't paid back a single krona; everything he earns goes on interest and mortgage repayments, and he feels ashamed to be in debt to his brother. Niklas knows Henke is getting by just fine without the money, but it still grates. As does the fact that he never told Bea about it. At first that was because Henke didn't want Sus to know, said they should keep it between themselves, and though telling Bea felt like the natural thing to do, that got harder and harder the longer it went on.

The loan is now practically a dirty secret between the brothers, something he would rather not think about. Niklas is also ashamed of the money he has since borrowed for the Volvo, the renovations, Alma's riding lessons and everything else he has bought on credit rather than trying to save up and pay Henke back. He wants to do it, but somehow it just never happened. Time marched on, and the total went up. Whenever he tries to bring up the subject of their finances with Bea, she always manages to put a stop to it, telling him that it's about their family. The loans are for the girls' sakes, for their future. An investment they can't afford not to make.

It was well-aimed, Henke's little dig about him finally earning enough money to get by. A grown man in debt to his own brother. That was one of the main reasons he wanted Bea to continue her studies, so that she could find a job that paid better and ultimately share the burden with him. But it was impossible; she was in no fit state after Jacob died. She lost all sense of direction, and once she finally found something that seemed to bring a little of her lust for life back, it felt natural to support her in that. Niklas had probably been hoping, deep down, that she would eventually move on from the Red Cross, but she showed no interest in doing so. The sums just didn't add up, which meant it was a no-brainer to accept the new job. He should be grateful and happy that things might actually be easier now.

He makes a promise to himself to start transferring a sum of money to Henke every month. It might not be a huge amount, but it's about damn time he started paying him back. One day, he will be debt free, and the feelings of shame and inferiority will lift. As will his uglier thoughts about the fact that Henke earns a fortune for seemingly no effort at all, whereas he works flat out on all fronts and is still struggling.

He spots Bea and Sus in the distance, making their way back from the kiosk. They wave to the teenagers, who have just climbed out of the water and run over to cool themselves down with the ice lollies and cold drinks their mothers have bought.

'What d'you think about getting dinner at Rökeriet later?' asks Henke. 'Haven't had smoked herring or fish soup all year . . . Gah . . .' He pretends to drool and lets out a longing groan.

Niklas has never liked fish, a fact that the rest of his family find strange. He would also prefer a bit of peace and quiet this evening. Maybe he and Bea could take the girls out to dinner somewhere, just the four of them. But it doesn't matter what he wants, because the others all want to spend every minute together. He needs to try to be a little more positive, to learn to say yes. To take the initiative, both socially and actively, and make the holiday an enjoyable one for everyone.

Niklas turns to his brother and gives him a thumb up. 'Sounds good, let's do it.'

MOMBASA, KENYA

September 2015

THE SCHEDULE IS PACKED, and the days pass in a blur. Niklas is sitting on the beach in Mombasa, looking out at the Indian Ocean after a barefoot run on the sand. He barely felt a single niggle in his knees, and the air is warm and velvety. The sun has begun to dip towards the horizon like a big orange ball – the way it does in films – and for the first time since he started the new job at Sophiahemmet, it feels as though he made the right decision after all.

If he had stayed in Sollentuna, he never would have been invited to this conference, and the past few days have been more interesting than he ever could have imagined. Listening to speakers from all over the world, hearing about the ways they work and what they have discovered through their research. As Henke said over the summer: it really is good to meet new people. It's exciting to stand in front of a group of strangers and tell them all about the new maternity ward at Sophiahemmet. He might have had to pop the odd beta blocker and painkiller when his knees started playing up, but only in the most high pressure of situations.

Right now, he doesn't need anything; he isn't in any pain at all. Right now, he is mesmerised by the deep red sunset, the ocean and the fact that he and the others are going on a study visit tomorrow, to a district outside of Mombasa. They have plans to go snorkelling afterwards, further down the coast, staying overnight there before continuing their trip inland. Niklas is expectant and nervous, but in a good way; it'll do him good to get out into the field after the past few days indoors.

The ball of fire sinks below the horizon and is gone in less than a minute. Just like that, the sky above him is pitch black, though the staff have set out hundreds of lanterns along the road from the beachside restaurant to the hotel. He toys with the idea of quenching his thirst with a beer before heading back to take a shower.

Much of the trip so far has been focused on work, but he has heard that there should be a lot of dolphins at the spot where they are going snorkelling tomorrow. Niklas almost feels guilty that he is experiencing these things on his own, rather than with Bea and the girls. Still, if everything goes to plan and he manages to put enough money to one side, he should be able to take them on a fantastic holiday next summer.

He is so unused to being alone, without his family, that it's almost intoxicating. Sitting here on the sand, in silence, without anyone needing him. Without anyone making demands on him.

Though surely that is how everyone feels? Everyone who works hard to keep themselves and their families afloat. You get so used to the stress and the pressure of paying the bills and giving your family what they need that you simply don't have time to stop and think. High on adrenaline from travelling and full of endorphins after his jog, Niklas feels happy and free for the first time in a long while.

*

He and around ten other doctors get up at dawn the next morning to take the bus to the new maternal health clinic in Msambweni, around sixty kilometres south of Mombasa. The roads are bad, making the journey a slow one, and when they get to Kilindini Harbour, the bus drives onto an enormous ferry which takes them over to Likoni on the mainland, along with hundreds of other people, heading to work on bike and foot.

The rest of the journey meanders down narrow dirt tracks through small villages. Niklas and Robbie, the American obstetrician, exchange a couple of nervous glances along the way. Where are they going?

Their tour guide and host, Doctor Mary Gwada, is chatting to the driver at the front of the bus, and she points at a cluster of shipping containers in the middle of nowhere.

The bus comes to a sudden halt and Niklas and his colleagues file out. There is a flurry of activity outside, hospital staff running back and forth between the rusty containers. Niklas turns to Mary with a look of confusion.

Weren't they supposed to be visiting a maternal health clinic?

The Kenyan doctor explains that the shipping containers – a container clinic, as it is known – are a temporary fix while they wait for the new centre to be completed. Women from across the district come here to give birth, but the doctors also deal with various illnesses. They have only limited resources and staff, and have already lost one patient that morning.

Mary asks whether the group would like to take a look around and inspect the near-complete building, but before they have time to answer, a desperate midwife in a bloody apron comes running, shouting that her patient is about to bleed out.

Niklas and Robbie exchange glances with their colleagues, Helle, Karsten, Mike and Pascale. No one speaks; there is no need. They don't want to take a look around the new clinic. They want to get to work.

*

It's dawn by the time the bus leaves the container clinic with its bloody, sweaty passengers. Robbie and Pascale have worked for Médecins Sans Frontières for the past few years, and both look pale, but neither is anywhere near as overwhelmed as Niklas. In light of what he has just experienced, the hospital in Stockholm is a luxurious dream, as far as staff, equipment, workload and stress levels are concerned. The entire group worked day and night to help one patient after another – mostly women in labour – yet they lost mothers and babies. They simply didn't have the resources they needed, the sorts of things that are considered standard back home.

A hollow-eyed Niklas gazes out through the bus window, at the dirt roads and thick vegetation passing by. Everyone is quiet, the relaxed chatter from the journey to the clinic, when everyone was looking forward to the study visit and their snorkelling session, now nowhere to be heard. Mary insists that the latter will still take place, but the group's response is lukewarm.

Niklas closes his eyes and sees the women. There were so many of them – Ivy, Joyceline, Rahab – and their faces have been seared into his memory. Their desperation. Rahab was so young, not even eighteen. Her daughter was born too early, and without the necessary neonatal care, she didn't stand a chance. Mary tried to arrange for transport to the hospital in Mombasa, but nothing arrived in time.

The competition for beds in the clinic was so high that many of the women had to share, lying back to back. Overloaded beds full of screaming babies and women who had just given birth, in shipping containers. It was impossible to maintain any sort of sterile environment, and the doctors simply did their best with the resources available to them.

Niklas jolts awake as the bus comes to a halt, and he realises he must have dozed off. The doctors file out again, walking a few hundred metres down a partially overgrown path. Without warning, the brush opens out onto an endless expanse of sand. There isn't another person in sight. Nothing but bowed palm trees laden with coconuts, hanging like snowdrops over the white sand.

A few metres away, an open-top boat with a sunroof is waiting for them. The contrast to the scenes they witnessed just a few hours ago could hardly be greater, and it feels strange and uncomfortable for them to suddenly have fun as tourists when there are people in need of their help nearby.

Robbie gives Niklas a thump on the shoulder. They have done what they can, given their all and then some. None of them is in any fit state to work right now; they need time to decompress and catch their breath. Niklas listens to what his colleague is saying and tries to give in. It doesn't help that he feels guilty about being here and not there, but he needs to try to take in the dazzlingly beautiful paradise in front of him. Anything else would be disrespectful.

The turquoise waves are crystal clear, the vegetation and fish so vibrant that he feels like part of their undersea world. Purple coral full of bright yellow and cobalt blue, fish dotted with intricate patterns and markings. Niklas is still slightly wired, but his heart rate slows with every minute he spends beneath the surface.

A large sea turtle swims nonchalantly by, its front flippers like wings as it sails through the water. Niklas is bombarded with new sights, and he reaches out to touch a pink starfish. The sheer miracle of nature hits him with full force.

He is gliding along the reef, as weightless as the sea turtle, floating as though he were one with the Indian Ocean and its underwater kingdom, when he feels a tap on his shoulder. It's the guide, signalling for him to come up, even though he has only been in the water a few minutes.

Short of breath, he clambers back up onto the boat.

'Phone call for you, sir,' the man says in English.

'A phone call?'

'Yes, sir. Your wife. Very important. Emergency.'

One of the crew holds out a mobile phone to him, and Niklas immediately starts catastrophising. Something serious must have happened. Alma might have fallen off the horse and broken her neck, or Alexia could have been attacked and raped on her way home in the dark. Someone must have died. As he reaches for the mobile, a flashback races through his mind, from the morning when Lillis handed him the phone and he heard Freddie's voice telling him that Jacob had been found dead in bed.

'Hello, Bea?' His voice is rough, his mouth dry. 'Is everything OK?'

'It's a complete disaster.'

He can tell from her voice that it must be bad.

'I've tried calling you a thousand times!'

His pulse has now reached the same heights as yesterday, and he switches to crisis mode.

'Are the girls OK?'

'I need to be able to get hold of you in situations like this, Niklas!'

'We were at a clinic in the countryside, we had to jump in and help. My phone died. What's happened?'

'Alexia's teacher called, they're worried about the film shoot . . . Apparently she did really badly on her latest tests.'

'OK . . . ?'

'We need to take this seriously if she's ever going to graduate.'

Niklas's sense of panic transforms into confusion. *Very important? Emergency?* This?

'Of course, but what do you want me to do about that right now?'

'Talk to her. I've tried, but she just gets in a huff. You're the only one she'll listen to.'

Frustration bubbles up inside him.

'I understand that, but I've spent the past day working, I'm on a study trip . . .'

'You're on a boat, they said.'

'Yes, right now, but—'

'It's complete chaos here. The builders have ripped out the old kitchen, even though the new one still hasn't arrived, which means we can't cook, and the delivery company isn't answering the phone. Then Alexia's teacher calls, and I just don't know what to do. Alexia locks herself in her room whenever I try . . .'

Bea sounded angry at first, but her voice starts to tremble, fading to a worrying silence.

'Honey, are you OK . . . ? Bea . . . ? Why don't you order something tasty from Broms? Or go over and see Lillis and Tore?'

'They've gone back to Gotland. It's so typical that you had to be away this week, and I . . . It's all just so hard without you . . .'

Bea bursts into tears, and Niklas feels an odd weight on his chest. He grips the rail with one hand. The women's cries are still echoing through him. Not the usual cries during the throes of childbirth, the kind he has heard countless times in Sollentuna and at Sophiahemmet; these were desperate roars that ricocheted off the cold metal in the rusty containers, made by mothers who would lose their babies purely because they happened to have been born a few dozen kilometres from a real hospital. Despairing howls and newborn babies screaming for their dead mothers.

The sound of Bea's tears crackles over the poor line. To one side of the boat, Niklas can see his colleagues' snorkels sticking up out of the water. Robbie and Mary climb up onto the desk, followed by Helle and Karsten. The engine rumbles, and the boat starts moving.

The guide waves to them, pointing out to sea. 'Dolphin! Dolphin!'

Niklas spots them in the distance, their pale grey fins breaking the surface for a moment before disappearing again. On the other end of the line, Bea is still crackling.

'You could call Freddie and talk to him; he promised the shoot wouldn't impact on Alexia's schoolwork. Please, Niklas?'

She sounds desperate, and Niklas is just about to reply when the dolphins suddenly reappear. The captain accelerates, and he almost loses his balance.

'Dolphins!'

He can barely hear Bea over the roar of the waves and the engine. The sleek, glistening creatures almost seem to be racing the boat, swimming alongside the bow and leaping through the water, playful and teasing, as though they know they will win but want to let the slow humans think they stand a chance – just for fun. He wishes he was experiencing this with Bea.

'You should see this, there are dolphins right by the boat.'

'Dolphins? I'm trying to talk to you about Alexia and . . .'

He knows how his words must have sounded. 'Sorry. I'll talk to Freddie.'

'This is really serious, Niklas. She might have to resit the year.'

'OK, I'll call him as soon as we're done here.'

'It'll be a disaster if you forget.'

Niklas tries to imagine what kind of disaster she means. What happened last night was a disaster. The so-called medical care being administered from a bunch of shipping containers outside of Msambweni – that is a disaster.

'Could you give the delivery company a call, too?'

The dolphins are now zig-zagging in front of the boat. Everything around him, last night's challenges, Bea's despairing voice: it all seems to be competing for his attention, a whirlwind of sensations.

'I'm in Kenya, Bea . . . Wouldn't it be easier if you—'

'I've been pestering them, but they don't listen and I just don't have the energy to chase them again . . .'

Bea sounds even more desperate now.

184

Niklas feels so far removed from her, and not just geographically.

'OK, I'll give them a call, as soon as I can ... Things have been so overwhelming here and ... well, it's hard to explain, but I've really been affected by everything I've seen these past few days and—'

The call drops, or did Bea just hang up? Whatever the cause, Niklas doesn't have time to finish his sentence. Not that it matters, because he can barely remember what he was about to say.

When he looks up, the dolphins are gone. All that is left is a vague weight on his chest.

GARDERMOEN AIRPORT

LAYOVER IN OSLO. NIKLAS walks aimlessly through the airport, looking for presents for Bea and the girls. His fingers brush scarves, necklaces and various beauty products, but nothing feels interesting or personal enough. It also seems odd to come home from a week in Kenya with a pot of Estée Lauder face cream.

The shopping trip they had planned was called off when the doctors decided to go back to Msambweni on their last day, but Niklas knows that Bea will be disappointed he hasn't brought home any pretty African fabrics or wooden masks to hang up in the living room.

In some ways, it will be a relief to get home. His euphoria at being left to his own devices for a few days gradually gave way to a sense of inadequacy, on all fronts. Both in Kenya and at home. The phone calls with Alexia, Freddie and Alexia's teacher. Chasing DHL and trying to comfort and support Bea from afar. Every missed call was yet another reminder that he had left her to deal with everything on her own. And it felt increasingly pointless to sit in a plush conference hall, listening to yet another lecture, when he could be out there making a difference.

He pauses in front of the perfume counter, and a woman in a white coat comes over to him. She could almost be mistaken for a doctor, if it weren't for the form-fitting cut of her coat and the waft of perfume that follows her.

'Can I help you with anything?' she asks him in English.

Judging by her accent and her name – Sigrid – he guesses she must be Norwegian, and though he knows she would understand him if he replied in Swedish, he switches to English too. It seems easier somehow.

'I'm looking for something for my wife and two girls.'

'How old are your daughters?'

'Sixteen. Twins.'

'I know just the thing. My own daughter is the same age.'

Of course.

Forty minutes later, he boards the plane with two duty-free bags of perfume and a burning hole in his wallet, but he knows that Bea will still be disappointed. His footsteps are heavy as he walks down the aisle, and he feels an odd sense of emptiness, bordering on hopelessness, as the plane takes off for Stockholm.

SOPHIAHEMMET HOSPITAL, STOCKHOLM

October 2015

HIS RUNNING SHOES HAVE been gathering dust in the cupboard in his office, his T-shirt and shorts still in the bag he used to carry back and forth between Banérgatan and Sollentuna. Niklas has much less of a commute now, and the whole of Lill-Jansskogen Park is just around the corner, but he hasn't been for a single run since he started his new job after the summer.

One of the benefits of the move to a new hospital was supposed to be the opportunity to go running more often. He knew he would miss the water in Sollentuna, but the proximity to Lill-Jansskogen and all its illuminated trails would make it much easier to work out, both before and after a shift. Despite that, the closest he has come to any exercise so far is walking along Valhallavägen, to and from work.

His original plan – that, as senior consultant, he would have more of an umbrella role – quickly fell by the wayside when he realised just how short-staffed they were. Rather than one job, he essentially has three, and in his capacity as a doctor, department head and administrative manager, he often finds himself running between meetings and medical emergencies, filling out paperwork late into the night. But today, for once, he actually feels slightly relieved.

It's Friday, almost the weekend, and it doesn't currently look like he will have to be on call. This will be the first weekend in months that he might actually get a bit of time off. Niklas has recruited a skilled paediatric doctor from another hospital, and the department is unusually calm. With a bit of luck, he might even be able to leave at a reasonable time today – it is currently just after five. Niklas toys with the idea of finally going out for a run, trying to convince himself that it could have done him good to give his knees a bit of a break; he isn't in as much pain anymore, after all.

He turns to look out of the window. It's cold and dark, much too cold to run in shorts, but the temperature is still above zero, and if he keeps up a decent pace, the chilly air will feel good on his bare skin.

He glances down at his desk. The stacks of papers are like a physical manifestation of his guilty conscience, but it has also been far too long since he last did anything for himself. If it isn't his work keeping him busy, then he has to hurry home at the end of his shifts. The kitchen reno-vations have dragged on, continuing in parallel with the launch of the new ward, and it has been utter chaos. The papers on his desk aren't going to die if he ignores them for another day, though that thought gives him another pang of guilt. Niklas knows better than anyone that people can actually die as a result of leaving the files – or, in his case, forgetting them entirely.

But there aren't any cancer patients in these stacks. These are all staffing issues, annual leave requests and overdue reports. No one is going to die just because he decides to go for a run. He'll even have time to take a shower and walk home afterwards. His only plans for the weekend are to sleep, read and do as little as he physically can in an attempt to recharge his batteries before Monday. Working sixty-hour weeks really takes it out of you, and now that he stops to think about it, he realises he is exhausted.

Still, this isn't the time to stop and think. Now that he's part of the game, all he can do is keep going and pray that the pressure will ease once they've found their feet and hired a few more staff.

Niklas laces up his shoes and hurries outside. The air is bitingly cold, and he has to start running immediately to work up some heat. He curses himself for his lack of reflectors and a headtorch now that he is heading for the woods, but it'll have to do. He keeps his eyes glued to the ground to avoid the slimy, damp leaves lurking like black ice on the pavement, just waiting to cause him to slip and fracture something.

It's odd, but the minute his feet leave the ground, the weight seems to lift from his chest. It doesn't matter that it's cold; Niklas fills his lungs and disconnects his brain. This is running at its best, and he has only just got started. Not long until he is among the trees now. Not long until he smells the soft trails and rotting leaves.

Niklas jogs past the old Olympic Stadium and is just about to run by the School of Sport and Health Sciences when his phone starts ringing. Bea.

He rejects her call, but he immediately feels bad and answers when she tries again.

'Where are you?' she asks.

There is no point in lying to her; he's far too short of breath for that, so why is he even considering it? Bea used to like the fact that he ran so much, thought it was positive that he kept himself in shape, but over the past few years, she seems increasingly irritated by it. It takes too much time away from her and the family, like some sort of rival, even though he never goes for long runs anymore.

'Lill-Jansskogen. I'm just going for a quick run, but I'll be heading home soon.'

'We were meant to meet at Daphne's.'

Niklas racks his brain. Did he and Bea have plans to meet there? Today?

'It's Friday, date night.'

'I'm sorry, honey. I completely—'

'You forgot about me.'

'No, no, not you, I just got the wrong day. I thought it was next week.'

'I reminded you this morning. I arranged everything with the girls so that we could have a nice evening together ...'

She sounds so disappointed and upset, and Niklas is ashamed. It isn't entirely true that he thought it was next week; he was just trying to rescue the situation. He does actually have a vague memory of her talking about their date night that morning. His only excuse is being completely overwhelmed, incapable of processing all the information that constantly seems to be bombarding him. Not that Bea understands any of that.

'There's such a thing as mobile phones, you know. People use them to keep track of important information. I've been sitting here waiting for you, all on my own. Should I just go home?'

'No, no, I'm coming. I'll be quick.'

Niklas does a 180 and races back towards Sophiahemmet.

*

Thirty minutes later, he is sitting opposite a glum Bea in Daphne's, his shirt clinging to his damp back.

'I'm sorry, I just have so much on right now.'

She sighs. 'We never have time to talk anymore. You're home so rarely, it's like I'm a single mother. But I have a job too, you know. And then there are the girls and the renovations.'

That is true. Bea is right. It has all just been so much, so fast. Both at home and at work.

'What do you want to talk about?'

'I want to order first,' she says firmly. 'I'm about to pass out from hunger.'

'Of course, good idea.'

Niklas scans through the menu and takes a sip of water. He isn't hungry. He is still sweating, despite the fact that he ran no more than 500 metres. It must be

down to the stress, he thinks, pushing any disappointment over his aborted run to one side. There is no room
for those sorts of feelings now. Fridays are for spending
time with his family, maybe even their friends, not for
running in the forest – especially not if you've been away
as much as he has, working around the clock. Bea is
right about that, too. Of course it's much better to be
here with his wife, with a good drink in front of him,
soaking up the atmosphere. Like the good old days.

Niklas tries to change his mindset. Accept, adjust,
adapt. Imagine if they got tipsy and checked into a hotel
for the evening? It's been so long since they last did
anything like that.

'What are you going to have?' asks Bea.

Niklas looks up. She still seems so sad.

'I'm sorry you had to wait for me earlier, honey.'

'It's not that. Or not just that, anyway.'

'So what's up?'

Bea seems to be steeling herself.

'I spoke to Lillis.'

'OK?'

'And she's worried.'

'About . . . ?'

'Me. Because I've been taking on too much and feel
like I'm about to hit the wall. We keep ending up in
these traditional gender roles, with me doing everything
at home – managing the renovations, taking care of the
girls, planning our meals for the week – while you just
run off to work.'

Niklas feels a searing, stabbing pain in his temple, like a sudden migraine. 'Ow, fuck.'

Bea stares blankly at him.

'You always change the subject the minute I try to bring any of this up,' she says.

'No, no, I just had a sudden pain in my head.'

'Maybe it's because you go out running so much? It's not good for you, you know.'

'I haven't been running in months.'

'Which is why you should probably take it easy.'

'It's not that.'

'No, but there's always something, whenever I want to bring up anything to do with equality.'

Niklas swallows. It doesn't seem entirely fair of her to accuse him of being unequal, though it's also hard to argue with her. It's true that she does almost everything at home, that he spends too much time at work. It was exactly the same when he was in Sollentuna, though things were calmer there. But it isn't his fault; they're both to blame that things ended up this way. He tried to convince Bea to go back to her studies after Jacob died, but she didn't want to. Couldn't. And he understood that. Her grief and trauma took a long time to process, which meant he had to shoulder the financial burden.

And then the girls came along. Bea wanted to stay at home with them for as long as she could, said she thought it was healing. Months passed, then years. Time marched on, and somehow they ended up here. With Niklas in a management position at Sophiahemmet and Bea working

194

for the Red Cross, a job she is passionate about but which doesn't pay very well. Their joint incomes only just cover their monthly outgoings.

'I'm doing my best,' he says, 'but things are particularly busy right now because the clinic has just opened.'

'I know that, but it's been almost six months.'

'There are staff shortages everywhere, but things should start getting better soon.'

'It's having an impact on Alma and Alexia, too. Plus I have to sort out the transport to and from the stables whenever you can't give Alma a lift.'

'I know, and I'm trying, but it's not like I can just leave when a pregnant woman comes in in labour and there are no other doctors on duty.'

'A few years from now, the girls will leave home and you'll regret that you were never there. I thought family meant more to you than this?'

Her eyes well up, a tear quivering on her carefully painted waterline, threatening to spill down her cheek.

Niklas clears his throat and looks down at the menu again. He fiddles with the painkiller in his pocket, trying to work out whether he can pop it into his mouth without her noticing. His heart is racing, and he wonders whether that is down to the stress of hurrying over here or all the shit Bea is giving him for working too much.

This was exactly what he was afraid of happening, exactly what he told her during the spring, when he was debating whether or not to take the job.

He looks up and tries to stand his ground.

'We both knew it would be tough when I took this job, didn't we? But we decided it would be worth it, so we could borrow more money and renovate the kitchen.'

'Yes, but we also need to have some sort of life,' says Bea, looking insulted. 'And now you're making it sound like I convinced you to take the job because of the money, when I was actually just trying to encourage you to develop in your professional role. It was as much for your sake as anything.'

'Absolutely, and I'm happy you did. I really appreciate it, honey.'

Niklas doesn't feel particularly happy, though surely that isn't so uncommon in the early days of a job like this, when you are more nervous and stressed than anything. Right? He doesn't know, it's been so long since he last changed jobs. His fingers let go of the tablet in his pocket, and he grips his glass instead, knocking it back in one go.

'Things will get better, I promise. I'll talk to my boss. You and the girls matter more to me than anything.'

He catches a weak smile at the corner of Bea's mouth, and his heart rate slows slightly when he realises that she is starting to soften. That his reassurances have worked. The alcohol is probably playing its part too, flooding through his veins and up to his head, calming his thoughts and making his body relax. His shoulders drop, and he feels happier than earlier. No longer quite so empty. This could end up being a good evening if he just makes an effort.

It's Friday, which means he can afford to treat himself to another drink or two. He might even get a chance to go out for a run tomorrow afternoon, the full loop around Djurgården.

He raises a hand to catch the waiter's attention and points to his glass.

'Do you want another?'

Bea shakes her head. 'You need to drive tomorrow, remember? We have to go out to Bromma to pick up the tap I ordered, and then I want us to stop off at the Kvänum showroom on Sibyllegatan to look at an island.'

'An island?'

'Mmm, I think it would be a great touch, and we do probably have space for it, so I'd like to take a look at the options.'

'Could we do that next weekend instead? I'd really like to just take it easy tomorrow.'

'But you might be working next weekend.'

Niklas has no answer to that.

'And I want to get this damn kitchen finished,' Bea continues, 'so we can get back to normal.'

'OK, so what about Sunday instead?' Niklas suggests. 'And that way we can relax a little tonight?'

'Alma has a competition on Sunday morning, and Emmy's parents have given the girls a lift every weekend while you've been working, so it's our turn. Alexia has to get over to Vänersborg for filming, too. I told Freddie you'd drive her over there so you have time to do some maths revision with her first.'

Niklas can feel the joy draining from his body, leaving him weak and empty. His entire weekend has already been planned out for him, and he will be nothing but a chauffeur. He doesn't get a say in any of it, not this evening, tomorrow or the day after. *Accept, adjust, adapt.*

This is what it means to have a family, he knows that. You step up. And he does want to be there for them, of course he does. He's Bea's husband, Alma and Alexia's father. He wants to drive them to their riding competitions and film shoots, help with their homework and be present in their lives. He wants to be that man. So why is it all such a slog?

*

His mouth is dry, and his eyes feel like they might pop out of their sockets each time one of his heavy feet hits the ground. Bea and the girls are walking ahead of him on Karlavägen. His wife is moving with quick, short steps, as though they are in a hurry. Alma is keeping pace with her, and he realises that her body and posture are becoming increasingly like Bea's. Gangly, with her legs and feet turned in slightly, slim hips and a flat backside.

Bea glances back over her shoulder at him and Alexia. 'Are you coming? Broms will be full if we're not quick.'

'Sorry.'

Niklas grabs Alexia's hand and speeds up. His apology was more for yesterday than for their dawdling. Bea woke him in the middle of the night with an elbow to the ribs. He'd been drunkenly snoring, apparently. Niklas eventually dozed off again, but not Bea, as she explained when she woke him again not too long ago. She spent all night lying wide awake, listening to him snoring, and it's his fault she is so tired today.

When they got home from Daphne's at around ten, he sat down in the living room with a whisky and his LPs. He thought he deserved it after the crazy autumn he'd had. Lustans Lakejer and old Depeche Mode records. Another whisky, another vinyl. Tore's Procol Harum record, featuring 'A Whiter Shade of Pale', which he used to play when Niklas was a boy. For some reason, Niklas has always associated that particular musical memory with autumn, with melancholy and lonely weekends in town. Henke had left home by that point, and Lillis and Tore would go over to Gotland with Hampus to rake leaves and do some work in the garden. Niklas occasionally proved rebellious enough to refuse to go with them, and he has fragmented memories of freedom, of zero responsibilities or demands on him. Procol Harum and lager.

Bea went to bed around midnight. She asked him to do the same, to stop drinking so that he'd be in a fit state to drive in the morning, but something made him keep going. Maybe it was some sort of subconscious protest on his part, the coward's way out, a chance to escape driving and kitchen showrooms and take it easy for once.

Niklas breaks out in a cold sweat and Alexia drops his clammy hand as they turn the corner onto Grevgatan.

*

It takes him a while to rescue the mood at their little table in the corner. He isn't sure whether the girls have worked out just how disappointed Bea is in him, but they must have noticed something isn't right – though they spend more time looking down at their phones than anything. He steps into some sort of clown roll to cheer Bea up, mimicking the waiter's voice once he has taken their order and hurried away.

'We've got a lurrrrvely croak monshurrr today.'

Alexia snorts. 'Thinking about becoming an actor, Dad?'

'Why not? I can do all the waiters.'

A slight smile from Bea tells him he is on the right track.

His head feels like it might burst, but he continues in the same jokey tone, driven by his guilty conscience and the look on Bea's face, which swings back and forth between sad and annoyed. It's been so long since they last had a free Saturday together, and he desperately wants everyone to be happy again, not least because he got them into this situation by drinking too much.

He doesn't have a drink problem as such, but Bea is right that he has gone overboard a few times this past year. It probably has something to do with the sheer amount of stress he is under, the fact that he hasn't been eating properly and isn't getting any younger. His body simply can't handle booze as well as it used to, but still. Surely he deserves a couple of whiskies after a hard week every now and then?

Niklas eats far too much. Hollandaise-drenched eggs Benedict and American pancakes with maple syrup. He isn't really all that hungry, more queasy than anything, but he needs to dull his hangover as best he can. He'll need energy if he is going to be able to function today, if he is going to act the happy dad and keep Bea in a good mood. And his efforts do seem to be working. Bea has smiled briefly several times now, and her sad eyes seem warmer and brighter than before. She is softening.

'This was nice,' she says, stroking Niklas's arm. 'But we need to make tracks if we're going to get to Bromma in time. Thanks to you, we have the infinite joy of taking public transport,' she adds with a teasing wink.

So, their plans haven't been cancelled, just tweaked.

Niklas wearily waves to the waiter, who raises an eyebrow and nods to let him know he has understood.

Bea gets to her feet.

'We'll just add it to the tab,' she says. 'That way, we'll be there when they open. I guess it'll be busy today.'

'The tab?'

She rolls her eyes. 'It's like I told Lillis yesterday: you really are clueless.'

Niklas confirms her suspicions, his face a question mark, and Bea explains.

'We have a tab because we're takeaway regulars, it's simpler for the girls that way. Haven't you noticed?'

She laughs at his confused face.

He doesn't know whether it's because of his hangover or because the penny has finally dropped, but Niklas breaks out in a cold sweat again. *Takeaway regulars?*

Broms definitely isn't the most expensive restaurant in Östermalm, but it's hardly the cheapest either.

'It was your idea,' says Bea. 'For us to have more takeaways while the kitchen was a mess.'

Niklas has zero recollection of that.

'Well, that really says something about how often you're at home, doesn't it?' Bea mutters with what seems like a triumphant note in her voice.

When the waiter comes over to their table, she smiles warmly.

'We'll add it to the tab.'

With a thanks and a nod, he turns and walks over to the till. Niklas knows what that means: the staff know exactly which tab she meant, and Bea and the girls really, *really* are regulars.

A moment later, they are out on the street.

'I just need to nip back inside to use the toilet,' says Niklas. 'You go on ahead, I'll catch up.'

Bea taps her watch and starts walking towards Karlaplan metro station, flanked by her daughters.

Niklas nods and turns back into the restaurant. Their waiter is busy with another table, but the maître d' is by the till, going through the day's reservations.

'Hi, excuse me. We just added our bill to the tab, but I was wondering if I could check the total.'

'Of course. What was the name?'

'Niklas Stjerne. Or it might be in my wife's name, Beatrice Stjerne.'

After a moment of scrolling, the maître d's face lights up.

'Yes, here we are ... Beatrice Stjerne, that's right. It comes to 13,543 kronor in total. Would you like to settle up now?'

It takes Niklas a few seconds to process the figure.

'No, an invoice will be fine.'

'No problem.'

Niklas turns around and marches towards the toilets, nausea rising up inside him. Eggs Benedict, maple syrup, coffee: all of it wants out.

*

He was reluctant at first, and will have to drive half the night to make it back in time for work in the morning, but Niklas is still happy that he gets to drive Alexia to her film shoot on the other side of the country. It gives them a bit of time together, which is great, though he is still tired after Alma and Emmy's riding competition and yesterday's hunt for a kitchen island.

Niklas hasn't had a drop of alcohol since Friday, but he still feels a little hungover. It's probably more the lack of sleep than anything. He remembers glancing at the clock at half-three in the morning, still wide awake, wondering whether he should dip into the money he has stashed away for their holiday. The big Christmas present. Because no matter how many times he runs the sums, it just doesn't add up.

There are days when he envies Calle and Charlotte, financially speaking. Two high earners who split the costs equally.

It's a different matter entirely to be single-handedly responsible for almost everything. He knows how important it is that Bea is happy and does something she enjoys, but sometimes he worries that the financial pressure might give him a stomach ulcer.

He tries to empty his mind and be present in the moment. To enjoy cruising towards the west coast with Alexia. It's only 3 p.m., but dusk has already begun to fall outside, and the Volvo is dark. His daughter's phone lights up her face.

'What're you doing?' he asks.

'Playing.'

'Is it that sweet game?'

'Mmm, Candy Crush.'

'What's the aim?'

'Of Candy Crush?' Alexia glances over to him.

'Yeah, what's the point of it?'

'You have to complete all these levels. Seriously, it's so addictive. It's like crack.'

'How do you know? Have you tried it or something?'

'Yeah, Freddie gave me some, why?' Alexia's face is stony, but her mouth quickly curls into a smile. *Got you.*

Niklas laughs. They have the same dark sense of humour, he thinks, so different to Bea and Alma, who don't appreciate sarcasm in anything like the same way.

Alexia turns back to her game, phone pinging as Niklas overtakes one car after another. She glances up as he accelerates past a lorry.

'You forgot to indicate, Dad.'

'Whoops, silly me. Well spotted, though. Do you want to take over?'

'Now?'

'It'll do you good to practise on the motorway. Besides, I'm tired. I just need to find a safe place to pull over.'

Alexia puts her phone down and scans the side of the road.

'I've missed you,' she says without warning.

Niklas feels a jolt in his gut. Alexia's film shoot has kept her away quite a lot over the autumn, but he has hardly been at home at all. He has spent far too much time at Sophiahemmet over the past few months.

'Sorry. It'll get better; it's just that everything is still so new.'

'That's what you said six months ago. Mum is so stressed over the stupid kitchen, it's all she ever talks about.'

'I know, but it'll be fantastic once it's done.'

'It's a kitchen.'

'True. It's a kitchen.'

Niklas feels slightly disloyal towards Bea, but he is also relieved that he isn't alone in thinking that a kitchen is a kitchen.

'Petrol station, Dad. Five hundred metres. Don't forget to indicate this time.'

*

They don't arrive in Vänersborg until eight that evening. Alexia drove well under the speed limit on the motorway, but it was worth the slightly longer journey to see her grow in confidence and to hear her shriek with joy as she overtook her first lorry.

Niklas is now standing in the doorway of the hotel room where she will be staying during the shoot.

'Freddie will be here in the morning,' he says, 'but it feels weird just leaving you here.'

'It's fine, I'll be OK.'

'Sure?'

'Sure, Dad.'

He is oddly emotional as he gives her a hug.

'Thanks for the lift. I know you didn't really want to.'

It's as though she has caught him red-handed, though he doesn't have time to say anything before Alexia continues:

'But I'm glad Mum forced you.'

'I'm glad too. Though she didn't force me to do anything. I wanted to drive you over here.'

'Nice try. Like everything else you're glad about? Bye, Dad.'

Alexia closes the door with a sad smile, leaving Niklas in the corridor outside. *Nice try? Like everything else you're glad about?* He isn't quite sure what she meant, but he has a sneaking suspicion that she is right. That he is just pretending.

ÖSTERMALM, STOCKHOLM

November 2015

IT FEELS A LITTLE odd to meet away from the hospital, without their white coats and their daily rounds to fall back on. Niklas hasn't seen Per Alvén since June, when the team on the paediatric ward saw him off with cake and a bottle of Glenfiddich, but, as he enters the restaurant today, his former colleague looks the same as ever. The same boyish gaze and teasing smile, forever young in an ageing body.

Niklas gets up. After a brief deliberation over how to greet each other, Per holds out a hand and gives him a gentle thump on the shoulder; they're more colleagues than friends, after all.

'I see you've jumped on the trend,' Per says with a nod to Niklas's head. 'Erika from X-ray has started dying hers grey, too.'

'Get yourself a new job, a couple of teenage daughters and a kitchen renovation project, and you can skip going to the hairdresser, too. Bea calls me the Silver Fox.'

'If you grow it a bit longer, you could start calling yourself Gandalf the Grey.'

Per laughs at his terrible joke, and Niklas can't help but join in. He has missed his colleague's childish sense of humour.

A few other diners – men in suits – turn in their direction, and Niklas has a sudden fond memory of the staff cafeteria at Sollentuna Hospital, where he and Per used to eat every day. It was like a noisy school dining hall, full of white coats, clicking wooden clogs and watery stew, yet he also remembers it being a much more pleasant place to be than the restaurant where they are currently sitting.

Once they have ordered their sushi, they go over everything that has happened since the last time they spoke. Other than Erika from X-ray having changed her hair colour, Bibbi has baked her way through autumn with such enthusiasm that the entire department has piled on the pounds. Tove and Lena have started exercising at lunch, jogging around Edsviken and doing strength training in the outdoor gym. Per has held off on joining them for as long as he can, he says, but Niklas still feels a rush of envy. Joar is due to go on paternity leave in the new year, and Niklas's replacement has finally arrived: a talented young doctor everyone seems to like. Life there has continued more or less like usual.

'Though we miss you, obviously.'

Niklas nods. The feeling is mutual. He steels himself and asks his question.

'Per, what would you say about working with me again? In town.'

The plan was to be a little more strategic, to start by telling his former colleague all about the new maternity ward at Sophiahemmet and the paediatric clinic they have planned. About the investment, the benefits. Brand new equipment, all cutting-edge; a light, bright environment. No 1970s corridors or shabby examination rooms. But Niklas feels like a dishonest vacuum cleaner salesman, because although it is true that the new department is great, it is also far from complete. They blew the budget months ago, and they are incredibly understaffed.

More than anything, Niklas is driven by the longing for his friend and colleague. For the everyday chatter and shared responsibility. He is lonely, and, as such, it doesn't matter that he has a big, comfortable office with views out onto the park.

'It's a flattering offer, don't get me wrong,' says Per, attempting to grip a piece of sushi with his chopsticks. 'But you know me, I don't like change.'

'I'm still the same colleague,' Niklas says, trying to talk him round. 'And the pay and benefits are great: seven weeks' paid leave, plus you'll be able to afford a summer house, a boat or caravan, whatever the hell you want. Your pension would be much better, too. Don't you think it's time to try something new? Develop a little, rather than just treading water in Sollentuna?'

He sounds just like Bea, which is the last thing he wants. He knows that Per has never been motivated by money or a drive to climb the ranks, but he can't help using her arguments. The truth is that Niklas needs his old workmate, more than he ever could have imagined, and so he forges on.

'I know that we could do great things together, shape the department the way we want it, without any bureaucrats from the local authority getting involved.'

'Like I said, it's very flattering, but I don't suit grey.' Per chuckles again, nodding to Niklas's temples.

Niklas smiles, but his face is tense.

'I'm not going to lie, it's a lot of work at the moment, but things will get better – especially once we've got the staff. These things take time, but it'll all work out. Please, Per. I need you.'

Did he just say *please*? Is he seriously begging his old colleague? Apparently so. Niklas can hear the desperation in his own voice.

Per's face turns serious. 'I'm sorry, buddy, but I don't need the stress. I'm getting by as it is, and my freedom is more important to me, always has been.'

Niklas is sorry too, more than Per could ever understand. The prospect of recruiting his old colleague had given him a flicker of hope all autumn, a chink of light in the darkness. If he could just tempt him to make the jump to Sophiahemmet, maybe everything would finally become a little more bearable? Fun, even?

He had imagined the pair convincing the others to make the move, too. Bibbi and Tove, Lena and Joar. Well, maybe not all of them, but at least one or two members of the old crew. They were a well-oiled machine, and though it would still be tough, they would have been able to make it work. Hire more people and, little by little, transform it into a good, tolerable workplace. Niklas now realises that none of that is ever going to happen, and even if he did manage to bring them over, it just wouldn't be the same.

It feels like he has set sail alone in the middle of a storm, without a life jacket. The others are safe and dry on the beach, but he is beyond saving. Even if things do calm down at Sophiahemmet, the fact remains that it's a private entity, with completely different demands and working methods to a public hospital. He is stuck on the hamster wheel.

Per has finally managed to get to grips with his chopsticks.

'God, this is good – a bit different to the old cafeteria, eh? Almost makes you want to change jobs just for the sushi,' he adds with another titter.

Niklas attempts to smile and puts down his chopsticks. It's definitely different, and yet he suddenly has no appetite.

HOGREPS, GOTLAND

December 2015

HOGREPS IS BLANKETED BENEATH a thick layer of meringue-like snow, illuminated by the garden torches that Tore ceremoniously takes out every Christmas Eve. He lights them as darkness falls, all the way through to New Year's Day.

Lillis is busy hanging gingerbread hearts in the kitchen window. She bakes them every Christmas, decorating them with 'love in icing sugar', as she likes to say. On each heart, she writes their names in florid, sugary letters. Niklas & Bea, Alma & Alexia, Henrik & Sus, Olle & Hedda, Lillis & Tore, Hampus & Jacob.

Niklas has always found the last pairing a little macabre, but Bea was incredibly touched the first time Lillis gave her brother a place among the hearts at Hogreps, and it has been tradition ever since. Hampus claims to be honoured to share a heart with Bea's late brother, and the others find Niklas's reaction odd – especially as Jacob was his best friend. But, to him, it is nothing but a painful reminder of his friend's death, though obviously he can't say that.

The grief is Bea's, not his. Losing a friend is nothing like losing a sibling, however much Lillis likes to say that Jacob was part of the family while they were growing up – in much the same way that Bea has become a bonus daughter to her.

Niklas looks down at Tore's old leather boots, which he has borrowed to smoke a quick cigarette in the ruins. They're probably about the same age as Niklas, and for as long as he can remember, the trusty old boots have had their very own place on the porch. He exhales a cloud of smoke and peers over towards Hogreps. With its brightly lit windows, it looks like a doll's house. He can see the hand-painted tiled stove and the enormous tree he helped Tore chop down the day before, now draped with tinsel and coloured glass baubles, Lillis's ceramic angels and generations' worth of home-made decorations.

The ruins are cold and dark, but they still feel like a sanctuary, and his cigarette seems to burn down far too quickly. Niklas pushes the spent butt behind a couple of rocks and lights another, hoping no one is wondering where he has gone.

He can see his family chatting and gesticulating as they wait to open their presents, and though he is invisible in the darkness, he crouches down and takes a deep drag. It's pathetic how scared he is that someone might see him smoking; he's a grown man, and he can do whatever he likes with his own body. Still, it does go against everything he stands for as a doctor. He knows the damage it does, and yet here he is.

His new-found smoking habit is only temporary, that's what he has decided, nothing but a few cigarettes a day.

Still, he really will have to quit once everything calms down. If his knees hadn't stopped him from running this autumn and winter, he never would have started in the first place.

Looking back on his year, there are a few things he knows for sure. Moving to a different workplace didn't help, and Lovisa's death still haunts him at night. Her parents have also talked to the press, which never seems to tire of that sort of tragic story.

Taking charge and helping to shape a new maternity ward hasn't been anywhere near as fulfilling as he expected, either. In some strange way, his life is exactly the same as before, only ten times more stressful. He has brought in two new doctors, but he still never really has time to come up for air. The problems just keep stacking up, weighing him down.

There simply isn't enough money, and it quickly transpired that the clinic is much less well equipped than he first thought. They have already had to send several emergency caesareans elsewhere, and the mothers' terrifying experiences make for worrying headlines. Niklas is being paid more for his efforts, but interest rates have also gone up, and with their mortgage payments rising, money is practically as tight as before.

Sweden could be heading into a recession. No one knows for sure, but things look shaky. The only glimmer of light is that he has managed to set a little aside every month to pay for the Christmas present currently in his inside pocket, warming his heart. When he thinks about that, it almost feels as though it might have been worth it after all. The hard work, the overtime, the stress.

This could be the start of a new era for his little family. Rather than coming to Hogreps every year, they can explore new countries before the girls get too old to want to go on holiday with their parents. He has dreamed of going back to Vietnam ever since Lillis and Tore took him there as a child. That trip made a real impression on him, and it might be naive, but he wants to recreate that now, to take his daughters to an incredible country that is economically poor but rich in so many other ways.

He can just picture the boat trips between paradise islands, eating Vietnamese pancakes on the bustling streets of Hanoi. The trip will create memories for life, something much more valuable than a new iPad, laptop or yet another bracelet Bea doesn't need. Imagine if this kind of present becomes a new tradition? Gaining experiences together, rather than buying each other things they don't need.

The porch door opens and he drops his cigarette to the ground, quickly stamping it out with Tore's boot.

'Dad?' The voice is Alma's. He can see her silhouette in the glow of the torches.

Niklas steps forward from the dark ruins. 'I'm coming.'

'We're opening the presents now.'

He reaches up to his chest pocket one last time to double-check the present is still there.

*

Niklas has been watching her all evening, trying to confirm his suspicions. Bea claims she is happy about the trip he has planned, really happy, but her eyes tell a different story. Her pursed lips, too.

She is now lying down in bed with the novel Lillis gave her, trying to pretend she hasn't noticed his eyes on her.

'Are you OK?' he asks.

'Mmm.'

'Sure?'

'I'm just tired.'

Her arms are tense, her hands gripping the book tight, and she is staring down at the page as though she is stuck mid-sentence.

Niklas pulls himself up into a half-sitting position. He knows he should keep quiet, at least for the moment, but he just can't help himself.

'We don't have to go if you don't want to. I can cancel the tickets.'

'No, you've bought them now.'

'I just thought it would be something fun for us to do together. Creating memories for life.'

'It's a really sweet thought.'

'But?'

Bea lowers her book to her chest and turns to look at him.

'You've wanted to go there ever since we got together, so we may as well go. It just seems a bit selfish.'

Niklas is speechless. He wants to argue, but he needs a moment to compose himself first. Bea picks up her book and starts reading again. From the attic, he can hear laughter and shrill voices from some Christmas film. Probably *Home Alone* or *Die Hard*.

'Is it selfish just because I think it'll be fun too?' he eventually asks.

'No, it's a really kind thought, I've told you.'

'It doesn't seem like you feel that way.'

Bea lowers her book and turns to him again.

'I would have appreciated it if you'd asked me first, that's all. We're going to miss out on an entire summer at Hogreps now.'

'But we always come here. Don't you think it'll be good to go somewhere new?'

'Sure, but it might be the girls' last real summer here, it won't be long until they're old enough to go off and do their own thing.'

'I thought they seemed excited about the trip?'

'Well, they didn't want to upset you. What did you expect them to say?'

Niklas tries to think. Is he really so far removed from his own children that he can't tell when they are disappointed? Were they just trying to look happy for his sake? He doesn't want to believe it, but ... what if Bea is right?

'It must've cost a fortune, too,' Bea continues. 'Can we really afford it?'

'The kitchen cost far more.'

'Maybe, but we discussed that first. We made a joint decision to invest in our home. But with this it's like you decided where we should go on holiday and then tried to wrap it up as a Christmas present.'

Her words leave Niklas utterly deflated.

'I just thought it would be fun to do something new as a family,' he says wearily. 'But I guess I was wrong.'

He slumps back against the pillow and closes his eyes. Feels them stinging beneath his eyelids. Maybe Bea is right and he is selfish for buying a Christmas present for himself. He just wants to experience something new with his children, his family. To do something different, rather than being stuck in the same old rut year after year.

'It was really thoughtful of you, it was.' Bea's voice sounds softer now. 'And I'm sure it'd be the perfect trip to take once the girls have left home, once we have a bit more freedom to do what we want. But if I'm really honest, now just isn't the right time.'

There is no point trying to make any changes, he has to accept that. They'll wait until the girls are older, until he and Bea are older. Right now, he just has to adapt. To do as his family wants. Cancel the trip. Everything Bea is saying sounds perfectly reasonable, but he can't help but feel profoundly sad and powerless.

'Did you like your sweater?' she asks him.

'What?'

'Your Christmas present.'

Niklas nods, though he barely remembers what it was like.

'It's great.'

'You can always swap it for a different colour if you'd rather, or a smaller size. But I thought you might like a bit of room for movement.'

'Good idea, thanks.'

He rolls over onto his side, with his back to her.

'Are you annoyed?' she asks.

'No, just tired.'

That isn't a lie. Niklas is exhausted.

Through the thick down duvet, he feels her change position, curling up beside the reading lamp and turning the page in the book his mother gave her.

STOCKHOLM

New Year's Eve, 2015

HE TELLS HIMSELF THAT it'll be good to do something different for a change, though this particular New Year's Eve party probably doesn't rank especially high on his wish list. Nor does the idea of driving back to Gotland tomorrow, a plan Bea sprung on him a few days ago.

'It'll be a bit hectic, but I still think it'll be good to be at the same party as the girls – just so we can keep an eye on them.'

Niklas suspects the girls would much rather their parents weren't there, though he doesn't say that. He has already given in. Even as he asked the question – whether it was really necessary for them to head back to Stockholm too – he knew Bea had no intention of discussing the matter. It was exactly the same when he tried to suggest alternatives: Did they really need to go to Gotland again on New Year's Day? Wouldn't it be easier just to stay in town?

Bea has already booked the return tickets, and it would be bad form to pull out of the party at such late notice. She is right, of course. Why let the tickets go to waste and be so rude? Rather than argue, he turns his attention to Candy Crush, which has proved to be a much better distraction than he ever could have imagined when Alexia first helped him download the app. Better than his painkillers, even. It's impossible to think about anything else when you're trying to complete a level.

'Hello? Could you put your phone down for a second, please?'

Niklas looks up from the game, where he has just managed to match five candies in a row, despite Bea's constant chatter. He knows what a lousy thing it is to do, how upset he gets when she does the same thing to him: pretending to listen when he starts talking about his problems at work, about which of his new colleagues annoy him and how lonely he sometimes feels.

It isn't that he is trying to get even with her – he wants to listen the way he usually does, to be as engaged as before – but his brain is just so tired. He is tired to the bone, unable to take anything in. Playing Candy Crush is about all he can manage.

'I don't know how you can waste so much time on that rubbish,' says Bea, nodding at his phone.

'It's nice not to have to think for a while.'

'Sure, but how are you going to feel on your deathbed? "God, I'm so glad I spent two hours a day playing Candy Crush so I didn't have to think"?'

She has a point.

Bea moves in front of him to catch his attention. 'What do you think?'

She spins around, showing off her dark green dress with a belted waist.

'Looks good,' he says, trying to sound appreciative.

'Do you think it's New Yearsy enough?'

'Yeah, I guess so.'

'You guess?'

'I mean . . . it is.' He has to make a real effort not to seem annoyed.

It's as though Bea always chooses to misinterpret what he is saying when it comes to the way she looks. If he says she is pretty, she wants to know why he doesn't think she is beautiful. And if he says she is beautiful, she questions whether he really means it.

'What are you going to wear?' she asks.

'A jacket or something.'

'It said tuxes on the invitation.'

'Then I guess I'll wear a tux.'

'Please, Niklas . . . could you try to show even a little enthusiasm?'

She looks sad, nodding to his phone before she turns back to the wardrobe and starts rummaging for a dress that is not only New Yearsy enough, but also goes with the tux he will soon have to put on, along with a friendly matching smile.

For Bea's sake, Niklas puts his phone down. She's right; it's ridiculous for a fifty-two-year-old to be playing a brain-dead game like Candy Crush, but it feels like cutting a lifeline.

*

Jonas and Maria Axelsson live just around the corner, on Wittstocksgatan. Niklas has never been into their apartment before, only ever the hallway, to pick Alma up or drop Emmy off after one riding competition or another. Bea claims that they once went over there for a drink, but he has no memory of that.

To Niklas, the whole thing is a little odd. A New Year's gathering taking place in parallel to some sort of teenage party in the shared space in the basement. Still, he is glad that the girls seem excited, despite the fact that he and Bea are essentially going to be at the same shindig.

Bea immediately switches to socialising mode, wearing a black wrap dress and the pearl necklace Lillis gave her when they got married – an heirloom that has been in the family for generations. Niklas has always been fascinated by Bea's ability to talk to anyone. She seems to find it so easy to connect with complete strangers, whereas he always hits a brick wall – and it has only got worse over the years, especially in private settings. The same is also true at work, but at least there he can step into his role and talk about a subject he knows. In settings like this, he can't help but feel awkward.

The large apartment is already crowded, the hosts flitting about saying hello to people as waiting staff carry trays of welcome drinks around.

Bea grabs his hand and pulls him after her, as though he were a child.

'We usually spend New Year's with family on Gotland, but it's so fun to do something different and come to a fantastic party like this. Isn't it, honey?'

Niklas nods as she jabs him in the side, Bea's signal for him to start talking, to take part in the conversation. Last time they were invited to dinner at someone's house, she gave him a telling-off afterwards.

'Everyone thinks you're really sulky, you know.'

'I tried my best, but—'

'You don't have to make such a big deal of it. Just be yourself.'

Oddly enough, that's the problem. Being himself. He knows how to behave when he is in a defined role, as a doctor, husband or father. His performance might vary, but at least the expectations are reassuringly clear. But in other contexts he feels lost and uncertain. Niklas is shy, in other words. And given that he is in his early fifties, a high-ranking doctor and a father of two, that is so embarrassing, he can barely admit it to himself.

People and faces flicker by. He is introduced to some and tries to introduce himself to others. The real disaster strikes when he ends up sitting beside Maria Axelsson at the dinner table, which means that responsibility for giving the thank you speech falls squarely on him. In all honesty, he would rather have a tooth extracted without anaesthetic than get up and thank his hosts for the venison they apparently hunted themselves. As they eat, all his energy goes towards agonising over what he is going to say and how he should say it. Fortunately for him, Maria doesn't seem to mind his lack of conversation. Aside from a bit of small talk about their daughters' shared interest in horses, she has been busy chatting to the man on her other side.

The minute the main course is over, Niklas excuses himself and hurries through to the bathroom. To his relief, he finds a beta blocker in one of his pockets. It must be a leftover from the conference in Mombasa, where he had to give a speech at a banquet.

As he takes his seat again, he notices Bea gesturing enthusiastically on the other side of the table. She is deep in animated discussion with her neighbour, who looks vaguely familiar. Another father from the girls' class, perhaps.

'Is it really so bad?' he hears Maria ask.

Niklas turns to her, confused.

'Having to sit beside the hostess, I mean.'

'No, no, it's an honour.'

She smiles. 'You look pale.'

Niklas's blood seems to rush to his feet. It's as though his body is holding him hostage, and he is embarrassed by his reaction. He is convinced that Maria will be able to see straight through him no matter what he says next.

'It's good to be sitting beside you,' he says quietly. 'I'm just not so great at giving speeches.'

There, he's said it now. Given her advance warning that she has picked a dud and that his speech won't be especially memorable.

'Look, I didn't even cook the food,' says Maria, 'so as far as I'm concerned you don't need to give a speech.'

'Don't you think people will be expecting one?' he asks.

She laughs, making her frizzy light brown hair shake. 'God, it's not like this is a state banquet. I honestly don't give a shit what people expect.'

With those words, she lifts a weight from his shoulders. Niklas sits tall, finally able to breathe freely again; he can forget about having to stand up, tap his glass and try to come up with something that ultimately just sounds forced.

*

Once the dinner plates are cleared away, the music starts. The bar in the living room opens, and the guests begin dancing. Niklas is waiting for a G&T when he feels a light nudge in his side. It's Bea.

'Did you have fun?' she asks.

'It was OK. You?'

'I ended up beside Sten Lewen, do you remember him? He was in my class in junior high.'

'No, not really.'

'Maybe you missed him, you'd already moved up to senior high by then. He's been living in Luxembourg for years, only moved back over the summer. His son is apparently the same age as the girls.'

Niklas gives her an absent-minded nod.

Bea is quiet for a moment, and she peers around the room before she continues.

'It was a bit weird that you didn't say anything earlier. Couldn't you have said a quick thank you for the food, if nothing else?'

'Is that kind of thing really necessary? It's not like this is a state banquet.'

She stares at him in surprise. 'No, but it's New Year's Eve, and it's probably a bit rude to your hostess.'

'She didn't want me to say anything. I asked.'

Bea seems tired. 'I'm guessing you told her you find that kind of thing hard?'

'No . . . I said that I'm not very good at it.'

She rolls her eyes. 'Then she was just trying to be nice.'

Bea looks embarrassed on his behalf, and Niklas realises that she might be right. Perhaps Maria simply read the signals he was giving off. Did she notice how nervous he was? Did she feel sorry for him and want to make things easier?

All he knows is that he has always been terrible at this kind of thing – unlike Calle and Freddie, who seem to have been born with a ready-made speech for any occasion, always funny and sharp.

'Have you seen Alma and Alexia?' asks Bea.

'No, I guess they're still downstairs.'

'I think I'll go and check everything is OK. Are you coming?'

'I'm just waiting for a G&T . . .'

Bea shrugs and walks away, leaving Niklas feeling disloyal for not going with her.

The barman sets down a glass in front of him, and he takes two deep gulps, wishing they had stayed on Gotland. He is thoroughly sick of spending every damn holiday with his family, but anything would be better than this party, which is just stressing him out.

For a split second, he toys with the idea of taking the lift downstairs and going home, but he quickly decides that would be impossible. You just don't do that sort of thing. Instead, he moves away from the noisy bar and the dance floor, down a narrow hallway and past a kitchen and bathroom. The apartment is bigger than he thought. One of the doors is ajar, and he spots what looks like an office on the other side, with a desk and a well-stocked bookshelf. He smirks to himself at the animal theme: a golden paperweight tiger, bookends shaped like dogs' heads, an armchair heaped with zebra- and leopard-print cushions. He slumps down onto it, leaning back against the savannah animals and sipping his G&T. There is a framed film poster on one wall, a vintage image of a furious King Kong crushing a plane in one hand and clutching a woman in the other. The room is calming, softly lit by an antique chandelier from the same period as the poster.

Niklas turns his head towards the window. On the far side, he can see the glowing Christmas star in his own kitchen. It feels slightly surreal, almost like he is spying on himself.

'Oh, hi.'

Niklas jumps. He hadn't heard Maria come into the room, and he feels like he has been caught red-handed.

'Sorry,' he blurts out. 'I just needed to give my ears a bit of a rest.'

'I can understand that, with someone like me as hostess.'

'That's really not what I meant.'

Right then, he notices that Maria's dress matches the décor. He was so nervous during dinner that he hadn't even noticed she was wearing leopard print. It's both flattering and touching somehow, he thinks, feeling slightly confused.

'Maybe you'd rather be left in peace?' she asks.

In all honesty, he would, but how is he meant to tell her that?

'But even if you would, how are you supposed to say so?' Maria adds, as though she has read his mind.

Niklas laughs. 'Exactly.'

'I'll just be a minute.'

'It's your office.'

'True.'

Niklas sips his drink, starting to become uncomfortable again. Fumbling for something to say.

'Very cool King Kong poster. Is it an original?'

'No idea, I bought it at a flea market in New York when I lived there.'

'Oh, wow. Cool.'

Did he just say cool again? Honestly, how can a man be so bad at small talk? It's even worse when Bea isn't there to cover for him.

'Any New Year's resolutions this year?' he asks, immediately regretting his question. So lame.

'I've actually stopped bothering with that sort of thing. It's not like I ever manage to keep them, anyway. You?'

'Nah, same. I don't know why I asked.'

'What else is there to ask on New Year's Eve?'

'I guess that's what I thought.'

'I've been trying to make everyday changes instead,' she says. 'But it's hard.'

He leans back in the armchair, trying to listen instead of focusing on his own awkwardness.

'What kind of changes?'

Maria seems to be thinking.

'It varies, but I suppose I just don't want to end up on the hamster wheel, going round and round in the same place forever.'

Niklas nods. 'You work and work, but there's no escape. You're stuck.'

Maria raises an eyebrow.

'It's more that I want time to think about the next step, to make sure whatever I'm doing really feels good. And that I have time to enjoy myself along the way, too. What you just mentioned doesn't sound so good, though. What are you stuck in?'

Niklas isn't sure why – maybe it's the alcohol starting to take effect – but he finds himself opening up, the words spilling out of him.

'Work. Everything. Nothing is fun anymore. I do things because I have to. A kind of weariness with life, I guess. It's probably just my age.'

He laughs in an attempt to play down his confession.

'You're a paediatrician, aren't you?' asks Maria.

Niklas nods.

'But that must be really exciting?'

'Yeah, it should be, but it doesn't feel that way.' Niklas is slightly surprised by his honesty.

'Then why do you do it?'

'It's my job. What else am I supposed to do?'

'Well, you could change careers, for example.'

Niklas laughs again, but Maria seems serious.

'That sounds like a great idea,' he says, slightly unsure whether he really believes it or whether he is just trying to be polite. 'But I've got a family to support. Bills to pay.'

'Anything's possible if you really want it.'

'Maybe if you're a millionaire.'

He knows that Maria's husband, Jonas, was involved in the dot-com bubble in the late nineties, that he sold his shares at the right time. But he also knows how what he just said must have sounded, and he is afraid she might be offended.

'I didn't mean anything by that, obviously.'

Maria shakes her head. 'I know what you mean, but some decisions are hard no matter how much money you have. I'm in the process of leaving my husband, for example. Not that he knows it yet.'

Niklas flinches, slightly taken aback by her frankness. 'Oh, I'm sorry to hear that.'

He knows that was a feeble response, but he can't think of anything better to say. He holds out his G&T to her instead, and she takes the glass and knocks it back.

'It's something I've been thinking about for a while,' she says. 'But, like you said, it's easy just to keep going round and round on the hamster wheel, living everyday life. He's the millionaire, by the way, not me. We've got a prenup.'

Niklas feels stupid for assuming that she was well off.

'What about the two of you?' Maria asks.

He shakes his head. 'We don't have a prenup.'

'I meant how are you doing,' she says with a laugh.

'Oh . . . ha . . . yeah, we're fine, I guess. Bea and I were pretty young when we met . . . we've basically known each other all our lives.'

'Yeah?'

'Her late brother was my best friend. We got together after he died.'

'Oof, I guess that must mean you've got a pretty special bond? That kind of thing really forges people together.'

'Yeah, I guess you could say we have shared trauma.'

'Was it an accident?'

'Suicide.'

'That's awful. It must be one of the worst things a person can go through.'

'It was incredibly hard on Bea.'

'And you?'

Niklas tries to think.

Maria hands back his empty glass. 'Given he was your best friend, I mean.'

'I guess it wasn't really the right moment for me to stop and think. In some ways, that might actually have been good for me, because I had Bea to look after and comfort. The best way to help yourself is to help someone else, as they say.'

Maria studies him with a look of slight astonishment. 'But that could also have been an excuse to avoid having to stop and think.'

Niklas swallows and raises his glass to his lips, shaking out the last few drops. He feels oddly moved, and has just decided that he needs another drink when he hears Jonas calling for Maria.

'It's almost twelve,' she says. 'But you're welcome to stay in here if you like.'

Niklas nods in gratitude. He isn't ready to go out and join the others yet.

Maria gives him a warm smile. 'You're not a slave, you know. You can actually quit your job if you're not happy there, even if you do have a family and bills to pay.'

She pulls the door shut behind her, leaving Niklas alone with the animals. He feels relieved and a little exhilarated. It was so refreshing and liberating to talk to someone the way he just talked to Maria. Totally unexpected.

She has only ever really crossed his radar as a figure in the background, as Emmy's mother, and yet during their brief chat, she managed to get right under his skin, surprising him with a thought he has never dared get near before. Niklas has never considered quitting as a doctor, not even as a joke. The idea has never crossed his mind, and the prospect of being free to do what he wants with his life, changing direction from one day to the next, sounds like utter madness. The forbidden nature of the thought leaves him with a rush of exhilaration, verging on intoxication – though that could also be the alcohol talking.

Niklas gets up from the armchair and walks over to the window, peering out at his family's balcony on the other side. It took him seven years to become a fully qualified paediatric doctor. He had discussed it with Bea, and she encouraged him to take a chance on the profession, even though the training was long and demanding and he was afraid of needles. They talked about how much good he could do, how it would open up a world of opportunity for him, enabling him to work wherever he wanted. Médecins Sans Frontières, all the ground-breaking research he could devote himself to. He could overcome his fear of needles if he really put his mind to it.

And she was right, of course. He found something good on the children's ward in Sollentuna, along with his little work family there; he was happy with it. But does he actually enjoy being a doctor? Is it exciting? Or is it mostly boredom, mixed with the constant dread of making a terrible mistake and having someone's life on his conscience – a fear that has come true more than once, though Lovisa's death is the one that troubles him most. In his new job at Sophiahemmet, he is trapped in a meat grinder of stress and responsibility, and no matter how fast he runs or how hard he works, he will never be able to escape. Some days are calmer than others, but only just.

Maria's words seem to have opened up some sort of window in him. Imagine if there is a way out after all? If he really could do something different with his life? What would that be? How would it feel? He has butter-flies in his stomach, though not from anxiety; this is

234

more a giddy feeling. A hopeful breeze, carrying the memory of something distant, from back when he was still young and curious. Hungry. Could he really do something just because *he* wants to do it, for his own sake? The thought is so dizzying and forbidden that he bursts out laughing.

Right then, he hears 'The Final Countdown' from the living room, followed by some muffled bangs outside. He pries the window open and leans out. One firework after another bursts across the starry sky above him, and down in the yard, the teenagers have begun to stream out of the basement. He sees his girls standing beside Emmy and a big group of friends.

On the living-room balcony, a group of guests have raised their champagne glasses. He spots Bea in the crowd, laughing with her old classmate Sten Lewen. Through the muddle of bodies, he also spots a hand waving. A pink glow lights up Maria's face, and she leans over the railing and waves again. Niklas reaches out to wave back as the others start counting down, the last second of the old year transforming into the first of the new.

'Happy – new – year!' she shouts, her messy hair blowing in the wind.

'Here's to 2016!' Niklas yells back, raising his empty glass to Maria with a smile. Not out of politeness or because that is what is expected of him, but because he is happy. Because, even though he is on his own at the other end of the apartment, away from all of the others, he doesn't feel like he is alone.

He has Maria there, on the other side, and she knows something about him that no one else knows. He promises himself not to make any damn resolutions this year. He won't stop playing Candy Crush, either. He is going to make changes to his everyday life. Real changes.

BANÉRGATAN, STOCKHOLM

New Year's Day, 2016

WHEN NIKLAS WAKES THE next morning, that feeling is still lingering in his body, despite the alcohol having left his system. The realisation makes him as excited and happy as he was yesterday. He is free. He can quit his job if he wants to. He can stop being a doctor, start over as something entirely different. Just like that, the new year looks unexpectedly hopeful and bright.

He pulls on his sports clothes and heads out. Though he is hungover and his knee is protesting, he feels almost weightless as he runs along Valhallavägen towards Gärdet. The endorphins his body produces as he sprints up the hill towards Borgen only add to his euphoria, and on the way home he stops off at the bakery to buy walnut bread and croissants.

He bounds up the stairs to their apartment on light legs, and for the first time in a good while, he takes a long shower, enjoying the cool water and letting the jets massage his shoulders. It's as though the first day of the year has added some new ingredient to his life, something that was missing during the last. Even the prospect of heading back to Hogreps later today, by car and ferry, no longer seems like a slog; if anything, it feels comforting, positive.

Bea slowly opens her eyes as he comes into their bedroom carrying a tray, fully loaded with croissants and freshly brewed coffee.

She rolls over in bed with the unmistakable groan of someone who had too much to drink the night before, and Niklas is both grateful and slightly surprised that he isn't worse for wear himself.

'What are you doing?' she mumbles, rubbing her eyes.

'New Year's brekkie. I woke the baker just for you.'

Bea's pained face transforms into a surprised smile. 'You're so sweet.'

She reaches out and kisses him, digging her fingers into his wet hair.

'Have you been out running?'

'Just to Gärdet and back.'

'I really don't know where you get the energy . . .'

'I feel pretty wide awake, oddly enough.'

Bea sits up and sips her coffee. 'Where'd you disappear to last night?'

'I actually had a pretty interesting chat with Maria.'

'Axelsson?'

Niklas nods.

'God, *what* did she look like in that leopard-print dress?'

'I thought it was OK?'

'Mmm, debatable. Bet it matches the ugly tribal tattoo at the base of her spine.' Bea laughs and takes a bite of croissant.

Niklas doesn't like her tone, and he has a sudden urge to defend Maria. Maybe it has something to do with the way he feels that morning, with the lingering excitement that he is so desperate to cling onto, but hearing Bea insulting Maria and her dress feels almost like she is insulting him, too.

'I've been thinking about doing something different this year,' he says. 'Changing jobs.'

He just blurts it out, without stopping to think, and Bea freezes mid-chew.

'But you've just done that?'

'Yes, I know, but it feels right.'

'Surely you just need to give it time, find your feet before you think about moving on again?'

'I've been doing this job for twenty years; I've found my feet. What I need is to do something else.'

Bea seems puzzled. 'What do you mean? As in you want to move to a different specialism? No longer work with kids?'

'No, as in I don't want to be a doctor anymore.'

It's slightly surreal to say it out loud, but it also feels good. Liberating, somehow. Right.

'Stop it, Niklas, this isn't funny.'

'I'm serious.'

Bea puts her cup down with such force that the coffee sloshes out onto the nightstand. Flakes of crisp pastry fall like confetti onto her nightdress.

'Just because I trained to be a doctor doesn't mean I have to do it for the rest of my life, especially not if it feels like a prison.'

Bea reaches out and touches his arm. 'When are you going to stop punishing yourself? You're a great doctor.'

'This has nothing to do with that,' he says, pulling away from her. 'I've felt this way for a long time. Maybe even since the beginning.'

'So you've been doing something you don't enjoy for the past twenty years?'

'Exactly.'

She bursts out laughing, and Niklas is confused.

'What's funny?'

'Charlotte and I were wondering when your midlife crisis might hit just the other day. I mean, what are the odds?'

Niklas's heart rate rises, but he sits up straight and tries to keep his breathing under control.

'Call it whatever you want, but that's how I feel.'

'One of Charlotte's colleagues went off on a weekend meditation retreat, and when he came home, he'd decided he wanted a divorce. Two weeks later, he changed his mind again.'

'This isn't the same.'

Bea gives him an amused look and takes another big bite of her croissant. She seems to have regained her appetite, but Niklas's has deserted him.

'OK, let's say you were no longer a doctor,' she says between chews. 'How would we be able to afford to stay here? And what about Alma's riding lessons? The car? All the trips to Vietnam or wherever you want to go?'

'I'm sure we could find a way if we really tried.'

'OK, but it's not like we have millions stashed away. We have to be realistic here.'

'I don't know, but there must be a way. I can't be a slave. Maybe you could find another job?'

'So I should leave the Red Cross just because you've decided you don't want to be a doctor anymore? I don't have a degree, remember. That was our deal.'

'Well, it's not too late to get one.'

'Of course not, but if I'm going to do that, we'll need to have this discussion again in five years' time, once I've finished studying for my incredibly well-paid new profession. I have to say, it doesn't feel great that you're belittling my job like this.'

With a wounded look on her face, she reaches for her phone and starts scrolling to let him know that the conversation is over.

Niklas gets to his feet. The lightness he felt earlier is gone, and with it the feeling that anything is possible. Bea is right, of course she is. He has to be realistic. Even if she did go back to school and tried to find a better paid job, it would take years to reach that point. Is he really going to force his family to move and Alma to stop riding because it's suddenly vital that he quits being a doctor? If they sold the apartment, they would still have debts to pay. They have to live somewhere, after all.

No, Niklas has already made his choice, many times over. When he first started studying to become a doctor, when he got married and had kids. When they bought the apartment. When they renovated the bathroom and

241

kitchen. When they bought their safe, expensive, environmentally friendly Volvo.

With every decision, his white coat has become increasingly difficult to take off. Of course he isn't free. That was an illusion, a gin-fuelled fantasy in the fog of the new year. He is a slave.

Bea seems to have composed herself again, and she puts her phone down.

'Don't you remember what it was like when you first took the job in Sollentuna? You hated it. You came home and said you wanted to quit every single day, but then things turned around. It'll be the same with your new job, I'm sure of it. And you might not think it has anything to do with it, but that damn death has been following you around all year and . . .'

Her voice fades away as he turns and leaves the bedroom. Niklas knows she is probably right, but he doesn't have the energy to listen right now. It feels like something has just been extinguished inside him.

DJURGÅRDEN RIDING CLUB

February 2016

THE GREAT CREATURE STUDIES him with pleading eyes. It's all in his mind, of course, but it feels like the horse is begging for help.

Save me. Let me go.

Imagine if he did. If he unclipped its muzzle, opened the box and sent the brown gelding galloping off into the distance with a slap on the backside. It would probably enjoy a few hours of freedom on Djurgården before it was caught. Either that or it would end up being hit by a car on Hunduddsvägen. A terrible idea, no doubt about it. Still, there is something in the horse's brownish black eye that seems painfully familiar.

'Can you grab the saddle?'

Alma lets go of the horse's heavy back leg and straightens up, with the hoof pick in one hand.

'And the bridle, too.'

Niklas gives her a thumbs up and walks over to the tack room.

It smells good in there, like leather and saddle soap. There is a little name tag by each bridle and saddle, just like a nursery, so everyone knows whose is whose.

Kilmore, My Lady, Walther, Figaro, Lucky Star, Stella, Avatar, Morris.

'I thought you must be allergic.'

Niklas turns around and sees Emmy's mother. Maria from the party.

'Because we never see you round here,' she explains, smiling softly at the confused look on his face.

'Ah, no, I usually just do the driving,' says Niklas, giving her a slightly embarrassed smile in return.

'Are you staying to watch?' Maria asks.

That wasn't the plan – Bea has asked him to run a few errands while Alma is riding – but he is pleased to see Maria again, and realises he wants to hang around.

'Think so,' he says. 'For a while, anyway.'

'See you in the stands, then.'

*

The arena is cold, but Maria has already bagged two blankets and she waves to Niklas from one of the benches at the top of the stands. Down in the manège, the riders are moving around while they wait for their instructor, Alma and Emmy chatting as their horses walk side by side.

'Next time, I think I'll have to wear my ski suit,' Niklas says with a shiver as he sits down and blows on his frozen fingers.

'Double long johns is the solution, otherwise it's just too cold.'

Considering how long Alma has been riding, Niklas should know things like this. He is embarrassed that he doesn't come out here often enough to know better. Maria is a seasoned pro in contrast, with a thermos of coffee and everything. She hands him a cup.

'Thanks.'

'You're probably at risk of frostbite otherwise.'

'Yeah . . . Hey, thank you for all your help ferrying the girls back and forth to competitions and that sort of thing. Bea doesn't drive and I often have to work evenings and weekends, so it's been tricky . . .'

'Are you still working in the same place, then?'

'Yup, I am. Sophiahemmet.'

'Is it still as awful?'

Niklas hadn't been expecting a cross-examination, but Maria doesn't seem to want to waste any time on small talk.

'I might have exaggerated a bit last time we spoke,' he says. 'These things come in waves; sometimes you're happy, sometimes you're not . . .'

Maria focuses her piercing eyes on him, and he feels a sudden urge to defend himself. Who is she to judge?

'How is everything with you?' he asks. 'With the divorce?'

Niklas immediately regrets his choice of words. What he just said must have sounded far too harsh, petty, as though he wanted to get his own back somehow.

'Sorry,' he hurries to add. 'I didn't mean . . .'

'No?'

Niklas is speechless for a moment, but then she flashes him a disarming smile.

'Don't worry. It's kind of sad, but mostly a relief. It's also pretty exciting, like the start of something new.'

'Ah, so have you already . . . ?'

'Yup, but these things take time. I'm looking at apartments at the moment. Jonas is too, but it's still an upheaval for everyone.'

Less than two months have passed since New Year's Eve, but Maria has already put her plans in motion. Made radical life changes. What has he done? Resigned himself to his fate at Sophiahemmet. Accepted the consequences of his earlier decisions. He is stuck, letting time march on rather than throwing himself into the unknown the way Maria has.

'Wasn't it scary, making the leap?' he asks.

'Yes, though the thought of not doing it was worse.'

He lets her words sink in, unsure whether it's the note of hope in what she is saying, the warmth of the blanket slowly thawing his frozen limbs, or the delicious coffee. But something makes him feel uplifted and yet oddly frustrated.

RUDDAMMEN, STOCKHOLM

May 2016

MARIA'S NEW APARTMENT IS on Körsbärsvägen, a stone's throw from Stockholm East Station, in Ruddammen. It's a quiet area, one Niklas has always found slightly depressing. As a child, he took piano lessons in a bunker-like building on one of the side streets they are now passing on the way up the hill in Freddie's van.

'I definitely owe you one for sorting out the van,' says Maria, 'but you know I could've easily rented something myself, don't you?'

'Why bother? This was just gathering dust over in Frihamnen.'

That isn't entirely true. It was actually pretty tricky to get hold of the vehicle, which was being used in a production somewhere out of town. Niklas had to convince Freddie to let him pick it up late on Friday night, all the way out in Ekerö, promising his friend he would have it back by eight o'clock on Monday morning at the very latest, when shooting is due to start again.

He and Maria have been texting a little since their meeting at the stables, mostly to arrange lifts for the girls, but he has also tried to check in on her from time to time, asking whether she needs any help. When she mentioned moving house, he immediately thought of Freddie's white van, which he and Bea have borrowed to transport large items a few times. He offered to check whether it was available, but forgot to mention that he was technically on call that day, meaning he could be dragged back to the hospital at any moment. He didn't want to worry her for no reason, and now he is trying to juggle the stress that comes with the prospect of being needed in two places at once. He also feels guilty about having taken on yet another extra shift to get out of going out to Hogreps with the others over the long weekend.

*

Her new apartment is in a shabby 1940s building, where the dirty yellow plaster has started to flake away from the facade. Things are a little better inside, with light flooding in through the many windows and views out across Roslagstull.

'It's a great space, isn't it?' Maria asks.

'Definitely,' he lies. 'Where do you want these?'

Maria points through to the living room, and he puts down another couple of moving boxes before heading back out for the next load. As he is making his way down the stairs, his phone rings. Of course it does. His responsibilities at work are calling, and he speeds up in order to grab the last few boxes.

When he gets back to the apartment, he finds Maria standing in the middle of a maze of boxes.

'I'm trying to find the champagne glasses for a little toast,' she says, 'and I'm starting to realise it might have been a good idea to label the boxes.'

'That's sweet, and I'd love to stay, but . . . I have to go to work.' Niklas feels stupid for not telling her about being double-booked, and now he has to desert her in the middle of everything. 'I forgot to say, but I'm technically on call today . . . I can come back and help again later, though. I just have to go in and check on a patient.'

'I'll be OK, but thanks for your help.'

Maria picks her way out from the boxes and gives him a hug. She smells like sweat and perfume, a scent that unexpectedly makes him want to bury his nose in her hair.

'I'll come back later.'

'No need.'

'It's fine, I won't be too long. Just save all the heavy stuff for me.'

Maria lets go of him and peers up at his face. 'OK, but I don't want you to come back.'

'Sorry, I understand if you're disappointed . . .'

'Seriously, Niklas. Stop.'

'I know I should've told you I was on call, and I'd really like to help you with the rest, but—'

She interrupts him with a laugh. 'I just want to enjoy unpacking my new home in peace and quiet, on my own. I was planning to ask you to leave soon anyway.'

Niklas feels a mixture of relief and confusion at her reaction, his sense of guilt still lingering. In his pocket, his phone starts buzzing again. He is needed at the hospital, but he also can't shake the worry that he has let Maria down.

'Well, just give me a call if you need me, because I can come over and help once I'm finished . . .'

'Don't worry. But you're very welcome to come over for a drink another evening, as a guest. Or is this some sort of fetish you've got? Do you need to help people to feel good about yourself?'

Niklas chuckles, though it seems to catch in his throat. Does he help people for their sakes or for his?

When he gets down to the street, he jumps into Freddie's van and tears off along Valhallavägen, skidding into the parking area outside Sophiahemmet. There is a desperate woman inside, someone who really needs him. Niklas is stressed, hates being on call, but at least he is serving a purpose. His life has meaning.

BANÉRGATAN, STOCKHOLM

June 2016

THE MINUTE HE HAS dropped off Bea and the girls at
the ferry terminal in Nynäshamn, Niklas drives back to
Banérgatan, parks the car in the garage and takes the lift
up to the apartment. It's the first time he has been there
in two weeks, and the first time in a long while that he
has had the place to himself.

One of the girls has left a bowl of cereal in the living
room, and the kitchen is a mess after breakfast. It isn't
like Bea to leave things like this. Could it be her way of
putting her foot down? Or maybe she isn't doing so well?
Niklas knows how much pain he is causing her right now,
and a part of him just wants to give up altogether. To stop
it from hurting so much, for everyone's sake. To comfort
her the way he usually does. That would be the simplest
thing: to catch the next ferry to Gotland and join them
at Hogreps, let everything go back to normal and continue
as before. But no, he seems to have reached the point
where he can no longer back out, though he also has no
idea how to move forward from here.

Other than the rumbling pipes when one of the neighbours
flushes a toilet or turns on a tap, Banérgatan is silent. The

air is stuffy, and he goes from room to room opening the windows. Bea's accusing eyes seem to follow his every step. From the photograph taken on the maternity ward right after the girls were born to the family snap taken in Costa Rica. There are framed pictures of him, Bea, Alma and Alexia all over the place, the walls plastered with images of familial happiness. He has never even stopped to think about that before, the photographs have always just been part of the décor, like everything else Bea brought in to make their home as warm and welcoming as possible. It feels like he is seeing them for the first time. Wherever he turns, their demanding, judgemental eyes seem to be watching him.

Even with a through-draught, it's as though he can't breathe in the baking-hot apartment. Niklas goes through to the bedroom to lie down and gather his strength, but he spots a note on the bed.

Come soon. We love you <3
Bea

As he reads those two short lines, everything suddenly seems so clear. Black and white. He can't live up to the expectation behind her words, to Bea's love, their home or their lives together. He needs to get out.

*

Niklas wanders aimlessly in the afternoon heat, and though he isn't quite sure how he got there, he finds himself in

Ruddammen. The area no longer feels quite so depressing, not that anything has really changed there since he helped Maria move in. The change is in him. The piano lessons of his childhood have been replaced by new experiences. His shoulders relax as he walks along Körsbärsvägen, and he finds himself smiling as he looks up to the fourth floor of the shabby yellow building. There is a light up there, a glimmer of joy that he hasn't felt in a long, long time.

They haven't arranged to meet today, and he didn't call ahead, but Maria still welcomes him with open arms, unconditionally and without any questions. He barely knows why he is here, as though he was just following some sort of internal compass that led him to her. He hangs his linen jacket on the brass elephant head Maria has mounted on the wall, its tusks perfect as hooks.

'Sorry if I'm not the most chatty today,' he says after a moment or two.

'It's enough just to want to keep me company,' Maria replies. 'Jonas has taken Emmy and Lukas to his place in the country for a few weeks, so there's plenty of room if you just want some peace and quiet.'

Niklas follows her through to the living room, where the floor is cluttered with Jiffy bags, pink tissue paper, different coloured candles and patterned cushion covers. There is a gentle breeze from one of the windows, and the summer air mixes with the soft scent of wax and perfume.

'I've started taking web sales from the shop, and the orders have been flooding in. Guess people need something to make the time pass while they're out at their summer houses,' Maria explains with a laugh. 'Sit down, take it easy,' she continues, pointing to the corner of the room. 'I'm just going through the day's orders, it'll probably take a while.'

Niklas moves a few boxes, spots a leather floor cushion and sits down with his legs crossed. He doesn't feel much of an urge to help her, he realises. That's unusual for him, but it really is OK just to sit quietly on the other side of the room.

He didn't come over to do anything, to sort or fix, comfort or tidy. He came over because he needs Maria. He wants to be wherever she is.

RUDDAMMEN, STOCKHOLM

August 2016

MARIA IS ALREADY UP when Niklas wakes, even though it was the middle of the night when she got home after dropping the kids off at Jonas's place. She spent last week in Milan with Emmy and Lukas, a combined work and leisure trip involving a visit to an interiors fair, and Niklas had her apartment to himself while she was away.

He listens for sounds from the kitchen and smells the aroma of coffee drifting through to the bedroom. Even though he has been here a while, it feels strange to hear someone else moving about in the morning; with Bea, he was always the first to wake.

Niklas makes his way through to the living room and finds Maria slumped on the blue velvet sofa, one half of which is much paler than the other after six months in her shop window. She has a notepad on her lap, and the pen in her left hand is dancing back and forth across the page as she sketches away, deep in thought.

His body almost seems to contract with longing. The apartment on Körsbärsvägen has been oddly empty without her, though staying here has also left him feeling surprisingly good. It's as though her relaxed energy has seeped into the walls, and some of that has rubbed off on him. Not that he dares say any of that out loud, of course. It sounds ridiculous enough in his head.

The fact that he is happier has also made it much easier to talk to the girls, both during his many calls to Gotland and since they got back to town a week ago. They might not be living under the same roof, but he doesn't think he has ever felt so relaxed around his daughters. It's as though he can be himself in a different way with them now, even if Alma is loyal to Bea and peppers him with critical questions he can't always answer. Niklas has never been less in control of his life, but he is strangely calm and hopeful about the future.

He curls up beside Maria and breathes in the scent of her hair as carefully as he can, trying not to disturb her.

'What do you think?'

She turns the pad so he can see it, still sketching away. An abstract pattern fills the page.

'Impressive.' His response sounds a little lame, so he tries to come up with something else to show her just how talented he thinks she is. 'Did you know that Picasso was left-handed too? And van Gogh.'

'Vincent also cut off his own ear and shot himself,' Maria says drily before bursting into laughter, her chest shaking.

He tries again, with another compliment. 'It'd look good on a cushion.'

'Thanks, but it's actually going to be my new tattoo.'

Maria already has four. One is a tribal pattern at the base of her spine, something she often pokes fun at but doesn't regret enough to have removed. She also has Emmy and Lukas's names written in cursive script on her wrists, and a leopard on her forearm. If Niklas is really honest, this is the part of Maria he doesn't really understand.

'Why are you getting another one?' he asks, with genuine curiosity.

'As a symbol of the divorce, my freedom.'

'Isn't the paperwork from the court enough?'

She lowers the pad and gives him an amused look. 'You think it's ugly, don't you?'

'No, I . . . I guess it's just not really my thing.'

'No?'

'I don't know . . . I think it's a bit . . .'

'Common?' Maria fills in.

Niklas is embarrassed, but that is exactly how he feels. He thinks it looks trashy. Still, he doesn't want to upset Maria.

Right then, a memory comes flooding back to him, something that must have been lying dormant for years, buried beneath everything that was too painful to think or talk about. Under different circumstances, he probably would have let it lie, but he wants to be open with Maria. He also wants to show her that they have more in common than she thinks.

'I actually thought about getting a tattoo once, a long time ago.'

'Oh yeah?'

'Jacob and I were planning it as some kind of friendship thing, but it all went to shit . . .'

He can just see Jacob, their awkward attempts to draw on each other's arms in ballpoint pen. And he can still hear Lillis's disparaging tone when she saw his faux tattoo.

If you're going to draw on yourself, you could at least make it look nice.

A burning shame washes over him.

'Tell me, what did it look like?' Maria asks.

'No, it's a bit . . . I don't know . . .'

He has to steel himself. Thinking about the design is almost more painful than remembering the sense of defeat he felt when his parents refused to sign the permission form he needed as a minor.

'Come on, you wimp,' says Maria, giving him a teasing glance. 'What could be worse than my leopard?'

'An olive branch,' Niklas blurts out, laughing and waving a hand in the air as though to bat the memory away. 'It was supposed to stand for bravery, victory and friendship . . .' Another embarrassed laugh. 'But, well, our parents wouldn't let us get them. Maybe that was lucky, because I'm sure Bea would've hated it; she thinks that kind of thing is so common.'

Hearing himself say it, he has a sudden realisation: it was Bea who thought that, not him. The idea that tattoos are common isn't his opinion, it's an echo of someone else's.

Maria gives him a warm smile, turns the page in her notepad and starts sketching. Little by little, an olive branch starts to emerge on the blank sheet.

SKANSTULL, STOCKHOLM

A BARE-CHESTED NIKLAS leans back in the leather chair. His back is sticky, dripping with sweat, though the tattoo artist hasn't even started yet. August has been one long heatwave, but the air feels, if possible, even stuffier today. Or maybe he is just nervous. He could still back out if he wanted to. The sketch on his forearm is just Maria's stencil; there isn't any ink beneath his skin yet.

Right up to the very last moment – even as he and Maria stood outside the tattoo parlour – he kept questioning his motives. Is this an attempt to exorcise his feelings of guilt over the separation? Is he in the middle of a midlife crisis? Slumped back in the chair now, he decides to listen to Maria's advice: as long as he is true to himself, he doesn't need to worry about how the outside world views his actions. If Niklas wants a tattoo, he should get one. Who cares what anyone else thinks or says? Who cares whether it's common, whether he is a cliché of a middle-aged man? He knows that this is about him and no one else. Maria manages to make all that sound true, but when he repeats it to himself, it seems more like a banal self-help tip from a glossy magazine.

He doesn't need to explain that this tattoo is so much more than a symbol to anyone who judges him – his wife, parents, siblings, patients and colleagues. He is doing it to defend the person he is, the core of him that's still in there.

He just wants to find his way back to himself. What else does he feel? What does he like? What doesn't he like? It's been so long since he really stopped to think about these things that he isn't sure. What kind of food does he enjoy? What sort of style does he have? More than anything, he wants to find the courage to go against other people's expectations of him. To stop paying attention to who he should be and everything he has tried to live up to. As Maria says: 'It's just a bit of ink. It's not like you're about to chop your arm off or something.'

Maybe that was why he asked her to wait outside, so he can be sure he isn't doing it for her.

It's time. The tattoo artist moves Niklas's forearm into the right position and lowers the needle to his skin. He doesn't want to back out; he wants to break free. The needle makes his delicate skin sting, and his eyes water because of the pain and emotion. An olive branch of freedom.

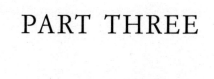

PART THREE

BEA

BANÉRGATAN, STOCKHOLM
November 2016

THE GIRLS ARE AT school, and the apartment is pleasantly quiet. Sitting at the kitchen table, Bea peers around the room. Everything turned out just how she wanted. Better, even. The matte green colour on the hand-painted ash cabinets – 'Atelier Mossa' – is exactly as the catalogue described it: 'artistic and natural, artless and exquisite'. The ugly white goods are all hidden away behind cupboard doors, and the island they eventually picked has pride of place, with open shelving in the same rich shade as the drawers and an enormous gas stove looming large in the middle. The inbuilt display cabinet seems to hover just above the skirting board, just as she imagined it, the cherry on top of the cake.

The kitchen is perfect, but now she has to give it up. And all because Niklas has given up on her.

Bea put her heart and soul into this project, and she has paid for it with her life. Literally. Niklas has mentioned the renovations as one of his reasons for wanting a divorce, or at least a partial explanation. A little odd, in her opinion, given that he was barely home all spring and didn't have anything to do with the project. She was the driving force behind the whole thing, and on the handful of occasions she did ask for help or input – for a lift to a builder's depot or a showroom, questions about the colours or materials – it was more to give him an opportunity to feel involved. It's always more fun to work together, after all, and though she provided the impetus for the work, she obviously wanted Niklas by her side. As support.

Bea has a moving box on the floor beside her, nothing but a cast-iron frying pan and a Smeg mixer inside. That was all she could bring herself to pack before she slumped down into one of the chairs. It just feels so wrong. Every fibre of her being is against packing up the kitchen; it's impossible. All these things belong together, just like she and Niklas do. The two of them, together with the girls. Their family.

Their entire shared history is here. The lemon-yellow yoghurt bowls they bought when they visited Henke and Sus in Brazil, the various orange Le Creuset pans they have collected over the years. Their wedding china, which Lillis made by hand. Twelve dinner plates, twelve side plates, twelve soup bowls. Are they supposed to split that in two, keeping half a set each? Their home is falling apart, broken just like their family.

At the same time, she is slightly ashamed. It's just an apartment, after all. Just a damn kitchen. Losing Niklas is a thousand times worse. But for Bea, the kitchen and apartment are also at the heart of everything she loves and has tried to build. It's the family's centre point, their base, a source of security for her, Niklas and the girls, and that is being ripped out from beneath them.

Would Niklas have stayed if they'd kept the old kitchen? Did she put too much pressure on him? Or is the kitchen just a pretext for leaving her? He has given her a number of hazy explanations in order to avoid the most obvious answer: that he is in the midst of a classic midlife crisis and projecting all of his disappointment onto Bea. Onto the kitchen, his job. Onto everything that doesn't have anything to do with him and *the incident*.

She gets up and tries again, attempting to sort through the cups this time. The *Best Dad Ever* mug that Alma and Alexia once gave Niklas for father's day is on the shelf. It's an ugly thing with a picture of Homer Simpson on it, but it also has real sentimental value to Niklas, who used to drink his morning tea out of it every day. A little further back, she spots the two cups Lillis helped the girls to make when they were younger. They decorated them themselves, and then Lillis fired them in her kiln. Alexia painted a gangly figure whose legs are attached to its head, and Alma drew something that was supposed to represent a flower and a sun. Those have even more sentimental value.

Bea sets the cups down on the counter and slumps back onto her chair. She doesn't want to pack them away; she doesn't want to do anything. It is as though her arms and legs are made of concrete. She feels like chaining herself to the round wooden table and refusing to leave.

Every cell in her body is screaming that it's happening again. A sudden, inexplicable loss; a cruel disappearance from her life, hitting her without warning or explanation. Just like with Jacob.

She has to force herself to keep going. The removal van will be here in a few hours, to take her half of their things to the new apartment in Örby, a suburb to the south-east. It'll be fine. She just needs to convince herself that everything will be fine, even if it didn't turn out how she expected or hoped.

It shouldn't have come as a surprise that she didn't have enough money to live anywhere close to Banérgatan. Inger was surprised, however, when Bea announced that she was left with 'just' two million kronor after Niklas bought her out. Not at the amount, as such, more over Bea's lack of gratitude at having a sum of money most people could only dream of. She was also troubled that Bea had such an 'irresponsible grip' on their finances that she hadn't realised just how in debt they were, nor how much she might get after a divorce.

Bea is ashamed by her lack of gratitude and mortified that she never took more of an interest in their affairs. Niklas had apparently taken out a second mortgage on the apartment without any security, meaning that virtually everything would go back to the bank following a sale – and he had made that calculation before the property market began to falter. How could she have been so naive?

Niklas has always had primary responsibility for their finances, for the money coming in and out; he earns more than she does, so that seemed natural. Especially during the tough periods, when Bea was depressed and couldn't work. He always said he understood. That he was there for her and that she could rely on him. It wasn't as though she forced him to take that responsibility.

She doesn't want to know how he managed to find the two million to buy her out when they couldn't get any more loans from the bank. As far as she is concerned, she just needs to lower her expectations – however much she would love to stay in the area where she grew up and has spent her entire adult life. It'll probably do her good to get out there and see something new. Her and the girls. Besides, this is nothing compared to the humanitarian disasters going on elsewhere, all over the world. She sees it daily in the tragic fates she comes into contact with through her work, and in light of that she is grateful just to have a roof over her head. At least she and her children aren't trying to cross some hostile ocean in a rubber dinghy – even if it does almost feel that way sometimes. She has to remind herself just how good she has it, to pull herself together. The glances Inger gives her help with that, if nothing else.

The concrete blocks around her feet seem to grow lighter, and she manages to get up, grabbing the girls' mugs. Those are coming with her.

NIKLAS

KAPTENSGATAN, STOCKHOLM

SITTING ON THE DAYBED in the office of his apartment on Kaptensgatan, Tore looks confused. For as long as Niklas can remember, his father has always taken a nap on the green chaise longue after lunch. It's narrow, hard and unbelievably uncomfortable, but Tore likes to have 'something firm' under his back, especially now that he is in such pain.

'Imagine you're doing a curtsey,' Niklas encourages him.

'Why do you want me to do that?' Tore asks grumpily.

'I just want to see how it looks. Come on.'

His father reluctantly gets up and gives him a quick curtsey. The pain is immediate, causing him to wince.

'How much weight have you lost?'

Tore pretends not to have heard him.

'How many kilos since the summer?'

'I never weigh myself.'

Niklas gives him a stern look.

'A few belt holes, maybe. But that's good at my age, with my cholesterol and everything.'

Niklas nods vaguely and continues with the rest of his questions.

'OK, and are you still going to the toilet like normal?'

'What a question . . .'

'Dad . . .' The choice of word surprises him; it is one he almost never uses. Niklas has been calling his parents by their names since he first learned to talk, all in line with Lillis and Tore's seventies' mantra that children and adults are of equal worth. 'Dad' sounds so strange, particularly while he has his doctor's hat on.

Tore mutters to himself. '. . . Takes a bloody age to go for a piss, I suppose. And that's if anything actually comes out – even though I'm bursting.'

'He's always so tired, too,' Lillis adds from the doorway. She can't help herself, though Tore gives her a dark look.

'That's not so bloody surprising when you're seventy-six.'

'Tired how?' asks Niklas.

Tore seems irritated, but he reluctantly answers the question. 'Weak, somehow. I can barely mow the lawn.'

Niklas clears his throat. 'Why didn't you say anything?'

'Pff, we've not seen hide nor hair of you lately.'

Niklas bites his tongue, and Tore realises he has gone too far.

'I didn't mean it like that. Just, well, you know . . .'

Niklas knows, but he doesn't have the energy to get into that debate right now.

'We'll start with a few tests, and then I'd like to get you booked in for an MRI.'

'Never. I'd rather die than get into one of those tubes.'

This time it is Niklas who pretends not to hear. 'I'll write a referral.'

'Aha, and what does that mean?'

Tore is sitting down on the shabby old chaise longue again. He looks like a child with his wide eyes and swinging legs.

'That a skilled, competent doctor who isn't your son will take a look at you.'

'Is that normal for lumbago?'

'Lumbago or a slipped disk, but those don't usually last this long. We'll see what they say. I can write you a prescription for more painkillers in the meantime.'

'Fine, but I want something with a bit of bite, not just paracetamol.'

He continues to grumble, and Niklas digs out the half-pack of co-codamol he happens to have in his pocket and hands it over. He then packs away his blood pressure monitor and follows Lillis through to the kitchen, where she has a stew bubbling away on the stove, ready for the girls coming over.

His parents' visits to Stockholm have become more frequent since Tore's back started playing up and he and Bea began their divorce proceedings, not that there is any explicit link between the two.

'Glass of wine?' asks Lillis. 'It's made from Hogreps grapes. We brought a case over; I'll give you a bottle to take away with you later.'

Niklas nods and watches his mother as she opens and closes the grubby white kitchen cabinets, taking out his granny's old glasses. They are covered in a thin layer of dust, and Lillis rinses them out beneath the ancient tap, which is probably an original feature from when the apartment was first built.

'So, what do you think?' she asks.

'We'll have to start with the tests and then—'

'Just tell me.'

She hands him the delicate glass, filled with buttery yellow wine.

'I'm a doctor, not a fortune teller. It's impossible to say.'

'But making qualified guesses is surely part of the job?'

Lillis's hand is shaking, and Niklas realises he needs to keep up the professional facade, to hide just how worried he really is. He is the backbone of the family, the rock, the son who always steps up. The one who lives right around the corner and comes over to help whenever he is needed, who races over to Gotland the same afternoon if duty calls. Who has to fill the void left by Henke's decision to be an expat on the other side of the world and Hampus's fun but disorderly life as the baby of the family, free from all responsibility.

And so Niklas holds back. He can't share his fears with Lillis; he needs to be there for her. Both as her son and as a doctor.

'It'll be OK, I promise.'

He says that, but the truth is that Tore's worsening pain, his tiredness and his sudden weight loss have all set alarm bells ringing. It's obvious something isn't right.

'I'm just so worried,' Lillis sobs, seeking out his embrace. 'I've been nagging him since the summer, but he won't listen to me. You have to help him, promise me you will.'

Niklas hugs her back, trying to reassure his anxious mother.

'And there's all this business with you and Bea, too,' she says. 'I can't sleep.'

He tenses, but Lillis continues.

'You need to let her in so that you can solve any problems you might have together.'

Just like his wife, his mother refuses to listen to him and what he wants. Refuses to accept that he has filed for divorce, that they are in the middle of dividing up their estate and that Bea is moving to a new apartment as they speak.

He reaches into his pocket, then remembers that he just gave the last of his co-codamol to Tore. It's tempting to have another glass of wine instead, but no. He needs to drive after dinner.

'We're getting divorced,' he snaps, 'you know that.'

'But you have six months to change your mind, to talk and listen to each other.'

'It feels like no one is listening to me.'

'OK, but surely you can see why we might wonder if you really know what you're doing. It's all been so quick. And considering Bea's past ... Don't forget about that, OK? This is going to be especially traumatic for her; you're the most important person in her life.'

As though he could forget. Not a single day goes by that he isn't acutely aware of his responsibility towards Bea – and not just because of Lillis's constant reminders.

He still remembers exactly how it all began, as though it were yesterday.

*

Narvavägen. The stairwell is familiar, the door the same as ever. Everything looks just like it always does, exactly as it has since the day Niklas first came over to Jacob's place after school, back in year one. They played at each other's apartments, though, more often than not, they went to Niklas's on Kaptensgatan. Not because it was closest, but because it was easier that way. There were always plenty of snacks, and Lillis and Tore liked it when their boys brought friends home. At Jacob's place, you always got the sense that his parents wanted to be left in peace. That Niklas was tolerated at most.

This time, it's Bea who opens the door to him. Her parents are nowhere to be seen. They might not even know she invited him over. Jacob's room looks different, and his bed is gone. That was where he did it, Niklas knows that, but somehow its absence seems worse than if they had just left it there.

The room is oddly neat and tidy, not at all how he remembers it – though it has been a long time since he and Jacob last hung out here.

Bea looks thin, almost invisible. Nothing like before, when she was a little chubby. There is barely anything to her now. She says she is glad to see him, though it looks like she is on the verge of falling apart.

On Jacob's desk, she has a few objects lined up. His Casio watch. His old leather wallet, bent from being shoved into his back pocket. The neckerchief he always wore. The belt he bought at the same time as his army jacket, from the surplus store; Niklas was with him that day.

Bea nods to the table and tells him to pick something, a memory of Jacob, but it feels wrong. Not just towards Jacob, but to Bea and her parents, too.

The betrayal.

He feels like a coward for not having the courage to tell her that he and Jacob weren't best friends at all towards the end. They weren't even friends. And he is afraid that Bea might break into a thousand pieces if he refuses to take one of the precious heirlooms she has set out for him. He has to, for her sake and for Jacob's; it's the least he can do now that it's too late to do anything else.

Niklas's eyes start to wander, landing on the Casio watch. He can see Jacob's tense wrist, his nervous hands.

Bea's pleading eyes. Niklas picks up the watch and fastens the metal strap with a click.

'Jacob would've wanted you to have it,' she says.

Her face lights up slightly, and the pressure on his chest eases for a moment.

When he gets home that evening, they have a goodbye dinner for Henke, who is going off to do an internship with a shipping company in Copenhagen. Lillis has cooked lamb steaks with cognac sauce and Hasselback potatoes. It's Niklas's favourite meal, but he can't manage a single bite.

Hampus curls up in his lap and fiddles with his wrist-watch. Lillis says it's lovely that he'll always have a little piece of Jacob with him, that it was kind of Bea to give him one of her brother's most treasured possessions. Why doesn't he ask her over for dinner one day next week? It's important they hold Bea close now, she says. Especially considering how cold and distant her parents are. After all, who else does she have?

Niklas tenses. He hadn't managed to think that far ahead. Now that Bea no longer has Jacob, she essentially has no one. With that thought, the weight on his chest is back.

*

'Hello? Anyone home? Can you hear me?'

Lillis holds out the bottle of wine and gives him a quizzical look.

Niklas shakes his head. 'No, thanks. I have to drive the girls over to Bea's place after dinner.'

Lillis looks pained.

'Are you really going to make the girls flit back and forth across town now?' she asks. 'Does the metro even go all the way out to . . . where was it, Örby?'

Niklas loses it.

'Do you really not care how *I* am? Are Bea and the girls the only ones who matter? Don't you think only seeing them every other week is going to be tough on me, too?'

'Of course I want you to be happy, Niklas. That's why I'm sticking my nose in. It just doesn't seem very well thought through, nor does all this business with Alma's friend's mother.'

For a split second, he thinks about leaving the car and catching a cab later; it suddenly feels impossible to get through Sunday dinner without large quantities of alcohol.

'Maria, you mean?' he snaps. 'You know her name.'

'Yes, yes, it's just that Alma is finding the whole thing very tricky. As I understand it, the girls have fallen out because of all of this.'

That hurts, because he knows it's true. Niklas is overcome by a sudden sense of powerlessness. Clearly his feelings are wrong. Unauthorised. Invalid.

'I'm sorry,' he says, 'but this isn't something I did just to cause trouble. All I know is that Maria is my best friend and I love her.'

He has never put it like that before, neither to himself nor anyone else, but as he says it, he realises just how right and true it feels. From the heart.

'Goodness,' Lillis says coolly. 'After only a few weeks?'

'More like six months, actually.'

'You know that infatuations fade, don't you?'

'And love dies.'

Lillis flinches, pursing her lips.

Maria has been branded, and her marking clearly reads 'infidelity' and 'betrayal' in big red letters. That's how Lillis sees her, everyone else too, all those who think she and Niklas jumped straight into bed together. But that isn't what happened. Niklas has been more emotionally unfaithful than anything, though he never expected to develop feelings for Maria. The idea that they might have anything in common had never even crossed his mind.

He isn't with Maria because he needs to be, or to make her happy. He's with her because *she* makes *him* happy. Because she refuels his lust for life.

Falling for another person . . . Does anyone really know how that works? Ignoring the purely chemical processes in the body, he has no explanation other than the most obvious. The fact that they met when they did probably plays a part, as does Maria's unique world view, which has given him a new perspective on what he can, dares and is allowed to do. On the responsibilities he has to himself and others.

She has liberated his mind somehow. Lifted the hundred-kilo weight from his chest. Sometimes he wonders what might have happened if they'd met earlier. Would he have been able to avoid all this? Would he have forgiven himself sooner? Realised that he isn't responsible for other people – other than his children, of course – or at least not in a way that makes him a slave.

The guilt is heavy. He doesn't want to hurt anyone, and yet that is the inevitable consequence of him choosing himself, his life and love. Does it make him a bad person to listen to his own needs for once? The answer to that might be yes, but he has no other choice.

'I know I shouldn't get involved,' says Lillis, 'but I can't just stand by and watch you put your entire family at risk. How can you be so sure you'll feel the same way a year from now? Or two?'

'I have no idea how I'll feel in a year. I don't even know how I'll feel next week. Do you? All I know is how I've felt with Bea over the past few years.'

The doorbell rings, and Tore comes shuffling out of the bedroom to answer. He hears the last few words, and the look he gives Niklas is hard to read. Is it pain or disappointment? Or both? Whatever the answer, his voice is sharp and irritated.

'The girls are here, so drop all that nonsense and let the poor things have a few hours of normality.'

*

Alma demonstratively gets into the back seat, but Alexia sits up front with Niklas.

'Can I drive?' she asks.

'Probably not the best idea tonight, it's a bit icy.'

'But you've been drinking,' Alma quips on her sister's behalf.

'Half a glass of wine, two hours ago,' Niklas says, glancing back in the rear-view mirror.

Alma purses her lips, just like Bea does whenever she is annoyed with him.

'You can stay at Banérgatan tonight, you know. We don't have to—'

'Might as well get it over and done with,' says Alma.

'D'you think you'll find your way out to the ghetto, Dad?' Alexia teases him.

'I don't think that's fair.'

'It's right in between Bandhagen and Östberga, so it's the closest to the ghetto you've ever been before.'

'You're probably right, yo.'

Alexia writhes in shame, and Niklas laughs at his own lameness. He casts another glance in the rear-view mirror, but there is no reaction from Alma.

Alexia plugs in her phone and starts playing a Kanye West track, which he thinks might be called 'Famous'. The suggestive chorus and electronic beat give Niklas the sense of sailing forward, and he and Alexia nod their heads in sync as they pass Gamla stan and Skeppsbron. He drives on, past Slussen and down into the tunnel beneath Södermalm.

Alma's phone starts ringing as they approach Gullmars-plan, and he turns down the volume. Her face softens as she answers, her voice too.

'Hi, Mum . . . Yeah, we're in the car now. OK . . . Yeah, no problem. See you soon. Bye.'

Another glance in the mirror.

'Was that your mum?' Niklas asks.

'We need to go back.'

Alma's tone is suddenly much colder, and Niklas tries not to let it affect him. She has every right to be angry and disappointed.

'Did you tell her we're almost there?' he asks.

'She wants us to pick up the TV and the espresso machine.'

'But she's already taken the big TV and the Nespresso?'

'Well, she says she needs them.'

Niklas wants to argue, to say that they've talked about this, that Bea has already picked out everything she wants. That they each agreed to keep one TV, and that she chose the Nespresso machine because she finds it easier to use. But he bites his tongue. It's just a TV and a fucking coffee machine, after all. It's not worth an argument.

'I'll run them over tomorrow.'

'Mum wants us to get them now.'

'It's really late, honey. We're almost there.'

'Seriously, how hard can it be? It's not like you had to move or anything.'

Despite the darkness in the back of the car, he sees Alma's eyes flash. Anger bordering on tears. It feels like a knife being driven into his heart.

'OK, we'll go back.'

Alexia sighs. 'For God's sake . . .'

'It won't take long,' says Niklas. 'Alma is right.'

'*Mum* is right,' Alma corrects him.

Niklas nods. 'OK.'

He turns at the roundabout by Gullmarsplan and drives back across the Skanstull Bridge. What he really wants is to stop the car, the world. Time. To reprogramme himself. To wish he had never met Maria, even though she is the best thing ever to have happened to him – after the girls. But is it really worth it? His children being upset? How can it be worth it?

BEA

ÖRBY SLOTT, STOCKHOLM

IT'S A SWEET LITTLE 1940s two-bed. A few original features, like the charmingly worn greyish-green Kolmård marble windowsills, the glazed interior doors made from wood veneer and the fishbone parquet in the living room. Someone must have ripped out the original kitchen at some point, which is a shame, because the plasticky replacement cupboards have all started to yellow and peel at the edges. Still, renovating the place is out of the question. Bea's monthly wage will only stretch to a fresh lick of paint and a few other bits and pieces once she has paid all the other bills.

First and foremost, she needs to get Alma and Alexia's rooms ready. Bea is glad she eventually managed to find an apartment big enough for her and the girls. Or almost, anyway; she will have to sleep on the pull-out sofa bed in the living room, but she can live with that. The key thing is that Alma and Alexia each have their own space, and that they aren't too far from central Stockholm.

She unpacks in a frenzy, not even stopping to eat. Everything has to be put into its rightful place, and the boxes have to go. Bea tries to make things cosier by spreading a rag rug across the grey linoleum floor, brightening up the kitchen with some of Lillis's colourful ceramics. Objects from her old life, which help to create a sense of security in her new one – though nothing looks quite right in its new home.

It takes her several hours to empty the boxes, but even that is much too quick, and once she is finished, she isn't sure what to do next. She finds herself standing in the kitchen with a gaping void inside her, a black hole of loneliness. It's a little like the time immediately after giving birth, when everything has been leading up to getting through that moment. The move is now over, and she is left all alone with her new baby, absolutely terrified about what comes next.

Bea has no idea what things will be like going forward. Life feels vaguely familiar, yet also completely alien. She has never lived alone before. She moved straight from her parents' house to live with Niklas, and they have been together ever since. Everything has always revolved around her home and her family, yet here she is, involuntarily single and alone in her very first solo home, with nothing but the slim wedding band around her ring finger to remind her of Niklas and her old life. Taking it off almost seems to give her phantom pains, like having a limb amputated. She has a habit of twisting it with her little finger and thumb, and whenever she removes it, she finds herself touching the bare skin where it should be. Wearing it is painful, and she wants to take it off, and yet some part of her also wants to keep it on. Doesn't want to make things permanent.

She hears water flooding through the pipes above her somewhere, racing past her apartment. It brings back memories of the sounds she is used to from Banérgatan, and Bea tries to cling on to the scrap of comfort that brings her.

She knows that she needs to try to accept her new reality. She has spoken to Charlotte, confided in Inger, but in those conversations it was always something in the future. Something that would happen at some point, something she would have to navigate when the time came. But this is the present, and it doesn't feel anything like she thought it would. She wants to be positive, but after the moving van left, it was as though this was all happening to someone else. Like she just tagged along for the ride, getting further and further away from everything she knows, and now she no longer knows where she is.

It isn't just her home and her life with Niklas that have been snatched away from her, it's her entire childhood with Jacob. For as far back as she can remember, she has trudged back and forth between Narvavägen and Östermalm School, kicked a ball in Gustaf Adolfsparken. As an adult, she pushed the double buggy along the same streets. She knows every single building, every last nook and cranny in the blocks around Karlaplan. It was where she experienced the great loves of her life: first her brother, then her husband. And also the greatest losses, over the same two men.

Both as a young girl and then later, with her own children, Bea has bought pick 'n' mix from Karlafrukt and Christmas trees from the stall by the fountain in the square;

she has gone for picnics in Gärdet and eaten ice cream and watched the boats on the Djurgården Canal. In some ways, Östermalm is like a small city within a city.

The same is true here at Örby slott, a small community with buildings dating back to the fifteenth century, a place where there was once a county store, a butcher, a hairdresser and a community centre. But all of that is now long gone.

There are no high-rise buildings in Örby slott; the area is dominated by villas and multi-residency blocks built from brick and plaster, wedged in between Huddingevägen, Östberga and Stureby. Årstafältet park is nearby, and according to the estate agent's brochure, there is even a pretty wood for walks between Gamla Enskede and Svedmyra. There are no sweet little canals, though, and the closest lake is twelve kilometres away.

Bea probably just needs time to adjust, which would have been much easier if the change was voluntary. Because the fact remains that this isn't where she *wants* to be; it's simply all she could afford. Though, on the other hand, how many people actually get to live exactly where they want? None of the millions of displaced peoples, in any case. Ironically, some of them have been placed not far away from her new apartment – at least according to a disgruntled note in the stairwell. The authorities have put up some modular housing in the car park opposite the big conference centre in Älvsjö, and there are around 100 recent arrivals living there. As so often lately, Bea is ashamed of her selfishness and her sense of entitlement. She is a first-world woman with first-world problems, as Inger always likes to say whenever someone dares complain about anything petty – broken washing machines or miserable weather on holiday – at work. And she is right. Bea needs to try to pull herself together.

She needs to find a way to feel at home here, for the girls' sake. She needs to find a foothold, something to cling on to. She could bake or cook; that usually helps whenever she is feeling stressed. Make Lillis's scones. Start a new loaf of sourdough, spend hours stretching and kneading it. She could put something in the slow cooker, the mutton with dill sauce dish everyone loves. Let the aromas seep into the walls. Give herself purpose, direction. But when she gets up and opens the cupboards, she realises she doesn't have any of the ingredients, and there isn't a supermarket nearby.

Instead, she wanders restlessly into Alma's room, then Alexia's. They'll be here soon, and she isn't ready for them, hasn't managed to make the place warm and welcoming enough. Not like back home, their real home. Why would they want to come and stay with her here? All she wants is to be back on Banérgatan, so why would her daughters feel any different?

A sudden fear shudders through her. What if they ditch her too? That thought alone is enough to make her panic, but as she heads back through to the kitchen for a cup of coffee, she has a sudden brainwave. She checks the time and digs out her phone. Have they left already?

As ever, Niklas doesn't pick up, but Alma answers after just one ring.

*

Bea hears the familiar rumbling of an engine outside, and when she peers out through the as yet undressed window she sees the family car – no, Niklas's car – pull up by the door to her building. She has only just finished making up both beds and lugging the Nespresso machine and TV into Alma's room. Alexia will soon have her own screen and coffee machine too, a little like a luxury hotel room for each of them. Snug dens worthy of two almost-seventeen-year-olds, giving them a sense of being grown-up. She desperately wants to offer them something they can't get from Niklas.

Bea heard him muttering in the background when she called, but if he's desperate for coffee, he'll just have to buy a new machine or scoot over to Maria's place. He earns over twice as much as Bea, and she isn't too proud to lay claim to anything that can make her new home more comfortable for the girls.

The little electronic doorbell unit above the door makes a soft, pleasant ringing sound, nothing like the shrill din of the brass buzzer at Banérgatan. Despite that, she still jumps when they ring it, taken aback by her own nerves.

Bea takes a deep breath and opens the door to her very first guests. Her husband and daughters. There they are, standing just outside, with a couple of bags, an espresso machine and a TV. It all feels so strange and wrong.

The threshold is like an ocean between them. Just a few months ago, they were a solid, comfortable family unit, but now they are four people who need to get used to their new, unfamiliar circumstances. Bea is overcome again by how surreal it all is.

They exchange brief hellos and then stand in silence, until Alexia says what everyone else is thinking.

'This is kind of weird, isn't it?'

'Yes, it's definitely a little different,' Niklas blurts out.

A little? Bea thinks, biting her tongue to stop herself from saying it out loud.

Alma quickly steps forward, as though she is crossing an invisible boundary. She stands by her mother's side in the hallway. That feels good, making it slightly less lonely on this side of the door. On the wrong side of the Atlantic.

Alexia follows her sister in, turning around to look up at Niklas. 'D'you want to come in and have a look?'

He gives Bea an unsure glance. 'Is that OK?'

'Maybe once we're a bit more settled.'

He nods. 'Of course. Cool area, by the way. It seemed nice as we were driving through.'

Anger bubbles up inside Bea.

It's not cool at all. Did you miss the noise barriers as you were turning off from Huddingevägen? Still, this is where you've forced me and your kids to live.

Niklas keeps making small talk. 'Is there a castle round here? Is that why it's called Örby slott?'

'It's an embassy these days, I think,' Bea replies wearily. 'Don't know how it got the name.'

She tries to hide her irritation at Niklas's faux interest in the area, telling herself just to grin and bear it. That's all that matters now; holding it together in front of the girls.

Once she has finally closed the door on him and his awkward waving, she turns to face the girls.

'Come with me, I want to show you something!'

She, Alma and Alexia are now alone in the cramped hallway, and in some ways it feels even stranger than being on her own. Bea feels a sudden pang of regret at insisting they came over so soon. Now, as she shows them round, she can see the apartment through their eyes and the contrast to Banérgatan is so clear. She tries to paper over the cracks.

'The kitchen's a bit drab, but there's parquet floor in the living room. And have you seen the marble windowsills? Pretty stylish, huh? It's all very functional, but I think the glass doors are pretty charming . . .'

Bea knows just how shrill and forced she sounds, she can hear the fear and uncertainty in her voice. She notices that Alma and Alexia are trying to be positive for her sake, but she can see her true feelings reflected in their eyes.

'. . . There's a bit still to do, of course, but I think it has potential.'

'Definitely,' Alma says quietly.

'Which is my room?' Alexia asks, failing to say a word about the apartment itself.

'One is a bit bigger than the other,' says Bea, 'but I thought you could swap at some point, to keep things fair . . .'

'It doesn't matter, I'll have the smaller one,' Alma quickly offers. Always so self-sacrificing.

'Then I've got a surprise for you . . . For both of you, actually. Come with me!'

Bea walks through to the smaller of the bedrooms, where there is a narrow Ikea bed pushed up against one of the walls, neatly made with the quilted blanket Hampus sewed years ago. Her jade plant is on the windowsill, grown from a cutting Niklas's parents gave her before the girls were even born, and on a chest of drawers by the foot of the bed – a flea market find from Gotland – Bea has positioned the TV beside the Nespresso machine and some of Lillis's cups.

The girls give her a slightly quizzical look.

'I thought you should both have your own rooms, so you can have a bit of peace and quiet whenever you bring friends over. This way, you won't feel like I'm cramping your style in the living room. I'll be sleeping on the sofa bed in there, but only at night. Otherwise you can spend as much time in there as you like.'

Alma attempts an appreciative smile.

'We can put the espresso machine in Alexia's room,' Bea continues, 'and the bigger screen, since there's a bit more space.'

'I usually just watch stuff on my computer,' Alexia says stiffly. 'And Dad probably has more use for the coffee machine, but thanks anyway.'

With that, she turns on her heel and leaves the room. Bea hurries out after her.

'You should think of yourself, love. Dad can buy a new one. I'm sure he'd rather you had it.'

'I don't even drink coffee anymore.'

Bea wonders if she is just saying so for Niklas's sake, but she doesn't want to push it and get into an argument.

'OK, then we'll keep it in the kitchen. But you just have to say if you change your mind.'

'Is this where I'm sleeping?' Alexia asks, peering into the larger of the two rooms, with a window out onto the yard.

'Exactly. Like I said, there's still a bit to do, but I've made up a bed for you.'

Her daughter nods and moves inside, looking around before dropping her bag to the floor.

'Anyone fancy going for a walk?' Bea asks. 'It might be fun to explore the area.'

She can hear how forced it sounds, but it's impossible to act normally when everything feels so strange and wrong. This fake, ultra-positive facade is currently all that is stopping her from falling apart.

'I'm pretty tired,' says Alexia. 'Maybe some other day.'

'Or we could watch a film together, if we can work out what to do with all the cables . . .'

'I'm pretty tired too,' says Alma, looking a little guilty. 'But definitely tomorrow. Sorry.'

'No, no, you're right, it's probably a better idea to save it for another time,' Bea hurries to reassure her. 'We're all tired.'

The girls close their doors, leaving her alone in the hallway. Somehow that seems even lonelier than it used to when they shut themselves in their rooms at Banérgatan. Back then, it was almost a relief when they wanted to be left in peace. Her new apartment may be smaller, but the void feels all-encompassing.

NIKLAS

BANÉRGATAN, STOCKHOLM

IT'S BEEN A LONG time since he was last at the apartment. He has been staying at Maria's place in Ruddammen whenever she doesn't have the kids, and at Freddie's when she does. Coming back now feels like visiting a museum where the remnants of his former life are on display. A collection of objects from an era that seems oddly distant. How is he supposed to be able to live here? Does he even want to? He knows he has no choice, for the girls' sakes.

Maria peers around with interest. 'I don't think I've ever been to your place before. It's nice.'

'Yeah, Bea is great at decorating.'

The parquet floor creaks underfoot as they walk through to the living room.

'Great amount of space. High ceilings.'

'Could do with a bit more furniture, though.' Niklas laughs, though he is more sad than anything. It felt odd to leave the girls at Bea's new place, but it's just as strange that Maria is now looking around what was their home for so long.

She moves over to the sofa, slumps down and tucks her legs up beneath her, the way Bea always does when she reads. A sudden wave of nausea rises up inside Niklas.

'Just need to use the toilet.'

He reaches the porcelain throne just in time and hears Maria following him down the hallway. Her footsteps sound different to Bea's, fortunately.

Without a word, she fills a glass with water and holds it out to him. She then crouches down and puts an arm around his shoulders.

'I must stink.'

'I still love you.'

A strange sound escapes from his throat, like a lament over everything he has lost. Over the divorce, Tore's illness, his own self-reproach and guilt. As that passes, an indescribable weariness hits him.

'Sorry,' he mumbles. 'This can't be much fun for you.'

'If you believe the other parents' gossip, I'm a narcissistic psychopath, so it's all good,' says Maria, bursting out laughing.

Niklas looks up at her in surprise. 'What's so funny?'

'I mean . . . what am I supposed to do, you know? Be miserable for the rest of my life, just so the other mums accept me? They'll only find something else to bitch about.'

Maria can't stop laughing, breaking down in hysterics that seem to rise and bounce off the bathroom tiles. Her eyes well up, making her mascara run. Niklas joins in, and before long, he has no idea what they are even laughing about. This mess, how fucking hard life is. He laughs at his own inadequacies and yet . . . He also feels a dizzying sense of relief that he dared make the leap. He took the plunge, hurling himself straight in at the deep end, hand in hand with Maria. It was an epic bellyflop that hurt like hell, but at least he did it. He survived, and he can do it again.

*

Once the laughter has petered out, Niklas takes a shower and gets changed. He is home again, even if the apartment now feels more like a hollow shell than anything. It's not just that half the furniture is gone; the people are too.

Maria is in the kitchen, pouring boiling water through a makeshift coffee filter made from kitchen roll. Niklas would rather have wine, but he doesn't say anything. Alcohol probably isn't a good idea right now. The kitchen roll coffee also tastes much better than he was expecting.

'It'll get easier once the girls are back,' she says. 'Or it did for me, anyway – not that I'm still living in our old place.'

'Maybe I should try to find somewhere else . . .'

'It probably doesn't make much difference where you are in the beginning, it'll be tough either way. The relief doesn't come until later.'

Niklas looks around Bea's kitchen. At the pots and bowls, the pictures and knick-knacks. Beside the sink, where the espresso machine used to be, there is a dishcloth that looks about as wrung out as he feels. Right then, it hits him.

'All of this is Bea's. She chose every single thing. Everything but the espresso machine, which is all I really wanted. A great coffee machine. And I drove it over to her place the other night. Anything that was mine is gone.'

'That's your mum's, isn't it?'

Maria points to a lemon yellow bowl on the worktop. There are more ceramics in the green china cabinet, all different shapes and sizes.

Niklas nods. 'Though I've never really been keen on Lillis's stuff.'

'So where are your things?' asks Maria.

*

It takes them a while to find the right storage cage in the attic, and Niklas is embarrassed that he doesn't even know the combination for the padlock, though the code turns out to be the girls' birthdate.

It doesn't matter that it's the middle of the night or that he has to go to work in the morning; once he gets started, he just can't stop. Maria helps, filling boxes with things that Niklas has never liked or that remind him too much of Bea.

In a dusty box, he finds his old school yearbooks and photographs from his teens. He shows Maria a spotty version of himself, and is busy rummaging through the other memories when he spots Jacob's Casio watch.

'Those are back in fashion now,' says Maria. 'Why don't you ask the girls if they want it?'

'I doubt it even works,' he says, putting it back without checking.

Maria gives him a slightly puzzled look, but Niklas doesn't have the energy to explain. He doesn't want to think or talk about the past. Instead, he puts all his energy into lugging an old leather armchair that Bea never liked down the stairs.

They push the sofa up against a different wall and swap the chest of drawers in the hallway for the one in the bedroom. Niklas has never given any thought to the way the apartment is furnished, but it is oddly enjoyable to move things around, giving the place a different feel, in a good way.

'Isn't this kind of unfair on the girls?' he asks, struck by a sudden doubt.

'It's not like you're throwing anything away,' says Maria. 'And they can help you sort everything out once they're back next week. Who knows, they might actually want to make a few changes themselves.'

'And what if they don't?'

'Worst-case scenario, you can just put everything back where it was. Everything that's not already at Bea's place, I mean . . .'

Niklas hopes Maria is right, because what he is doing right now feels almost illegal. Moving things Bea positioned so carefully. Packing up objects she bought and approved. Putting away the things that she loves and taking out others that she hates. But he's not doing it to be difficult; he's just trying to be true to himself.

They make one last trip up to the attic, searching for anything else that he could take downstairs. How does he want his home to look? Does he even have his own style? Niklas isn't sure, but he is oddly curious about what that style could be. Maybe he and the girls could come up with something together?

His mouth curls into a smile.

'I think I just felt it,' he says.

'What?'

'The sense of relief you were talking about earlier.'

As the words leave his mouth, the timer on the lights runs out and they both notice a pale blue glow through the window overhead. Niklas and Maria look up and see it at the same time: the moon, shining in on them like some sort of soft floodlight. They hold each other in its pale light, and for a brief moment, he thinks that it was all worth it after all.

BEA

ÖRBY SLOTT, STOCKHOLM

THE FIRST SNOW FELL overnight, and it looks like a blanket of whipped cream as Bea runs to the bus stop. She searched high and low for her thick down jacket, but it seems to have vanished in the move. She'll just have to make do without it, she thinks, trying to keep warm by stamping her feet while she waits for the bus. There is a newsagent and a dry cleaner on the ground floor of the apartment building on the other side of the road, a dentist a little further down the street.

The number 165 bus to Liljeholmen is already packed when it eventually swings around the corner onto Huddingevägen, and Bea only just manages to squeeze on. The route meanders through the area, which mostly consists of detached villas and rows of houses. The streets all have some sort of connection to St Lucy's Day, which seems fitting for the time of year.

The roads are slippery, the bus full of weary people packed in like sardines. They gaze up at the roof with blank faces, no doubt dreaming of teleporting somewhere else. The bus passes Brännkyrka Church and leaves Bea's new neighbourhood behind, continuing through Västberga

Industrial Estate and up onto Södertäljevägen, where the traffic is heavier, before finally turning off towards Liljeholmen and the metro station.

Bea's new neighbourhood. That's what it is, but it still feels surreal, like she is on a brief sojourn in some far-flung country.

*

Emerging from Karlaplan Station forty-five minutes later, Bea feels like she can finally relax, as though she has just returned from a long trip abroad. If the weather were better and she wasn't already running late, she would sit down on one of the benches by the fountain and just enjoy being *home*. Each and every building around here is like a trusty old friend. Even the Fältöversten mall, an ugly 1970s monstrosity, seems friendly and welcoming today.

She squints over towards Narvavägen. Are her parents still in Stockholm, or have they already left for Mjölby ahead of Christmas? They've started spending more and more time in their little forest cabin there since they retired, leaving them even more shut off and distant. It strikes Bea that she still hasn't told them about the move or the divorce. They rarely ever speak, but she knows exactly how they will react. Her mother will make the divorce all about her and how sad *she* is, and her father will make sure Bea understands that they lack the means to support her financially.

She sets off along Karlavägen, towards the Red Cross office. Towards the crossing with Banérgatan and her old home. It could be any other day, as though she has just left the apartment and is making her way to work. If she's in a good mood, she might take a detour down to the Valhalla Bakery to buy some sweet buns for Inger and the others, a latte for herself. She could pick up some of the walnut bread Niklas likes so much, then cross over to Gustav Adolfsparken, past the church and the playground where they always used to take the girls.

What she really wants is to call the office and let them know she won't be coming in, then head home instead. To her real home. She wants to take the lift up to the fifth floor and lie down on the soft double bed by the window onto the yard. Niklas will come in and curl up beside her, smelling like Dior aftershave, his cheeks soft and smooth. His lips are warm and delicious, and he'll hold her until she falls asleep in his arms. Until she wakes up from this nightmare.

The light turns red at the crossing, and Bea stops to wait. On the other side of the road, a gaggle of children are making their way towards Östermalm School, just like Alma and Alexia once did. She gazes longingly at her old building, at the pretty red facade and the bone-coloured embellishments around the windows, the oak garage doors. As she is standing there, the doors open and the family car rolls out. Niklas is behind the wheel, and in the seat beside him . . . Maria. With that, Bea's daydream shatters into a thousand pieces. Today isn't just any other day after all.

The car turns towards the crossing, where Bea is frozen to the spot despite the fact that the light is now green. Niklas brakes and comes to a halt. They see her. She sees them. There are other people walking by, and the traffic lights keep ticking, but Bea can't bring herself to move.

Niklas and Maria are now staring straight ahead, as though she were invisible, though she knows they have both seen her. Her legs refuse to move, and the lights eventually turn green for the cars. Bea remains where she is on the pavement as Niklas accelerates and tears away.

The light on the pedestrian crossing turns green again, ticking to let her know she can cross. Bea knows she should keep going, make her way to the office, to work. Ticktockticktock. But instead she turns and walks down Banérgatan.

*

Bea pushes her key into the lock and stops to listen as she steps inside. She can't hear a sound. There is no one home, she knows that. Niklas just left with Maria, and the girls are in Örby, a late start at school. But here she is.

Just twenty-four hours ago, this was her home, the address where she had lived for almost twenty years, so why does it feel like she is doing something wrong by being here? Her surname is still on the door. *Stjerne.* She has no intention of giving that up. Niklas can take a lot from her, but he can't stop her keeping the same surname as the girls. That's just the way it is.

Bea lingers in the gloomy hallway, breathing in the scent of her home. She closes her eyes for a moment and tries to trick herself into daydreaming again, but something isn't right. What she can smell isn't Niklas's aftershave but the faint, almost imperceptible aroma of women's perfume.

When she opens her eyes and makes her way through to the living room, she sees that the scent isn't the only thing that has changed. The furniture is all in the wrong place, and some of it has disappeared completely. The sofa is up against a different wall, dolled up with a couple of ugly cushions and a blanket she has never seen before. Those must be Maria's.

Bea moves through the apartment with wide eyes and a half-open mouth. The pictures have been taken down, things she hasn't seen in years set out here and there. In one corner, Niklas's ugly leather armchair from his boyhood room on Kaptensgatan has made a reappearance.

In the bedroom, someone – Maria, she would guess – has hung an awful mirror with a tacky golden frame, and there is a toiletry bag she doesn't recognise in the bathroom. Bea sniffs the air again. The same fragrance as out in the hallway.

In her wonderful kitchen, they have put away all the beautiful bowls and vases she left for the girls. The china cabinet has been gutted of all its lovely objects, and Niklas has shoved a load of books inside in their place, as though it were a bookcase.

The green kitchen table, which matches the new cupboard doors, has been moved through to the dining room, and someone has spread a wishy-washy tablecloth over the top. By the kitchen window, there is now a white plastic table she has never seen before, and all the cookbooks that fit perfectly in their little inbuilt nook are now stacked on the floor.

Bea deliberately tried to make her departure from Banérgatan as invisible as she could for the girls, taking pains to ensure that it still felt like home, but clearly she needn't have bothered. It's as though Niklas and Maria have pissed all over her efforts. The whole point of him buying back Bea's share was so that the girls' safe space would be kept as consistent as possible, that was what he had said when he icily explained that she couldn't afford to stay. But it was all just bullshit. It feels like he could hardly wait to bring Maria over and have her wreck everything Bea poured her heart and soul into creating.

With shaking hands, she brings up Niklas's number on her phone. He answers after a couple of rings.

'I've got a patient in a minute.'

Bea's heart is beating so hard, she can feel it pounding in her throat, which seems to constrict, preventing the words from coming out.

'Bea? Has something happened?'

'How could you . . .' she eventually manages to hiss.

'I'm at work, I've got patients . . .'

'She's moved in, redecorated, brought all sorts of stuff over!'

'What? No. It's all mine . . .'

'I'm barely out the door, but you've already moved Emmy's mum in. How do you think that makes me and the girls feel?'

'She hasn't moved in.'

'I can see with my own eyes what she's done!'

'Hold on . . . Have you gone over to Banérgatan when I'm not there?'

'I came to pick up some things.'

'But we've already split everything; you've taken more than half.'

'One of us has to think about the kids, and you certainly don't seem to care. This is crazy, Niklas.'

'You know I could file a police report, don't you? Do me a favour and don't go over there when I'm not home. Those things are all mine, and—'

Bea hangs up on him, gasping for air. It's as though her throat is about to burst. She wanted to say more, but she was so angry, her brain seemed to short-circuit. Niklas's tone shocked her, too. File a police report? The man really has lost his mind. She has a sudden urge to get away as quickly as she can, and never come back. Though first she plans to save as much as she can.

Bea takes out her phone to call in sick at work. She'll be much too busy for that today.

NIKLAS

SOPHIAHEMMET HOSPITAL, STOCKHOLM

IT'S HALF EIGHT IN the evening, and Niklas has mixed feelings as he emerges into the cool November air in his workout clothes. The news that the maternity ward will be shut down came as a shock to most of the staff, and the same is partly true for him, though he had heard the chatter about the hospital's finances in meetings and in corridors. Talk about how strange it is that the hospital can be understaffed, overcrowded and still unprofitable. There are rumours of investments that were too big from the outset, figures that don't add up. When he was first told what was happening, a few hours before the main meeting, he couldn't quite bring himself to listen.

One part of him is relieved, but another is terrified. His finances are entirely dependent on his job here. He had to take out additional loans to buy back Bea's half of the apartment, and the bank was clear that he was nearing his limit. What they don't know is that he passed it a long time ago, that he had to borrow money from Henke to get Bea her two million – on the understanding that he would stick to the repayment plan he and his brother had agreed on.

Henke isn't tight; on the contrary. This is the second big loan he has helped Niklas with – all without Sus's knowledge – and Niklas knows that he needs to start paying his brother back, but it just isn't that simple. Even if he managed to sell the apartment right away, there would still be a real risk that it wouldn't be enough to cover the second mortgage, never mind the money he owes Henke.

Against all odds, property prices have fallen while interest rates have risen, and he is also tied into the lease for the Volvo for another two years. But with what money? His only option is to keep paying off his debts at a steady rate and hope that the market picks up again.

The news of the closure slightly overshadowed his conversation with Bea that morning, which is probably just as well, because Niklas doesn't want to fight with her. What upset him most wasn't that she had gone to the apartment, but that she hadn't bothered to ask him first. The sheer lack of respect in just barging in. And for her then to have the nerve to complain about what he has done to the place, when she has already taken everything she wanted and more.

The cold air stings his cheeks as he turns off onto Valhallavägen. The snow that fell that morning has already melted, and it splashes up onto his running trousers and makes them unpleasantly damp. But that isn't all that is bothering him. Something about Bea's behaviour seems to be irritating him on a deeper level. Niklas can't quite put his finger on it at first, but once he allows his thoughts to drift, it comes to him: the way she is acting reminds him of Lillis. The condescending pat on the head, talking to him as though his choices are reprehensible. As though it's him who is in the wrong, who is unhinged, when all he is trying to do is be true to himself. The clear subtext is that his feelings don't matter, and nor do his choices or wishes.

Bea's claims that Maria has moved in and taken over couldn't be further from the truth. All Maria has done is encourage him and help him with the boxes. Offered him a few bits and pieces to fill the gaps until he gets round to buying new things of his own. They worked together to move the furniture around last night, and for the first time in his life, he actually enjoyed decorating the place.

Niklas feels brave and liberated for having tried. There were no rights or wrongs, no all-important matching colours that trumped his thoughts on where the kitchen table should go. His taste is fine. If Niklas thinks it looks good to have books in the kitchen, then that's OK. And if the girls disagree, then of course he'll listen to them. But, for once in his life, doesn't he have the right to decide how his home should look? Or should Bea, his ex-wife, continue to govern where he puts his fucking cups and glasses?

He hesitantly speeds up, getting further and further from the hospital with every step he takes along the near-deserted Valhallaallén. By New Year, his department will no longer exist. No one knows what will happen to him and the rest of the staff, not to mention where all the pregnant mothers will go. Lots of people cried at the staff meeting, others got angry and started shouting. Niklas has seen it all before, in his old job, and now it's happening again.

Despite all that, he is light on his feet. The closure of the department will force him out of a job where he isn't happy, a job he never really wanted in the first place. A workplace that was on the verge of breaking him, both physically and mentally. Just the thought of no longer having to go there every day fills him with a huge sense of relief – even though he still has no idea how he will cope with the financial blow.

It'll be tough, but this could be the start of something new. His break from Bea was painful, but it set in motion a change inside him. What's happening to Tore is another kind of change, one he would rather not have to think about. It's too difficult, almost too big to fit among the rest.

His foot hits a pothole, and his trainer plunges down into the filthy water, causing the melted snow to spray up onto his face. Niklas can make out the dark expanse of Gärdet park in the distance, Kaknäs Tower flashing like a beacon in the winter sky. He imagines pouring himself a big whisky when he gets home, digging out Procol Harum's 'Whiter Shade of Pale' and lowering the needle on Tore's old record player before relaxing in a hot bath.

*

Fifteen minutes later, a sweaty, muddy Niklas is standing in the middle of his living room, struggling to process what he can see. Or rather: what he can't. The pictures are gone from the walls in the dining room, as is the dining table and Maria's tablecloth, which they moved through here last night. The kitchen chairs and whisky glasses have all vanished, as have several rugs and side tables. The blankets and cushions Maria lent him have all been dumped on the floor, and on the windowpane in the kitchen, Bea has left him a Post-It note.

Took some things for the girls. The removal company will send you the bill.

Niklas barely has the energy to get angry; he feels more empty and sad than anything. Maybe it's just as well that he gets rid of all the old junk, starts over from scratch.

Right then, a sudden thought hits him, and he hurries through to the library.

As he suspected, the desk and chair they bought from Svenskt Tenn are both gone, but she has left the most important thing, right in the middle of the floor: the record player and the blue crate of LPs. Niklas sits down beside it with his legs crossed. His trousers make the parquet floor muddy, and a little pool of water starts to grow around his damp trainers. He rummages through the records and breathes a sigh of relief when he spots the tatty black and white cover. Procol Harum is still here.

*

Alexia starts laughing, but Alma doesn't seem quite so amused.

'What have you done?' she blurts out, peering around in despair, on the verge of tears.

Niklas doesn't know what to tell her. In one sense, he is already the villain, so it seems easiest just to continue along those lines. But there is also a part of him that wants to fight back, to explain that Bea has really outdone herself this time. That it's partly her fault the apartment looks the way it does.

'I moved some things around, and then your mum came over and took a few bits and pieces too.'

Alma's face turns red. 'Are you seriously going to blame this on her?'

'What d'you mean blame?' Alexia snaps back. 'You just want everything to be Dad's fault, don't you?'

'Mum's not the one who had an affair with Emmy's whore of a mum!'

Alma keeps shouting, and Alexia shouts back, even louder than her sister. Niklas is left standing between them like some sort of gutless referee.

'OK, girls ... let's just ... Can't we ... JUST BE QUIET!'

His daughters immediately stop shouting and look up at him in surprise. Niklas never usually raises his voice, or at least not like this.

'OK . . .' says Alexia, holding up both hands. She almost looks amused.

'I've got a suggestion,' says Niklas.

Alma uses the sleeve of her sweater to dry a tear from her cheek, and Alexia folds her arms. Both are staring at him, waiting for him to go on.

'Can't we try to make this into something fun?'

'Fun?' Alma spits out the word, as though he just said something disgusting. 'What's fun about any of this?'

'I just mean that the place is like a blank slate. Maybe we can try to start over somehow?'

Alma glares at him with a look of disdain. Even her sister seems sceptical.

Niklas takes a deep breath and tries again.

'I know you're disappointed in me, but I didn't plan any of this, for us to get divorced and for me to fall in love with someone else – especially not your friend's mum. But that's what happened, and I'm sorry. Can't we try to . . . make something out of this? What do you want it to look like round here? You two can choose.'

He gestures to the empty walls in the dining room.

'Like before,' Alma mutters.

'Maybe we could repaint?' Alexia suggests.

'Exactly,' Niklas agrees. 'Good idea. We can repaint. And get a new table for the living room. What do you think?'

'We could look online, get something second-hand,' says Alexia.

'Perfect. What do you think, Alma?'

She shrugs. 'What about our rooms?'

'We can repaint those too, if you like. Get new furniture, throw things away . . . whatever you want.'

Alexia holds up her hand for a high five, but her sister ignores it.

'Alma? I'm sorry, honey.' Niklas moves over to her and tries to give her a hug, but she pulls back.

'Do you think everything's going to be OK just because you've said sorry and want to buy some paint? Mum spends all her time crying, and you and Emmy's mum, you . . . Seriously, it's so fucking gross . . .'

'Alma, it's OK.'

She stares at Niklas. 'What is?'

'You don't have to like any of this, and you don't have to like Maria. I'm not going to force you to do anything; you can be angry with me for however long you want. But can't we try to sort this damn place out, so it's a bit more homely at the very least? Buy some fun colours? Or does everything have to be white?'

Alma thinks for a moment and then nods.

*

The girls wanted to take down the crystal chandelier, and it is now lying in the middle of the parquet floor. A rice paper lampshade has taken its place, illuminating the dining room with a soft yellow glow. A dark November rain is lashing against the windowpanes, so rhythmically it almost sounds like a drum, keeping pace with the vinyl spinning on the record player. There are LP sleeves scattered across the floor around Alexia, who seems to have stepped into some sort of DJ mode and is playing Pink Floyd. Alma is perched at the top of a stepladder, ready to paint the stucco pink.

312

'Are you sure?' she asks uncertainly before dipping her brush into the tin, as though to check her father hasn't completely lost his mind.

'Go for it,' Niklas replies. 'Whatever you want.'

And his daughters really do go for it. Their work probably won't make the apartment any easier to sell, but with the girls' slightly mad artwork on the walls and his shabby old armchair in the middle of the room, he doesn't think it has ever looked better.

BEA

ÖSTERMALMSGATAN, STOCKHOLM

IT WAS KIND OF Charlotte and Calle to invite her over for dinner. The weeks when the girls are with Niklas are always hard, and it is just so depressing and lonely to take the red line to Liljeholmen after work, then catch the 165 bus back to Örby slott.

She hasn't started calling it 'home' yet. Örby still feels like some sort of temporary stopping point, and her ultimate aim is to move back to the neighbourhood she knows best, possibly once the girls have flown the nest and she can get by somewhere smaller. Though Östermalm also feels more hostile now, largely because of the constant fear of bumping into Niklas or Maria. That's one benefit of living miles from the centre, at the very least: the risk of running into them outside the local dry cleaner's is minimal.

Calle is by the hob, throwing together a spaghetti vongole, and Charlotte pours Bea a glass of wine as she takes a seat in their sweet little kitchen. It's strange how quickly her perspective has changed. She used to think their apartment felt cold somehow, almost like it was a reflection of their decision not to have kids. Pared back and slightly unwelcoming. But in the wake of her separation, Calle and

Charlotte's home now seems like a warm, comforting embrace. It's as though she is desperately clinging on to anything that can numb the sense of longing for her old life.

'Thank you for inviting me over.'

'Of course! We miss you,' says Calle, testing a piece of spaghetti to see whether it is ready.

'Niklas has really lost it,' Charlotte adds. 'He's not his usual self at all.'

Calle nods in agreement. 'This impulsive, angry version of him only seems to have emerged since Maria came into the picture.'

Bea sips her wine, which quickly settles like a soft, warm blanket around her. But it isn't just the alcohol helping her to relax. All the harsh words and actions lately have left her exhausted, and the feeling of being among friends who really care about her and understand what she is going through is such a relief that she could almost start crying. Lillis has had so much on her plate with Tore lately – all the tests and bad news have been taking up almost all their time – and Bea has felt increasingly isolated.

'Have you heard the latest?' she says, taking another sip of her wine.

'What, has something else happened?' Charlotte asks. 'Wasn't getting a tattoo and changing the locks enough?'

'Apparently I'm not allowed to go out to Hogreps anymore.'

'What?!' her friends blurt out in unison.

'Yup. Lillis says I should just ignore what he says, but it doesn't exactly feel great.'

'But, I mean . . .' says Calle. 'It's their house?'

'True, but Niklas and his brothers will eventually inherit it.'

'And so will your girls,' Charlotte points out in her most lawyerly tone. 'I'm pretty sure Alma and Alexia will want their mum to be able to visit.'

'It's a shame he won't just talk to someone,' Calle says as he tips the mussels into the vongole and transfers the pan onto a brass underlay.

'He refuses,' says Bea. 'Just sends long, angry messages about me taking the pictures and the kitchen table.'

Charlotte starts dishing out the spaghetti.

'Legally speaking, of course, he does have a point,' she says. 'But it's petty of him not to just let you take the things you want, especially since he gets to keep the apartment on Banérgatan.'

Bea nods eagerly. 'Exactly, and I was just trying to save a few things for the girls to inherit one day. They're all in the basement at my place. Maria probably wouldn't hesitate to sell the whole lot at auction,' she adds with a note of distaste.

'He told me you'd pretty much gutted the apartment,' says Calle, spearing a mussel on his fork.

'That's what he's been telling everyone, trying to make me look crazy, even though he's the one who's lost his mind. First he bought me out of the apartment for the girls' sakes, and then he changed all the furniture so the place is barely recognisable. He'd already moved a bunch of stuff up to the attic, so I really don't see what the big deal is. I just took a table and a couple of pictures.'

'Weird,' Calle agrees. 'He won't listen to me either, unfortunately. I've tried.'

'He won't listen to anyone. Just look at what Alma sent me.' Bea holds up her phone and shows them a picture of the dining room at Banérgatan.

Calle and Charlotte both seem shocked as they study the pink stucco and the abstract patterns on the walls.

'Has he started taking drugs or something?' asks Calle.

'Do you think so?' Bea replies anxiously.

'No, but it does make you wonder.'

'He's started taking Maria,' says Charlotte. She sips her wine. 'From what I've heard, it isn't the first time she's gone after someone else's husband.'

Bea gasps. 'Really?'

'I can't remember who it was, but someone at Broms mentioned that she'd been flirting at some party – and it went further than that, I think.'

Bea lowers her cutlery, a wave of nausea washing over her.

Calle gives his wife an irritable glance, and Charlotte immediately blushes.

'Sorry, that was tactless of me.'

'Yeah, incredibly tactless,' Calle agrees. 'We don't even know if it's true or not . . .'

Bea shakes her head. 'You don't need to apologise, Charlotte. The whole thing is awful . . .'

'Maybe it's just as well you're really pissed off now, however hard that is for you. That way, he can't just come crawling back with his tail between his legs once his little midlife crisis is over.'

Bea glances up at Charlotte with a look of hope on her face. 'Do you think he will?'

Charlotte rolls her eyes. 'Would you seriously want him back after all this? After everything he's done?' She gives her friend an encouraging look, but to Bea the choice is a simple one.

'I just want my old life back.'

Now that she thinks about it, she would do almost anything to win back Niklas and everything else she has lost.

ÖRBY SLOTT, STOCKHOLM

December 2016

THE CLOSEST REAL SUPERMARKET is on the other side of the conference centre two kilometres away. Bea has plans to start cycling over there as soon as the roads are a little less slippery, but it's not like she would be able to balance a Christmas tree on her handlebars anyway. She decides to try to lug one home on foot instead. This will be her first Christmas in her new apartment, and it seems extra important to try to make it special.

Bea tells herself she is doing it for the girls, but the truth is that she baked the huge gingerbread hearts with their names on them as much for her own sake as theirs – just like Lillis always does at Hogreps. Feeling Christmassy has never felt so vital before, and since Niklas seems to be doing his best to change as much as possible, Bea will have to try to keep their traditions going alone, however hard it might be.

The tree is wrapped in a plastic net to make it easier to carry, but it is still heavy and awkward, and as she comes out on the other side of the footbridge by the conference centre, she has to stop to catch her breath. Despite the low roar of the traffic on Huddingevägen, she feels oddly cut off from the world around her.

In the distance on her left, she can see Brännkyrka Church. It looks so idyllic, perched on top of the little hill where people go sledging in winter. The idea of the children's laughter among the graves seems beautiful somehow. She tries to ignore the busy roads around her, but the noise of the cars makes it hard. Hard too not to make comparisons, even though she knows she shouldn't. It isn't fair on the area to compare it to the tranquillity of Gustav Adolf Church, or to Jacob's quiet grave in Skogskyrkogården, and yet she is powerless against the negative thoughts, constantly finding fault instead of emphasising the positives.

Like the fact that it feels wrong for her to be lugging this tree home on her own, for example. The four of them should be buying one by the fountain in Karlaplan and carrying it home together. She misses that, just like she misses being able to stroll down to the shops in Fältöversten in under five minutes. Life and movement. Not like here, where the majority of people seem to drive to the supermarket to do a big shop for anything that's not scratch cards and ice lollies, the few things available at the newsagent.

The sharp needles work their way in through the thin gloves Alma made in home economics, pricking her fingers, and Bea curses herself. She should have bought a smaller tree, but she wanted one that actually looked like a Christmas tree rather than a pathetic little shrub. The real question is what sort of state it will be in by the time she gets home.

She passes Örby slottspark and glances up towards the 'castle' from which the area takes its name, a manor-like building that, ironically enough, is currently being rented out to the Vietnamese embassy: a constant reminder of last year's Christmas present that Niklas eventually cancelled.

Bea's coat pocket starts to buzz, and she lowers the tree to the ground and digs out her phone.

An incoming call from the number she once had saved as 'My Love' but which she changed to 'Niklas' a few weeks ago. Other than a short message to say he would report her to the police if she ever entered the apartment without him again, he has refused to speak to her since she went over to Banérgatan and got the movers to pick up some things for the girls. Bea doesn't doubt for a second that he meant it, given everything else he has done lately. Like banning her from Hogreps, for example – her favourite place on earth. Thinking about that is almost too painful, and yet she knows it will be even harder come summer, as the girls' school holidays get closer.

Niklas is still trying to get through to her, which means he must really want to talk. It's usually the other way around, with her chasing him. What if something has happened to Alma or Alexia? Bea feels a deep sense of unease as she takes off her glove and answers the call.

'Hey, what's up?' he says.

What's up? As though he is talking to a vague acquaintance.

'I've just been to buy a Christmas tree.'

'Ah, OK . . . It was actually Christmas I wanted to talk to you about.'

'Haven't we already decided everything?'

'Yeah, but I need to change the plans a bit.'

Bea knew she shouldn't have answered. Her legs start to shake.

'The fact is that Tore isn't well.'

'I know.'

'His doctors say this will be his last Christmas. The cancer has spread, and he has metastases everywhere.'

Bea's legs practically give way beneath her. She manages to take a few steps, slumping down onto an icy bench by the fountain, which is blanketed with snow. Darkness is falling quickly around her, and there aren't any street lamps in the park.

Tore. The girls' grandfather. Her second dad. The man who has been more of a father to her than her own ever has. Who was there for her when Jacob died. Bea has always been closer to Lillis, but Tore feels as much her parent as Niklas's.

'Are you OK?'

His voice is soft, like the old Niklas. Her Niklas. He is still in there after all, beneath all the threats of police reports, new locks and decisions to ban her from family gatherings. Bea breaks down in tears.

'I know this is really hard for you too,' he says.

'How are you doing?' she manages to ask between sobs.

'So-so, I guess . . . But it . . . it would be nice if I could have the girls over Christmas. Tore would love it, and everyone will be at Hogreps because . . . well, it's his last . . .'

Everyone. Everyone but Bea.

'I understand. I could also join you . . .'

'Bea . . .'

She can hear it in his voice: he doesn't want her there.

Bea swallows. There is nothing she can say, nothing she can do. She knows he is right, even if this was the lifeline she had been clinging on to: having the girls over for Christmas in her new apartment. Making it their own together. She needs to let go of that now, for their sakes. For Tore and Lillis's sakes. For Niklas's, too. She will have to make the sacrifice.

'OK.'

'Thank you, Bea. Thank you, I really appreciate it.'

Really appreciate it. The dissonance between his soft voice and such formal words.

Niklas says that he will buy tickets for the girls, tells her to take care and then he hangs up. Bea drops her phone back into her pocket. Her hands are stiff and numb, as though they have frozen into position. The tree is still lying on the floor nearby, wrapped up in its nylon net, and she gets up and walks away, leaving it there.

NIKLAS

HOGREPS, GOTLAND
Christmas 2016

NIKLAS IS TIRED AFTER the journey, but he has spent the past few hours lying awake. The room is cold, frost on the windowpanes and darkness outside. He should get up and throw another log into the stove, but, oddly enough, Maria seems to be sleeping deeply. He doesn't know how she can be so calm and peaceful given the terrible atmosphere in the house, something they both felt the minute they arrived.

In some ways, he regrets asking her to come to Gotland. As Henrik and Lillis said, it probably was 'selfish' of him. It's Tore's last Christmas with the family, and Niklas drags along this new woman no one likes – not even the girls. Or not Alma, at least, who still refuses to accept that he is in a relationship with Emmy's mum. Perfectly understandable, really, though he hopes she will soften with time.

It wasn't exactly fair on Maria, either, bringing her into this hornets' nest – however much she says it's OK and that she wanted to come, no matter what the rest of the family think. She has no idea what she is getting herself into or how Lillis treats people she doesn't like. Ice cold, ignoring them completely. Even Otis seems sceptical, giving Maria a brief sniff when they arrived and then curling up by the stove again.

Who knows, maybe it was selfish, but her presence, for him, seems to make everything just a little bit easier. Like Henke's criticism of the fact that Niklas brought her here, claiming it was nothing but a childish protest. Saying that no one wants Maria here. That it should have been Bea.

Bea.

Everything still seems to revolve around her and what she is going through. The fact that Niklas rejected her. He needs to prove to himself – and everyone else – that he has the right to choose who he spends his life with.

Tore has said that he wants to get to know Maria, and the fact of the matter is that this will probably be his last chance. He has given them his blessing, though it was probably naive of Niklas to think that would be enough to convince the others.

He spends more time brooding than sleeping that night, and feels like he is only running at half-speed until he takes a nap after lunch the next day – ignoring Lillis's protests. It's the day before Christmas Eve, which means everyone has to help dress the tree and prepare the ham and the Jansson's temptation casserole. By the time he makes his way back downstairs, dusk has started to fall, and everyone but Maria is busy in the kitchen.

'Seems like the jet lag from Stockholm is worse than from Brazil,' Henke mutters, looking up from the worktop, where he is in the process of liberating the ham from its rind.

'That was out of order,' says Sus. 'Would you like some mulled wine, Niklas?'

He nods gratefully.

'Where's Maria?' he asks.

Her jacket is no longer hanging by the kitchen door.

'She took Otis for a solo walk,' says Lillis, emphasising the word *solo* to make it clear just how odd – suspicious even – she finds it that someone would want to go for a walk on their own.

Right then, Niklas hears Maria stamping her feet in the porch, followed by Otis's cheery barking. Her cheeks are rosy as she comes into the kitchen, and she doesn't seem to notice the tense atmosphere. Instead, she walks straight over to Niklas and gives him a hug.

'God, it's so beautiful down by the water. Big pieces of ice right along the beach, and not another person in sight.' Her eyes are glittering, her entire face radiating energy, as though the cold sea breeze and the barren landscape have reinvigorated her. 'And look what I found!' she says, holding out a pebble that has been worn down into the shape of a heart by the water.

Niklas is almost teary-eyed at her enthusiasm, at how blissfully unaware she seems of the atmosphere – as though her cheery fascination with the wonder of nature is enough to protect her. She doesn't seem the least bit annoyed that he spent several hours asleep that afternoon, either. If anything, she seems to have appreciated the alone time. For a brief moment, he hopes the others will realise just how incredible she is, and that the sour mood will turn.

*

The evening proves to be just as much of a disaster as he feared, of course. The teenagers head up to the attic to watch a film, and the adults gather in the kitchen for the traditional present-wrapping session – complete with wax seals and a little rhyme on each tag.

Everyone makes a real effort to keep the mood light, for Tore's sake. Almost as though it were any other Christmas. His family is polite towards Maria, but Niklas can tell that their friendliness is forced. After just half an hour, Tore is in too much pain to sit upright any longer, and he heads upstairs to lie down. Lillis starts crying and follows him up not long after, and then Sus gets upset and claims she has a migraine, leaving just Niklas, Henke and Hampus in the kitchen. Plus Maria, who doesn't fully understand what is going on. She notices a shift in the mood, of course, that the pleasantries disappear as the brothers drink their Christmas beers and schnapps.

In the end, it is Henke who fires the starting shot.

'Just because Tore says it's OK doesn't mean it is, you know. He's just being nice.'

'I asked him and he said yes,' Niklas responds. 'That he'd be *thrilled* to see her, in fact.'

Hampus immediately speaks up in Henke's defence. 'What did you expect him to say, though? When you asked him.'

'Maybe we could talk about this later?'

Niklas is attempting to protect Maria, but he can see that it's too late. She now understands exactly what they are talking about.

'When? On Christmas Eve?' Henke snorts. 'No, you've only got yourself to blame; you're the one who put us all in this situation. I'm sorry, Maria, none of this is your fault. It's Niklas who screwed up.'

Henke tries to make it sound as though he likes her, but Niklas can hear the disdain in his voice. The anger.

'Screwed up how?' Maria asks, with genuine curiosity.

'I think we'll head up to bed,' says Niklas, but Henke doesn't hold back.

'How? Our dad's dying, and Niklas dragged you along, practically a complete stranger. All we know is that you're the reason for his divorce. The girls are upset and Bea, who is basically as much a part of this family as anyone else, wasn't allowed to come out here and spend one last Christmas with her father-in-law. But, apart from that, everything's just dandy.'

'I understand,' says Maria. 'It can't be easy for any of you.'

'No, you don't say.' Henke's voice is dripping with booze and self-pity.

Maria excuses herself, but Niklas stays behind to tell his brothers what he really thinks. He can't remember them ever having argued like this before, not even when they were younger and every disagreement felt deadly serious. This is something else entirely. They're all grown men now, and their relationships are on the line – for real. It's as though they all know nothing will ever be the same again after this. They will be brothers on paper but not in spirit. Does Niklas even want to stay in touch with them? It doesn't feel that way. It doesn't feel like he will ever want to come back to Hogreps, either. If it wasn't for the girls and for Tore and Lillis, he would leave right now.

*

When he gets to their room, he finds Maria reading in bed. Amazingly calm, even now.

'How'd it go?' she asks.

'So-so. How are you?'

'I'm OK.'

'I'm sorry, I shouldn't have dragged you into this. I thought my family would know how to behave, at least towards you.'

'It's not so strange. Bea practically grew up here, and your dad's really ill. Everyone's just upset. You should've seen Jonas's family when I told him I wanted a divorce. This is nothing.'

'Is that even possible?'

'They hate me, even though Jonas is totally cool about the divorce. Mind you, I'm kind of used to it; they never really liked me in the first place.'

She laughs, loudly. Niklas knows that the sound will carry through the walls and that the others will probably think it shows a lack of respect, but he doesn't care; it feels good somehow. He doesn't want them to think they have beaten her.

'Don't you ever get angry or upset?' he asks.

'Of course I do,' Maria says, now serious. 'But I grew up with divorced parents who still don't know how to have a civil conversation with each other. People can fight however much they want, but I'm not going to join in.'

Niklas feels a rush of gratitude that Maria is here. Yet again, it's as though she has given him new insight, a solution that had never occurred to him. He doesn't have to argue, not with Henke, Hampus, nor anyone else. No one will benefit from them shouting at each other.

Silence slowly descends over the house, and once everyone drifts off to sleep, a quiet snow starts to fall. Untouched drifts pile up during the night, blanketing the battlefield with a soft white calm.

When Niklas wakes the next morning, he realises that the best Christmas present he could ever have hoped for is already lying by his side, her hair like a knotty crown around her head. The minute she wakes up, he'll tell her the truth: that she makes him a better man, however much everyone else claims the opposite.

BEA

ÖRBY SLOTT, STOCKHOLM
Christmas Eve, 2016

HER PARENTS ASKED WHETHER she wanted to celebrate Christmas with them at their place in the country, but Bea told them she had to work. She has signed up to hand out food parcels and porridge to anyone who is lonely or homeless over the holidays, volunteering for Christmas in the Community, a charity event put on by the local authority and the Swedish Church close to Kungsträdgården park. That seems far more tempting than three hours of her mother's latest miserable diatribes in the car, followed by a couple of days trapped in the darkness that inevitably descends over her parents at the thought of *yet another Christmas without Jacob*. Besides, she knows they are happiest when they don't need to take anyone else's feelings into consideration. It's always been that way, even when Jacob was still alive.

She and Jacob were the product of societal norms and expectations at the time, the idea that getting married and starting a family was simply what one did. Her mother had explained that once when Bea questioned her parents' lack of interest in their children and grandchildren.

Deep down, Bea had been hoping for an invite to Hogreps until the very last minute. The softness in Niklas's voice when he asked to have the girls over Christmas had woken a glimmer of hope in her that they might finally be able to start over. Perhaps not as man and wife, but as happily divorced parents and good friends at the very least. People who were still capable of spending time together, as a family. But when she called and tried to talk about it all, it was as though a steel door came crashing down – despite the fact that everyone else wants her there. Everyone but Niklas.

Calle and Charlotte are going away for the holidays, otherwise she would have been very welcome to join them. Inger invited Bea to celebrate with her parents and siblings in Bålsta, but that didn't really feel like an option either. She doesn't know Inger especially well, not to mention her family. Spending Christmas with the other volunteers will be better than sitting alone at home. This way, she can do some good and possibly even be a source of comfort and help to someone else.

Still, Bea has a heavy heart as she gets dressed and makes her way to the metro station that morning. She keeps checking her watch, imagining how far they have made it through the usual Christmas schedule over at Hogreps. Lillis's almond porridge for breakfast, followed by board games in the kitchen, lunch preparations and walking down to the sea at eleven. Tore setting out the burning torches as dusk starts to fall. Eggnogs and dinner at one, before they all sit down to watch Christmas TV.

As Bea's train pulls into the station at Slussen, the rest of the family will be walking along the gravel track towards the beach. She can just picture them, their arms linked, thick coats on. Hot breath forming clouds in the cold air, escaping in little puffs as they laugh and chat. Lillis and Tore directing their traditional Christmas song to the sea. Lillis and Tore. Henke and Sus. Alma and Alexia. Niklas and . . . Bea's heart feels like it might break, but she can't just sit here on the red line, thinking about them. Alone in a noisy metro carriage heading for Central Station. On Christmas Eve.

It isn't until she arrives at Kungsträdgården and spots Sankt Jacob's that the name really sinks in. Saint Jacob's Church. Bea isn't religious, but she has always loved churches, all the beauty and atmosphere. Right then, it hits her: Jacob is with her today. She isn't alone after all.

There is a sign pointing to the congregation hall next door – *Christmas in the Community – Welcome!* – but before she heads inside, she briefly nips into the church. Jacob's church. She sits down on one of the pews and closes her eyes. Fiddles with Jacob's neckerchief, which she has in her pocket today, the way she does every Christmas. As she did on their last Christmas together.

*

His neckerchief flutters in the wind as they walk along Karlavägen. He has a piece of silver tape on the arm of his pale blue Moncler jacket, covering the black crater where

Freddie stubbed out a cigarette on the nylon. Jacob claims it was just a joke, but Bea can tell from the look in his eyes that he is upset. She says it was a terrible joke. Wants to say more, but can't think of the words.

His wallet has worn a hole in the back pocket of his jeans, and it looks like it might tumble out at any moment. They are teenagers, but they are on their way to Nobel Park to ride their snowracer. Jacob's idea, of course. To get out of the house, where their parents are busy moaning about all the stresses and strains of Christmas.

He is pulling her on the sledge because he wants to, not because she nagged him, and Jacob is the only person who won't judge her for opening her mouth and catching the snowflakes on her tongue the way she used to when they were little. She turns the little wheel this way and that, and not once does he complain that she is heavy or annoying or whiny. In fact, he tells her when they get to the park, which is quiet, full of untouched snow, if it wasn't for her, then he would have given up a long time ago.

When she asks what he means, he just says, 'Pff, don't worry about it' and then jumps onto the snowracer and grabs the wheel. For a brief moment, they teeter on the brow of the hill, then they rock forward over the edge.

*

When Bea opens her eyes, she realises her cheeks are wet. The sense of loss is as great as ever, as is the guilt. She should have understood what he meant.

As she is leaving the church, she lights a small candle for Jacob and whispers *sorry* and *Merry Christmas* and *I love you*. The ritual and the candles flickering in the stand suddenly seem meaningless. The presence she felt earlier is gone, and the void it has left behind is greater than ever. The loneliness and the longing. Not just for Jacob, but for the girls, for Niklas and Hogreps, too. Lillis and Tore's comforting words. Everything seems even harder to bear.

*

Not long later, Bea is busy handing out food and Christmas presents. It feels good, forces her to think about something else. There is a steady stream of people coming in through the doors: the homeless, the lonely, families with young children. The poor. The porridge quickly runs out, and new bags of presents and food have to be prepared. Time races by, and for the first time in a long while, Bea feels like she is needed, almost excited to be doing something useful.

Her work with the Red Cross is important, but it doesn't give her this sort of close contact with people. Being a web editor is more technical than emotional, but by volunteering like this, she gets to meet the people who are actually in need, right here and now. It also gives her a chance to work with her hands, to stop thinking about what is happening on Gotland.

At the far side of the room, she spots a familiar face. Something about the woman's eyes, or possibly her hair.

Is she one of the mothers from the girls' school? Someone she used to work with? A neighbour?

The woman ends up in the queue for Bea's table, and when she reaches the front of the line, Bea hands over a bag of food before any of the other volunteers have a chance.

'Merry Christmas.'

'Thank you.'

'There's porridge in the next queue, if you'd like some.'

The woman nods, but she quickly looks down and hurries towards the exit with her bag. Bea hesitates for a moment, then runs after her, catching up with the woman by the doors.

'Excuse me!'

The woman turns around.

'Sorry,' says Bea. 'I'm not sure . . . I just wanted to say that there are tables inside, if you'd like to stay and eat . . . Or if you need a place to sleep this evening, we can help with that, too.'

The woman gives her a shy look, eyes burning with shame.

'I'll be OK, but thanks . . . Bea.'

With that, she turns and walks away, leaving a confused Bea by the doors. How did she know . . . ? Right then, the penny drops, and Bea is the one who is ashamed. That was Frida, from Skin Care on Linnégatan. How could Bea have forgotten her?

When she last tried to make an appointment with her six months ago, she found out that Frida had moved away following a divorce. She booked a session with Josephine instead, which was perfectly fine, but nowhere near as good. Josephine was incredibly chatty, telling Bea all about how Frida's ex was an arsehole who forced her to write a prenup and then dumped her for some other woman, throwing her out despite the fact that they had three young kids together.

What could have happened since then to force Frida to queue for a bag of Christmas food with her face down-turned in shame?

*

'Hi, Mum! Merry Christmas!'

Bea covers her free ear in order to hear Alma's voice over the rumbling of the metro.

'Hi, sweetie. How's it going?'

'Good. What about you?'

'I've been handing out food to people who might be homeless or alone all day. It felt good to be helping, but it was still a bit sad to see so many people on their own.'

'But . . . aren't you celebrating Christmas?'

'I'll be OK. What matters is that you're having a nice time.'

'Yeah . . . but I miss you.'

Bea feels a pang of longing. However good it was to have been useful, it has also been a sad, heavy day. Full of love and gratitude from all the people she has met, but also a lot of pain.

'Have you done presents yet?' Bea asks.

'Yeah . . .'

Her daughter sounds slightly anxious, though maybe that isn't so surprising; it's her first Christmas apart from Bea, too.

'Did you get what you'd been hoping for?'

'A laptop from Dad and . . . Maria.'

'Maria?'

'Yeah . . .'

Bea makes a real effort to keep her voice steady, but it proves tricky.

'Is she there too?' she asks.

'Yeah, but they're leaving tomorrow.'

'What?'

'It's some present she gave Dad, a stay at the hotel in Furillen or something.'

'So he's leaving on Christmas Day? While you're all at Hogreps?'

'Think so . . .'

Alma's voice sounds delicate, almost like she is on the verge of tears. Bea gets up from her seat, unable to sit still. She paces back and forth in the near-empty carriage until the train reaches Liljeholmen, where she has to change to the bus.

'Are you and Alexia going with them?'

'No, just Dad and Maria . . .'

'OK, and how does that feel? What does Alexia think? And Granny and Grandpa?'

The doors open, and Bea steps out onto the platform, making her way over to the bus station to wait for the 165 to Örby.

'Dunno,' says Alma. 'They don't exactly seem happy about it . . .'

Bea's brain seems to short-circuit, and she realises she needs to say goodbye and hang up before she loses it completely. Niklas has taken Maria to Hogreps. So utterly disrespectful to the girls, to Lillis and Tore and everyone else who has gone there to celebrate his last Christmas. Bea wasn't allowed to join them, but apparently it's fine for his new girlfriend to be there – and then he decides to run off to Furillen on some sort of romantic minibreak on Christmas Day? Leaving the girls, who he insisted on taking with him, while Bea is stuck at home celebrating Christmas with Stockholm's homeless?

A wave of powerlessness, rage and despair washes over her. Just like Frida, she has been brushed aside by a complete arsehole. A selfish bastard who clearly only cares about himself and his dick. She feels like throwing up and crying.

Bea eventually manages to compose herself enough to call Lillis. Partly to wish her a merry Christmas, but also because she wants to find out what is going on.

Her former mother-in-law tries to keep up the facade, but it comes crashing down as soon as Bea asks her what is happening.

'I didn't want to say anything, I thought it'd just upset you. And he refuses to listen to me.'

Lillis's voice barely holds as she tells Bea just how important this Christmas is to Tore, and how awful it is that the girls are stuck in the middle.

'Everyone has tried talking to him, but he just loses his temper. I can't understand what he's thinking, Bea. I just don't know what he's doing.'

Lillis wanted everything to be like normal, but instead the whole thing is a mess. Tore has spent most of the holiday in bed, in too much pain to really join in. And it doesn't help that Maria, practically a complete stranger, is there with them – nor that they're going off to stay at some hotel.

The girls seem disappointed, Henrik is furious, and Hampus is almost as upset too. The only ones managing to keep their cool are Sus and the cousins. The cheery teenagers have been trying to maintain a bit of festive cheer despite all the changes.

Bea listens until Lillis says she has to go, and when she looks up at the board in the waiting room, she realises that her bus has been cancelled. The next isn't due for another forty minutes.

It's Christmas Eve, and she is stuck at the bus station in Liljeholmen. Without her beloved daughters, without her beloved family, without Lillis and Tore. Booted out of her old life. It isn't right, and it isn't right that Niklas keeps getting his own way, that he is being allowed to spiral out of control like this – at everyone else's expense. She needs to do something.

NIKLAS

FURILLEN, GOTLAND
Christmas Day, 2016

NIKLAS IS IN SOME kind of borderland between waking and sleeping, his head resting against the passenger-side window. Every now and again, when he opens his heavy eyelids, he sees the landscape racing by outside. Snow-covered trees interspersed with flat, frozen ground.

Maria is in the driver's seat beside him. It's strange not to be behind the wheel – in a good way. It means he can let his mind drift into disjointed thoughts and fragmented memories. The gravel roads remind him of childhood, of the annual bumpy drive over to the snowy stack of rocks known as Old Man Hoburg in the days between Christmas and New Year. Tore and Lillis up front, Niklas and Henke in the back seat of the Jeep, before Hampus came along.

He remembers them bickering about the bar of Marabou chocolate Henke wanted to take as payment – with interest – for the sweets he gave Niklas. Tore barked, 'Enough of that capitalist nonsense!' from the front seat and banned them from borrowing from each other – though, of course, it has always been Niklas who borrows from Henke, never the other way around.

More than forty years have now passed, but very little has changed. Henke now lends money to Niklas instead of sweets and seems to think that gives him some sort of veto over his brother's life. And Niklas hates himself for getting trapped in Henke's debt, for being dependent on him to maintain a standard of living he might never have even wanted.

Everything that happened yesterday is still eating away at him. The fact that the girls are back at Hogreps, that he and Maria are on their way to Furillen, even though it's probably Tore's last Christmas. It just doesn't feel right. Yet again, it's as though he has been tying himself in knots to please everyone, only to get more and more tangled up. A sudden wave of anxiety leaves him wide awake, and he straightens up in his seat.

Maria glances over to him before turning her attention back to the road.

'We're not there yet; go back to sleep.'

'I can't.'

'If this is all too much, we can always head back.'

'It does feel like . . . a lot.'

'Shall I turn around?'

'Maybe. I don't know.'

He takes out his phone and brings up Alexia's number.

'Hi, Dad.'

'How's it going?'

'Good. Just playing cards with Hedda and Hampus.'

'OK. Is Alma there?'

'She's gone for a walk with Granny.'

'What about Grandpa?'

'He's resting.'

Niklas tries to process her tone of voice. Is she OK?

'I just wanted to say that we can come back if you ...
if you and your sister want us to.'

'Uh, OK. Why?'

'It just feels a bit unfair that I've gone off and left
you.'

'But me and Alma didn't want to come?' Alexia sounds
genuinely confused.

'True, but you might not have wanted to come because
of ...'

'Maria?'

Niklas glances over to Maria, who turns to him and
smiles. She can probably hear every word Alexia says.

'Exactly.'

'I guess Alma's pissed,' says Alexia, 'but I just wanted
to stay here. Been there, done that, you know?'

'But not in winter?'

'Right, Furillen in the snow ... So what? Haha.'

Niklas hesitates for a moment. He knows he shouldn't
offload his guilty conscience onto his daughter, and yet
that is precisely what he does.

'Does Grandpa seem ... annoyed that we left?'

'If you asked Granny, she'd say yes, but if you asked
Grandpa, he'd say no. He's muttering to himself like usual,
but that's mostly because he doesn't have the energy to
play cards with us.'

Niklas can hear the smile in her voice, and he can't help
but smile too.

'OK, well, we'll be back before too long anyway. Just give me a call if you need anything, or if you want us to come back. We're only a couple of hours away.'

'Yeah, yeah. Bye.'

He hears Hedda and Hampus's voices in the background, something about who played the last card and whose turn it is next.

He and Maria are driving along the coast road, and the windswept nature reserve opens out in front of them, falling snow blowing away before it has time to land. Alexia was right: it's as barren as ever, just colder.

'Better now?' Maria asks.

Niklas nods. His guilty conscience is still bothering him, but he can't deny that it is a relief to get away for a day. A brief break from all the tension.

'I thought it seemed like a cool thing to do with the girls between Christmas and New Year,' says Maria. 'Something a bit different. But I guess I was wrong.'

'No, you were right. It's just that my stubborn family are allergic to change. Everything has to be the same as it's always been, otherwise there's a huge fuss.'

Maria gives him an apologetic smile. 'I've kicked the hornets' nest again, haven't I? Sorry.'

'If it wasn't for Tore, I probably wouldn't feel so bad. And Alma, obviously. But at the same time . . . It's like I can't breathe there, so . . . yeah, it's good to get away.'

'Look,' says Maria. 'We've got another week at Hogreps once we get back. You'll have plenty of time to hang out with everyone then.'

'That's true, but leaving on Christmas Day – is that even allowed?'

'I'm pretty sure you're allowed to be happy and enjoy yourself, even though it's Christmas.'

Niklas laughs when he hears how absurd it all sounds, and he winds down the window. They're close now. Through the snowy haze, he can see the brutalist factory building by the old limestone quarry looming in the distance. The freezing air smells like salt and freedom.

BEA

THE GOTLAND FERRY

EVERYTHING SUDDENLY FEELS SO simple and obvious. After months of fear and doubt, it's good to have finally reached this point. Bea has let go of Niklas. She no longer knows who he is, who he has become. Maybe he was only ever playing a part during all their years together, but he has gone way too far this time. He hasn't just let Bea down; he has also let his daughters, Tore, Lillis and everyone else he knows down, too. No one understands him anymore.

In all honesty, she no longer cares whether he is going through a midlife crisis or not. It would be one thing if it affected only him, if it lasted no more than a few months, but his crazy behaviour has extinguished any feelings she might have had for him. Her husband is gone, and she has absolutely no interest in being with this new version of him. She might have been able to forgive his infidelity, but what he is doing now is just cruel. Spurred on by Maria, no doubt, who has abandoned her own husband and kids to go on some sort of luxury getaway to Furillen on Christmas Day.

In some ways, Bea is relieved. She doesn't have to worry about what he thinks anymore, no longer needs to hope that she can fix things or think about playing her cards right. She can do whatever she wants. For her kids, her family. Because even if she and Niklas are in the middle of a separation, she hasn't divorced Tore and Lillis. Or Henke, Hampus or Sus. And, above all, she isn't getting divorced from her daughters.

Bea is both exhilarated and expectant as the night ferry sails into Visby harbour on Christmas morning. No one knows she is coming. Her arrival will be a kind of Christmas present no one was expecting. Since she first set off from Stockholm, she has been picturing the moment when she gets off the bus in Gammelgarn and walks along the snow-covered track to the white limestone house, the warm glow from the lamps in the sunroom and Tore's welcoming torches outside.

Lillis will come out onto the porch and her face will crack into a big smile – she might even let out a little hoot of joy. The girls will come running, followed by the rest of the family. The vision makes her eyes well up, and she reaches for Jacob's neckerchief as the ferry finally docks with a shudder.

*

The stress of the journey, her anger at Niklas's behaviour, all of it fades away when she catches sight of the house from the bus stop by Gammelgarn Church. Hogreps is blanketed beneath a layer of snow like something from a fairy tale, and it looks every bit as Christmassy as she imagined on the ferry. Bea's bag is light on her shoulder. She barely packed anything, not even a change of clothes; she already has plenty of things here, suitable for both summer and winter, and she can always borrow something from Lillis or the girls if necessary.

The snow crunches beneath her boots as she walks, and with every step she takes, she is increasingly sure that she did the right thing by coming out here. The prospect of surprising her family makes her a little jittery, but the feeling is a good one. Expectant nerves.

Almost there now. Just a few more metres around the corner. To Bea's relief, she sees that there is no sign of the Volvo. She knows Niklas is in Furillen, but it still comes as a relief to be sure.

She notices that the light is on in the studio and feels a sudden rush of warmth. Lillis.

'Hello! I'm here!'

The words just come spilling out of her, and Bea can't help but smile. Yet another sign that coming to Gotland was the right decision. This is where she belongs. Hogreps is hers just as much as it is Niklas's, if not more. The man doesn't even have the good sense to appreciate it.

Bea hurries over to the studio door, practically tearing it open.

The first thing she sees is Lillis's face, more confused than happy. Bea feels a sting of disappointment, but she quickly brushes it aside. It's no wonder Lillis is taken aback, almost shocked to see her; she has turned up without warning.

'Oh, love . . . what are you doing here? What a surprise . . .'

Bea walks over and gives her a long hug. 'Merry Christmas, Lillis. I just wanted to celebrate with you all, despite everything.'

Lillis nods and smiles, then bends down to pick up a few broken cups from the floor.

'Sorry, I dropped these . . . Let me . . . Welcome, love.'

*

Henke, Sus and Hampus are all sprawled around the fire, eating nuts and reading their new books when Bea and Lillis come into the room. There is the same mix of surprise and shock, but Sus immediately runs through to the kitchen to grab a bottle of wine to celebrate, and Otis starts leaping around her legs. Henke and Hampus both hug her and tell her how much they've missed her. Tore is the only one who is too tired to get up, and Lillis explains that he has been in bed all day.

'Christmas Eve really took it out of him. Out of all of us.'

Bea nods. She understands what Lillis means.

'Where are the girls?'

'Where do you think?' Henke replies with a smirk.

Bea holds a finger to her lips. 'Shh . . . I want to surprise them.'

Alma jumps and Hedda lets out an involuntary shriek when Bea pops her head around the curtain by the stairs to the attic and shouts, 'Merry Christmas!' Alexia just stares at her, as though she can't quite believe her eyes.

Bea can't hold back, running over to her girls and giving them both a big hug. She then does the same with Hedda and Olle, who are busy playing on their phones. The energy in the room is oddly low, but that's probably just their age, she thinks.

'Late night last night?' she asks, curling up on the sofa between her daughters and putting her arms around them.

Alma gives a hesitant nod. 'What are you doing here . . . ?' she asks.

'I thought it might be nice for you to have at least one parent here for Christmas.'

'Yeah, but . . .' Alma begins, only to be interrupted by Bea.

'Dad's over in Furillen, I know. I'm only going to stay a couple of days.'

'Does he know you're here?' Alexia asks in her usual pointed tone.

Bea realises that she should have dampened her expectations, because she is slightly disappointed that the girls don't seem happier to see her. They're probably just surprised like everyone else, need a bit of time to process her sudden arrival.

'No, but it'll be fine,' Bea says firmly. 'Granny and Grandpa know I'm here, and so do you.'

'But Dad said you weren't allowed to come?'

Alexia's tone is slightly harder now, making Bea uneasy. It's almost as though Niklas has brainwashed the girl. Still, Bea needs to try to keep calm; it isn't Alexia's fault.

'I'm allowed to be here. That isn't up to your dad. It's Granny and Grandpa's house, and they've said they're happy to have me here.'

Alexia gets up and walks away without another word. Hedda and Olle wander off too, both claiming they need to use the toilet. Alma is the only one left, sitting with an anxious look on her face.

'Aren't you even a little bit glad that I'm here?' Bea asks.

'Of course I am.'

Alma gives her a hug, though it seems a little dutiful, nowhere near as heartfelt as the one Bea gives her back. She tries to shake off the sense of unease that Alexia's words have stirred up inside her, about not being allowed to be here, but a seed of doubt seems to have taken root in her, and nothing feels quite like it usually does.

NIKLAS

FURILLEN, GOTLAND

THE GRAVEL HEAPS LOOK like snow-covered mountains, the barren landscape even harsher and more desolate without all the usual tourists and day trippers. Maria's friend owns the hotel in Furillen, which is currently closed for the season. She and Niklas have borrowed one of the cabins, which means they are currently the only people there.

The waves crash against the pier as they walk along the concrete breakwater.

'I could live somewhere like this,' says Niklas, gazing out towards the hazy horizon. 'God, it would be great. No one to argue with for miles.'

Maria nods as the wind tugs at her frizzy hair, messing it up even more.

'If we weren't both divorced, we probably could've afforded it.'

'You might've been able to,' Niklas says with a smile. 'I'd only be able to manage some hermit's cottage.'

'I don't think Jonas would've liked the isolation; he likes being around other people too much, part of a group.'

'Then Hogreps is perfect. Maybe we should set him up with Bea and Lillis?'

He lets out a bitter laugh. Maria studies him.

'What's the deal with them, by the way? What was it your mum said . . . ? Oh, right: that she and Bea were like peas and carrots.'

'Sorry,' Niklas mumbles. 'But if it's any consolation, Bea also comes before me. Sometimes it's like handyman and doctor are my only real functions.'

'What was it like before Bea came along? Was Lillis the same with your other girlfriends?'

'I didn't have many before her, but no. Their relationship is pretty special. I guess it's partly because Bea's brother died. Lillis probably felt an extra layer of responsibility towards her because Bea's parents have never been very . . . Well, they're a bit emotionally unavailable, or whatever it's called.'

'Lucky she had your parents, then. And you.'

Niklas nods. He can feel the chill starting to seep in through his clothes.

'What was he like?' Maria asks. 'Bea's brother, I mean. Your friend.'

'I didn't really know him all that well.'

'I thought you were best friends?'

'We were, for a while, but then it kind of fizzled out. Hey, aren't you cold? Should we head back?'

'Sure.'

They start walking towards the shore in silence.

'Sorry,' Niklas says after a moment or two. 'I'm just not used to talking about him.'

Maria seems surprised. 'Really? He seems so central. You know, with the gingerbread hearts in the window . . .'

'Yeah, I know, but that's mostly down to Bea and the others wanting to make sure he isn't forgotten. I don't want to forget him either, obviously, but I . . . just find it kind of hard to think about all that stuff.'

They walk quietly for a moment, and Niklas gazes out across the water.

'We actually came here on a school trip in high school,' he says.

'To Furillen?'

He nods. 'The plan was to go cycling and camping, but it was a total nightmare. It rained all week, everything was soaked. I was sharing a tent with Jacob and Freddie, I guess it must've been somewhere over there . . .'

He points to the other side of the bay.

'Anyway, we decided to sneak in here one night, even though it was a military exclusion zone. We egged each other on, but we were actually terrified of getting shot . . .'

'So what happened? Did you get in?'

'There was a big fence, and when Jacob tried to climb over it, he got a nasty electric shock.'

'Shit, that's awful.'

Niklas nods.

'It was a close shave. None of us ever would've guessed this place would end up becoming a luxury hotel.'

'I'm not so sure about luxury,' Maria says as they start walking back towards their simple, stylish cabin. After a moment or two, she pauses and turns to Niklas. 'You don't have to tell me if you don't want to, but I was wondering . . . why did he kill himself?'

*

The Stall. The playground on Styrmansgatan that also func-tioned as an unofficial youth centre at night. It's hard to imagine there were ever stables in the old barracks where there is now an after-school club.

Niklas is sitting on the edge of a blue sandbox. Jacob takes out a hip flask he stole from his father and offers it to him, pulling it back at the last second. Niklas sighs. He is running out of patience with Jacob, barely recognises the person he once became friends with. These days, he's constantly acting up and being an idiot.

Jacob promises to stop and holds out the flask again. Niklas reaches for it, but just as he is about to take it, Jacob yanks it away with a laugh. Niklas gives up. Jumps down from the box to leave.

Please.

I'm sorry.

Come back.

Jacob promises. Keeps his word and hands over the hip flask. Niklas takes a swig. Then another. It makes his throat burn, but it's worth it when he feels the sense of calm spreading through his body. One more swig. He can keep it if he wants, says Jacob. As a reminder. Niklas stares at him. What a weird thing to say. A reminder of what?

They are sitting side by side on the edge of the sandbox when Jacob suddenly leans in and kisses him, hard. Stale breath and the taste of whisky on his tongue. His neckerchief smells like smoke.

'Love you,' he whispers.

Niklas pushes him away and asks him what the hell he thinks he's playing at. Is he drunk or something? That's not even funny.

But I'm not joking, says Jacob. I'm deadly serious. That's how I feel.

Niklas jumps down from the box. 'You're messed up,' he hears himself say.

That would be the last time they ever spoke.

*

'Wow,' Maria says after a moment. 'That's a lot. Incredibly sad. I can understand why you find it so painful.'

Niklas nods. 'I've never told anyone before, not even Bea.' *Especially not Bea.*

When they get back to the cabin, Maria unlocks the door. They add more wood to the fire, make coffee and pour a couple of whiskies before curling up on the sofa.

'It sounds like he'd already made up his mind,' Maria says once they have both thawed slightly and she has had time to process Niklas's story. 'As though he knew what he was going to do.'

'Maybe. But the last thing he ever got from me was disdain, and the worst part is that I thought he was such a pain in the ass that whole last year. I didn't even like him towards the end, and I think he knew that . . .'

Niklas's voice falters, and he breaks down in tears. He finds himself almost surprised; he can't remember ever having cried over Jacob before.

'Sorry, I'm not much fun right now,' he says once he has managed to pull himself together.

Maria wraps her arms around him. 'I'm not with you for the fun.'

'Why are you with me?' he asks, genuinely curious.

'Second-hand is good,' Maria says matter-of-factly. 'It means you've already made your worst mistakes and want change. Plus you're brave, trying to be true to yourself.'

Niklas smiles at her, but his eyes drift through the doorway into the small second bedroom where there are two unmade beds. The room where Alma and Alexia were supposed to be sleeping. He feels a sudden pang of longing for them.

'Is it OK if we head back? Not because I don't want to be here with you, or because I'm not allowed, I just think I need to be with Tore and the girls.'

His body tenses in anticipation of her disappointment, prepared for her to be annoyed that he wants to cut their trip short.

'Why wouldn't that be OK?' Maria asks with a shrug. 'Get dressed and we'll head back to the battlefield.'

Niklas gives her a hesitant glance. 'Are you sure?'

'Of course I am. I miss Emmy and Lukas just as much as you miss the girls, even though I know they're having a great time with their dad in the mountains. Sometimes you just have to admit when a present wasn't quite right. That's the way it is.'

Niklas starts crying again, out of gratitude this time. Because she listens to him. Because she doesn't just dismiss or belittle his needs, doesn't show even a hint of irritation at the fact that he wants something other than her. But he is also crying out of joy, at the fact that he is managing to take his own needs seriously rather than simply staying put to keep Maria or anyone else happy. And though one part of him wants to stay here with her, escaping the terrible atmosphere back in Hogreps, a bigger part of him needs to be with Tore and his daughters.

BEA

HOGREPS, GOTLAND

'. . . THERE WAS SUCH AN incredible atmosphere among the volunteers and the people who turned up, everyone was so grateful for a bowl of Christmas porridge, and they all got a bag of food to take away with them. You could really feel just how much it meant . . .'

Bea is in her usual seat at the dining table, gesturing enthusiastically as she tells the others about Christmas in the Community.

'. . . I really should do it every Christmas,' she continues. 'It felt so good to think about someone other than myself.'

'A bit like going for a jog before Christmas lunch, to dull your guilty conscience?' Henke jokes, pushing a piece of gravadlax into his mouth.

'Henrik . . .' Sus warns him, giving him the evil eye.

'What? Come on, don't try to tell me she did it for the homeless people.'

'Not everyone's like you, Dad,' Hedda speaks up, clearly ashamed of his comments. 'Some people actually have a heart.'

'But, Hedda,' Bea begins, 'if there's anyone who has a heart, it's your dad. Unlike his brother . . .' She meets

Alexia's eye and bites her tongue. Too late to take it back now.

She tries to catch Lillis's attention instead, desperate for support, but her mother-in-law continues staring stubbornly down at her plate. In the seat beside her, Tore squirms uncomfortably, and even Sus seems troubled.

'I didn't mean it like that,' Bea says in an attempt to smooth things over. 'It was just a joke.'

'Was it?' Alexia asks coolly. She has been distant ever since Bea arrived, and this is hardly going to build any bridges.

Alma comes to her mother's rescue: 'Stop being so horrible to Mum all the time!'

'Maybe *she* should stop spouting so much crap about Dad, then?'

'I didn't mean anything by it, Alexia,' Bea butts in. 'It was just a bad joke.'

'Yeah, terrible.'

'Anyone for dessert?' Lillis asks in an effort to calm the waters. 'And then maybe we could watch a nice film together?'

'No idiot box at Christmas, thank you very much,' Tore mutters.

For a brief moment, everything is like normal again. Or almost, anyway. If it weren't for the intangible thing hanging over them, or their kind, well-meaning looks. There seems to be something else lurking underneath, another feeling that everyone is trying to cover up, and Bea can't work out what it is.

'More wine?' Henke asks, pouring her a generous top-up.

Bea drinks far more than she usually would, as do the others.

Right then, they hear a bark from over by the sofa. Otis had been fast asleep, but he has lifted his head and pricked his ears.

'Is there someone outside?' Olle asks in his croaky teenage voice.

'Huh?' Tore peers over to the door.

'I think I heard a car,' Hedda agrees.

Everyone stops talking and listens tensely. Hedda is right: they hear an engine approaching, and a car pulls up in the yard. A door slams, and they hear a voice.

A familiar voice.

Footsteps on the porch, two pairs, then someone opening the door and coming in without knocking.

Niklas and Maria appear in the doorway. Silence, two shocked faces, a mirror image of how the others looked when Bea first turned up.

'Are you back already?' Lillis asks after a moment. 'We thought you'd be gone a few days.'

'Changed my mind,' Niklas mutters as Maria takes his hand and squeezes it reassuringly.

Niklas turns to look at Maria, and his gaze is like a thousand knives to Bea's chest. She recognises that look. That was how he looked at her once, a long time ago. He then turns to the girls, as though he wants to apologise for what is about to come.

'I'm sorry, but this really isn't OK, and I'm talking to all of you here. This crosses the fucking line, Bea. And you . . .' he says, fixing his eyes on Lillis and Henke, 'what are you playing at? All this crap about family and about stepping up, but it's clearly only on your terms, and only when it suits you. Don't I also have a right to be happy?!'

'At everyone else's expense?' Bea explodes. '*You* need to be happy, even if it makes our kids miserable? No one knows who you are anymore, Niklas. Your entire family feel like you've had a personality transplant and you don't even seem to have noticed!'

'Then maybe you should marry my family instead? Because that's the thing, isn't it? This is what you want?' Niklas shouts, gesturing around the room. 'Not me?'

There is a moment's silence, followed by a loud thud. Everyone turns around and sees Tore lying lifeless on the floor by his chair.

*

Standing in the yard, Bea watches the ambulance roll down towards the main road with Tore in the back. Otis is by her feet, whimpering anxiously. Niklas and Lillis are with Tore, and Henke's BMW is right behind them, Sus in the passenger seat and Hampus and the cousins in the back.

'We need to go too!' Alexia shouts, tugging at Bea's jacket. 'Hello, Mum! Come on!'

'It's probably best if we stay here, love. We can't do anything for him right now.'

362

Bea is trying to take control of her inner chaos, but she can hear from her own voice that she hasn't managed it particularly well. She sounds shrill and weak, and Alexia is staring at her like she is some sort of madwoman.

Right then, Bea notices Maria step forward.

'I can give you a ride, if you like?' she says with a kind smile.

Her generosity is like a punch to the gut, and Bea immediately turns back to face Alexia.

'I think it's best if we stay here, honey. Grandpa is getting the help he needs, and—'

'We're going!' Alexia shouts, hurrying back into the house with Otis in her arms. She reappears a moment later, jumping into the front seat of the Volvo. 'Let's go, Maria!'

'Mum?' Alma looks up at Bea with pleading, despairing eyes.

Bea swallows. She knows she is defeated, but the prospect of getting into the same car as Maria makes her feel physically sick. Emmy's mother, the woman she used to chat with at the stables, who she saw at parents' meetings and New Years' parties, who drove her daughter to competitions, is now going to give Bea a ride in what used to be her car. There's just no way. She'll let the girls go and stay here on her own, she decides. Though perhaps the thought of watching Maria drive off with her daughters is even worse.

Without a word, she takes Alma by the hand, marches over to the car and gets in.

In front of her, in the driver's seat where Niklas usually sits, she can see Maria's messy hair. Alexia is in Bea's old place beside her, while she herself is stuck in the back like a child, face hot with humiliation.

Maria turns around.

'Belts on, everyone.'

*

Forty kilometres is a long way when you're trapped in a car with the woman your husband ditched you for. They drive in silence. Uncomfortable silence. Alma lets out a sob every now and again, and Bea fumbles for her hand.

Maria seems to be dealing with the situation by pretending everything is absolutely fine, as though they are still just supportive parent friends heading off to yet another riding competition. But her small talk eventually transforms into some sort of apology.

'I'm so sorry, Bea . . .'

Sorry? That's the kind of thing you say when you accidentally break a glass or give someone a cold, not when you've destroyed another person's life.

Bea stares angrily into the darkness, gripping Alma's hand tightly.

'I know what it's like,' Maria continues. 'When your father-in-law—'

'You'll have to excuse me,' Bea interrupts her, 'but I really don't feel like chatting right now.'

No, Maria has no idea what it's like. And Tore is more than just Bea's father-in-law; he's like a real father to her.

'Of course, sorry . . .' Maria replies, turning on the radio just in time to hear 'Some Die Young' by Laleh.

'Please, could you change—' Bea begins, but Alexia cuts her off.

'No, leave it. I like this one.'

When the song first came out, it had reminded Bea of Jacob. As though it had been written specially for him, for Bea, to help keep his memory alive. In the same way that Tore and Lillis have kept him alive by refusing to stop talking about him. With their gingerbread hearts with Jacob's name on them in the window, their photographs of him and Niklas – and Bea and her big brother – both here and at their place on Kaptensgatan. 'Uncle Jacob', as Tore always called him when he was talking to the kids.

Tore. He might not be physically young, but Bea has always thought of him as a young man, possibly because he was such an important part of her youth. One half of the anchor point that he and Lillis represented.

The music goes on and the girls start sobbing. Why hasn't Maria turned it off? Doesn't she realise how painful it is?

Bea tries her hardest to block out the words and the music, as well as all thoughts of Tore and Jacob. She doesn't want to cry in front of Maria, doesn't want to lose control in front of the girls. Once she opens that door, anything could happen.

VISBY HOSPITAL, GOTLAND

BEA TRIES TO AVOID hospitals wherever possible, though she has been to see Niklas at work a few times over the years. Before the girls were born, it felt important to try to change her thinking, to learn to associate hospitals with something other than Jacob's death. Jacob in a hospital bed after a suicide attempt gone wrong, brain-dead after a shot from Dad's hunting rifle, with a body that was somehow still alive. Several days passed before they eventually switched off the machines, but Bea stayed by his side, next to her parents. Niklas was there too, and Freddie and Calle came by. It was a different time, a different hospital, but the smell is always the same. The smell of death.

She notices it the moment she sets foot inside. It's there in the waiting room, where the others are sitting. Niklas, Henke and Hampus are talking in low voices over by the coffee machine, and Bea watches from the corner of her eye as Maria goes over and takes Niklas's hand. The girls follow her. Someone says something about Tore being in surgery, that it was a problem with his heart. Not the cancer, as they had assumed.

Lillis is sitting beside Sus, and she looks so small and fragile, in a way Bea has never noticed before. As though, over the space of just a few short hours, she has shrunk. Lillis, always so strong and comforting, everyone's mother and granny. She needs to be allowed to be weak now; she needs their support.

Bea sits down beside her, takes her hand and squeezes it. Lillis flinches and pulls away, as though Bea just gave her a shock.

'Sorry, I . . .' Bea begins, though she trails off when Lillis looks at her. Her former mother-in-law's eyes are full of sorrow, but there is also something else in there. Something new, almost pleading.

'It might be best if you left, Beatrice.'

Beatrice. No one calls her that, not even her parents.

Bea looks up at Sus in confusion, but her sister-in-law pulls a sympathetic face and then puts her hand on Lillis's arm and repeats what she just said.

'It might be for the best.'

Lillis seems oddly absent and distanced, but when Alexia and Alma come over, she opens her arms to them the way she always does. She needs her grandchildren, but she doesn't need Bea.

Bea gets up, unsteady on her feet, and staggers over to the coffee machine where Niklas, Maria and the others are standing. She needs to talk to Niklas. Alone. She pauses a few metres away from them and tries to make eye contact, but he looks away. Ignoring her completely, the others too. Only Hampus gives her a brief, sad glance.

'Niklas, can we talk?'

He turns to face her at last, but makes no attempt to move any closer.

'Can we . . . ?' Bea tries again, with a discreet nod off to one side, but he just stares blankly at her. 'Please . . .' she whispers.

He finally peels away from the group and takes a few steps towards her. 'What?'

'How is Tore?'

'Critical.'

Bea swallows. The words catch in her throat. She is on the verge of tears, knows she can't do this on her own.

'Lillis wants me to leave . . . It seems like she's in shock, but I'd really like to stay if Tore—'

'I think it would be best if you went too, Bea.'

Niklas studies her with that new look of his, the one that has become so familiar since all this began. The hardness she just can't get used to.

'Please . . .' she whispers, her voice unsteady. She needs to stay here with the others. She could sit quietly in the corner if that's what it takes, but she needs to be here, otherwise she will fall apart. She looks up at Niklas with desperation in her eyes.

'You'll have to take care of yourself now, Bea,' he says, giving her a sad shake of the head.

Bea lets out a sob as her eyes well up. Where is she supposed to go? She has been pushed out of everything that was hers, and the people who have always represented comfort to her no longer want her around. The floor seems to give way beneath her as Niklas turns around and walks back over to the coffee machine. All alone, squinting out through a haze of tears, Bea feels herself falling head first.

Lillis, Sus and the girls are still sitting on the bench, holding one another. Hedda and Olle are crouched on the floor, eyes closed and with their heads tipped back against the apricot-coloured wall, as though trying to sleep. Maria and the brothers remain beside Niklas, all looking away from her.

As though she were invisible, Bea slips out of the room.

*

When Alma approaches him a while later, Niklas is hunched over in one of the blue vinyl armchairs with his head in his hands.

'Where's Mum?'

'She left.'

Alma stares at him with a look of despair. 'What? Why?'

'Everyone is sad, honey.'

'Did you tell her to go?'

He doesn't want to lie to Alma, though at the same time, he has no idea how to tell her the truth, without it coming out all wrong.

'Everything got a bit silly earlier, and now everyone is upset . . . I think everyone just feels . . . Mum too . . . that we all need a bit of peace and quiet, so we can be here for one another.'

'But what about Mum? Why does she have to be on her own?'

'She's got other people . . . your grandma and grandad.'

'That's not true and you know it. We're the only ones she's got!'

Something inside Niklas seems to break, not just because he knows that Tore is going to die soon, but because he can see himself in Alma. He always thought that he and Alexia were most alike, but he realises now that the opposite is true.

'It's not your responsibility, Alma. Your mum is a grown woman. She'll be just fine, I promise.'

His words feel empty, and he isn't entirely sure why he is saying them. He can't promise that Bea will be just fine at all, and he sees the disappointment in Alma's eyes before she runs off towards the exit. He should go after her, try to convince her to stay. But when Niklas looks up, he sees the surgeon come out into the waiting room with the counsellor, and he already knows what they are going to say.

RIGOLETTO CINEMA, STOCKHOLM

February 2017

STANDING IN LINE OUTSIDE the cinema, Bea feels nervous, even though Alma is right beside her, protectively holding her hand. She worries sometimes that her daughter is taking on too much responsibility, though she also has no idea how she would cope without her.

Ever since Alexia decided to live with Niklas and Maria full-time, Bea and Alma have been alone in the apartment in Örby. Bea has told her that she can stay with Niklas however much she likes, that it must be exhausting to have to commute to school and the stables in Djurgården, but Alma has stubbornly refused to sleep at Banérgatan since Alexia moved in. Maria also seems to be living there more or less permanently now, and despite her guilt, Bea can't help but feel grateful for Alma's loyalty, particularly on evenings like this.

Tore's funeral a month ago was an utter nightmare. Having to sit at the very back, away from the others. She wasn't sure she should go at all, but at the very last minute, the girls had convinced her.

During the memorial afterwards, Sus told her that Lillis thought Bea had shortened his life, despite the fact that he was battling cancer. It's as though the old Lillis also died that night, and Bea has never felt more isolated and cut off.

When Niklas first announced that he wanted a divorce, she still had the rest of the family's love and support to fall back on, but after Tore's heart attack that also crumbled. She doesn't want to blame them, but it hurts so much that there are days when she can barely function, as though she has lost half of herself.

They are slowly getting closer to the entrance to the cinema now, and Bea can see Alexia smiling for the throng of photographers inside, Niklas and Maria on either side of her. Further back, Lillis is standing beside Hampus. They look about as awkward as Bea feels, and she has a sudden urge to go over and talk to them, but Niklas and Maria turn and move over to them before she has a chance. Alexia stays where she is in front of the photographers, alongside Freddie and a woman Bea guesses must be the director.

'Hello? Are you going in or what?' someone in the queue behind them asks.

There is a gap in front of Bea. Alma has already started moving forward, and she turns back and holds out a hand, as though she has noticed Bea's reaction.

'It's OK, Mum.'

Bea and Alma decide not to walk the red carpet, sneaking in behind the photographers instead while they wait for Alexia to finish. Alexia says a quick, cheery hello to them and then hurries off to join Niklas and Maria. Emmy is there too, and her little brother Lukas. The new family.

When they get to the foyer, Bea spots Calle and Charlotte drinking champagne and studying the film poster. She is relieved to see a couple of friendly faces, and she hurries over to them as Alma drifts off to talk to Lillis and the rest of the family.

Calle and Charlotte both hug her, and for a brief moment, Bea decides that the evening might be OK after all. That, despite everything, she still belongs here among them.

'What a talented daughter you two have,' says Charlotte.

Bea smiles for the first time that evening. Just hearing her friend say 'you two' about her and Niklas makes her warm inside.

'I haven't seen it yet, but Freddie says she's great.'

'If Freddie says she's great, then she must be fucking outstanding,' Calle says with a laugh. 'You know how hard that man is to please.'

Bea laughs too, allowing herself to get carried away in the excitement of the moment. It works well, at least until she spots Niklas and Maria again. They too are laughing and chatting, and she has to force back the tears rising up in her throat. Bea can feel her friends' sympathetic glances, and Calle reaches out and touches her arm.

'I know this probably isn't what you want to hear,' he says, 'but I actually think she seems quite sweet.'

Bea tenses, and Charlotte joins in the praise.

'I was pretty sceptical too, at first, but I think you should give her a chance. She's perfectly fine. They came over for dinner the other evening, and we had a great time.'

With that, Bea's mouth turns bone-dry. She knows her friends mean well, that they are just trying to be encouraging, but, unfortunately, their words have the opposite effect. She attempts to smile, but she knows her lips must be twisting into an ugly grimace.

Yet again, Calle and Charlotte exchange a glance. They seem to be looking to each other for support, as though they find it odd that she is having such trouble moving on.

Bea hears herself say that she needs a drink, and as she walks away, she sees her friends making their way over to Lillis, Niklas and Maria.

Calle and Charlotte. Just a few months ago, they told her they thought Niklas's behaviour was terrible. That he was going through a midlife crisis and that he'd had a personality transplant. And yet here they are, having couples' dinners with him and Maria. Bea has been replaced. Nothing strange about that. She needs to learn to normalise all these things. Everything that still hurts so much that she finds herself bursting into tears without warning, it's all just part of everyday life for the others.

*

It comes as a relief to be able to slump down in the darkness of the screen a few minutes later. As they were

374

about to take their seats, of course, she bumped into Niklas and the others, making their way over to the reserved VIP section. It took every ounce of strength Bea had to say hello to Lillis, who gave her a reserved nod as she walked between Maria and Hampus. Thanks to Alma, Bea managed to put on a brave face and act like it didn't bother her, but the whole thing is absurd. It's dizzying to remember they had talked about this day less than a year ago, about the big film premiere where they would walk the red carpet together, as a family. All a joke, of course, but there was a hint of seriousness about it too.

The film finally starts, and Bea turns her attention to the screen, grateful to have something other than her own messy life to think about for a while.

Alexia.

Born two minutes before her twin. That's her up there, and yet not. She plays a teenager from another family, taking part in a drama that isn't theirs, so powerful that it makes Bea ache. She is so gripped by the young woman on screen that she has to squeeze the armrests with both hands, laughing and crying. Alexia is *acting*. When did that happen? When did her big, clever girl – who is still only sixteen – become an actress, so confident that it's hard to believe she has ever done anything else?

The camera zooms in on Alexia's face, and Bea realises she can taste salt on her lips. From the corner of her eye, she notices Alma give her an anxious glance.

'I'm fine,' Bea whispers. Because she isn't upset now. These are tears of pride and melancholy.

*

Niklas feels like his bladder is about to burst. He shouldn't have had that last glass of champagne to calm his nerves before they went in. After squirming uncomfortably for what seems like an eternity, he gives up and gets to his feet, ducking down as he squeezes past the smartly dressed legs of his fellow cinemagoers. He can feel their irritated glances in the darkness and just hopes Alexia hasn't noticed him sneaking out.

When he reaches the foyer, it's as though a weight has lifted. Not just because he will soon be able to relieve himself, but because it's nice to get away from the suffocating family drama playing out on the screen. He wasn't remotely prepared for how serious the film would be, and he realises that he never really asked Alexia what it was all about.

The Dream Catcher. He had assumed it was a comedy, maybe even a romance of some sort. But this Lars Norén-esque darkness? That was unexpected. Divorce, a teenager being admitted to psychiatric care for self-harming. Jesus Christ.

Why didn't Alexia say anything? Or Freddie? All those days when he drove her to the shoot and asked how it had gone, she never said a word about all these difficult scenes. There is also quite a lot of nudity in places – so much so that he should probably have a word with Freddie afterwards. He and Bea should have read the script, of course, but they were both too preoccupied with their own problems. Still, he feels guilty about not being more involved.

'She's fantastic, isn't she? Our girl?'

Bea comes out of the ladies' toilet just as Niklas is about to make his way into the men's. He flinches when he hears her voice, but he quickly manages to compose himself and feels an unexpected rush of warmth towards the woman who is, after all, the mother of his children. To think that they managed to raise two such wonderful daughters together.

'Yeah, what a performance, huh?' he says. 'Hard to believe that's our baby up there on the screen.'

Bea nods. She looks hollow-eyed and tired, despite her makeup. Worn out in a way he has never seen before.

'It's pretty nice to see that there are people out there having a worse time of it, too,' he adds, giving her a wry smile in an attempt to lighten the mood. But his joke falls flat, he realises that immediately. A new hardness appears in Bea's eyes.

'Hits a bit too close to home, if you ask me. Alma is still having a really hard time with everything. She's incredibly disappointed in you and Maria.'

Niklas snorts, as much out of pain as anger. He has had enough of this now. Enough of protecting Bea, and enough of keeping his promise to Alma not to say anything, though he knows she is suffering as a result of becoming some sort of comfort blanket to his ex-wife.

'Alma doesn't want to live with you. She's only doing it because she's afraid of what might happen if she leaves you on your own. She doesn't think you can cope without her, because you spend all your time crying and dwelling on everything. So, great job, Bea. Guilt-tripping your kids into loyalty, just like you did with me all those years.'

The transformation from accusatory mother to wounded little girl takes no more than a few seconds, but it is one he knows all too well. Playing the sympathy card. But this time he isn't going to back down. It's time she heard the truth.

'Alma doesn't even dare talk to you about how she feels, but do you know who she does tell? Maria. The only person in this entire fucking mess who doesn't just think about herself!'

Another toilet-goer walks past, staring at them with wide eyes, perhaps wondering whether this is some sort of performance piece linked to the film. In the end, Niklas has to stop his tirade. His bladder just can't cope with any more, and he hurries through to the bathroom.

*

Bea returns to the dark cinema screen and slumps down beside Alma, who turns to her with a look of anxiety. *Is everything OK, Mummy?* Bea nods and tries to smile.

Is everything OK? Do you need help with anything? Can you manage?

It's the kind of thing parents are supposed to say to their kids, not the other way around.

Alma turns back to the screen with a look of focus, but Bea continues to study her daughter. Is what Niklas said true? Does Alma really want to live with him, but doesn't dare tell Bea? The realisation hits her like a punch to the gut.

ÖRBY SLOTT, STOCKHOLM

ONCE THE FILM WAS over, Bea skipped the after-party, telling Alma she would have to sleep at Niklas's place that evening. She was coming down with something, she said, probably the flu, and she didn't want to infect anyone else. Especially not Alma, who has a competition at the weekend. The girl reluctantly agreed to let her mother head home without her, and Bea is now all alone in her shabby white kitchen, a six-pack of beer from the shop by the bus station on the table in front of her. Her shabby white kitchen from 2004 that she can't afford to renovate. A kitchen she hates with almost the same intensity that she hates Maria and Niklas.

Is this what it's like to hit rock bottom? Was this how Jacob felt? That it was better to give up; that there was nothing – or no one – left to live for?

She could tell from the way Alma looked at her that what Niklas said was true, that her daughter was both afraid of letting her go home alone and relieved to get away.

Alexia was radiant on stage after the film was over. Someone gave her a bouquet of flowers, and Freddie lifted her arm in victory as the audience clapped. She is making her way out into the world, towards a life of her own, and Bea wants Alma to feel the same way: like she is free to throw herself into life and follow her own desires, needs and wishes. And yet that is precisely what hurts most: the fact that Alma is seeing to those needs by turning to Maria for support. What kind of a mother is she, begrudging her own daughter for talking about whatever is weighing her down? For being incapable of letting go of her feelings of humiliation the minute she remembers Maria exists. Maria, the perfect bonus mother. The woman both her children have turned to, who her friends and Lillis all seem to love. Because that is now an indisputable fact: Maria has taken over her life.

Hogreps.

Lillis.

The kids.

Niklas.

Her home.

Bea's kitchen.

And instead, Bea is left with this. Yet another empty can of beer. She throws it into the sink on her way into the bathroom and hears it rattling around inside. She doesn't even have the energy to close the door, meeting her own eye in the long hallway mirror as she sits with her knickers around her ankles and mascara running down her cheeks.

Who is that?

What the hell has she become?

Bea wipes and pulls up her knickers, getting to her feet and moving over to the mirror. The hatred she feels for

381

the self-pitying woman in front of her causes her to lash out at the glass with all her might. One of the shards slices her palm, and it hurts so much that she cries out in pain. With that, she suddenly realises that she has had enough. Enough of everything. Of herself, this apartment, the kitchen, all of it.

She quickly wraps a tea towel around her bloody hand and walks over to the cupboard in the hallway where she keeps her toolbox. She drags it out, turns it upside down, grabs the hammer and turns back into the kitchen.

The first strike leaves a big hole in one of the cupboard doors, and she is taken aback by her own strength. Bea keeps going until every single inch of the grubby white melamine is lying defeated on the floor. It feels so liberating to resort to violence, to get the sweat flowing and the shards flying. She yanks out all of the drawers, then hacks at one corner of the linoleum floor and starts pulling it up. She doesn't care how it looks or what might be underneath; it simply has to go. To change. It makes no difference how much it hurts. She can't keep waiting for life to start feeling kind or fair. She has to start living again.

FIVE MONTHS LATER

July 2017

BEA IS SLUMPED IN one of the soft deckchairs from Paola Navone, wearing nothing but a bikini. Her apartment is on one of the lower floors in her building, but her balcony isn't overlooked, and if she peers up over the railing and the geraniums in the hanging baskets, she can see a small sliver of lawn on the other side. The balcony above provides just enough shade for her to be able to sit and read out here, though a bead of sweat rolls down her forehead and lands on one of the pages.

It's warm today, at least thirty degrees, and Bea makes her way through to the bathroom to take a quick cold shower. She has just headed back outside to dry off on the sunlounger when her phone starts ringing.

'Hi, Mum!' She hears Alexia's voice first, followed by Alma's. 'We're in Berlin! What are you doing?'

'Just sitting on the balcony.'

The girls are quiet for a moment. They don't need to say anything; she can already hear their guilt down the line.

'Poor you,' Alma says in a small voice, as though it is her fault that Bea is stuck at home while they are out exploring the world.

'I'm fine, I promise,' says Bea. 'Reading and enjoying the sun. Are you having a nice time?'

'We've been on so many trains, so you can count yourself lucky for avoiding that. We're moving on again tomorrow,' says Alexia.

'To France. And we might ride Camargue horses,' Alma adds. 'And learn to surf, in the Atlantic.'

There is a noise down the line, and someone shouts.

'Yeah . . . we're coming, Dad . . .'

Bea hears Niklas's voice in the background, then Maria's. Possibly Emmy's, maybe Lukas's. The line crackles, and Alma and Alexia tell her they have to get going.

'Have a great time, and say hel—' Bea manages to blurt out before the call drops.

She puts her phone down and pauses to see how she feels. It's a bit like falling off a bike, she thinks, trying to work out whether there are any broken bones before you dare move. Oddly enough, she really did mean that last part. She wants the girls to have a great time and to say hello to Niklas and Maria. Possibly not in the way you'd say hello to the people you love most, of course. More like a polite greeting to acquaintances. Still, that feels like real progress.

Now that she thinks about it, she realises his pathetic little olive branch tattoo no longer bothers her, nor does the fact that Banérgatan is up for sale, or that he, of all people, is now studying to become a psychologist. She just hopes she never has to go to him for therapy.

Bea no longer feels much at all when she thinks about Niklas. Nothing is broken. She is whole – possibly even more whole than ever.

She wants the girls to have a good time in Europe, and she isn't the least bit jealous of their interrailing holiday, however nice it looks in the pictures on Maria's Instagram page. Having to schlep around on busy trains – through four countries, with as many kids – sounds like a nightmare to her. She would much rather be at home, doing the sorts of things she enjoys, though, of course, she misses the girls. Alexia's old room is now an office. Bea sanded the floors herself, and the whole apartment smells like freshly oiled wood.

Summer has been perfectly OK so far. Not great or brilliant, but perfectly OK. Relaxing, even – at least every now and again. As though something has finally clicked. There are times when she finds herself feeling relieved that she no longer has to go to Hogreps, though other days she misses it so much that it hurts. Maybe it isn't the house she misses as much as the island, but Gotland is still there, and she can visit whenever she likes. Nature belongs to everyone, after all.

She misses her family, of course. As it once was. Lillis and Tore and the atmosphere in the house. The sense of belonging, of being one of the Stjernes. But she isn't one of them anymore; she has sent off the paperwork to revert to her old surname.

Lillis's letter made her cry. Not because it was unkind, on the contrary. Her former mother-in-law wrote that she was sorry for everything, that the loss of Tore had hit her so hard that she simply couldn't manage any sort of contact – unfairly, of course. Lillis just wanted Bea to know that, and to say that she would always be welcome at Hogreps. She's family, after all.

Bea tries to picture that, to gauge how it would feel to go back there. To stay in the room she and Niklas once shared, drinking her morning coffee on the beach with Lillis and walking arm in arm along the shore. Barbecuing with Henke and Hampus, Sus, Olle and Hedda in the evenings. But the fact is that although she knows she can, she is no longer sure she wants to.

In some sense, it feels like that part of her life is over. It's a little sad, but also a relief. She was so dependent on Niklas and his family that she didn't think she would be able to survive without them, but she now knows she can. Bea is stronger, confident that she can handle almost anything. Some days, anyway. Other days are much tougher. But it's as Inger always says when Bea complains: first-world problems dreamed up by first-world people. She has a point there, her dear colleague who has now become some-thing of a friend – especially since they celebrated an unusual, if entertaining, Midsummer together in Bålsta.

Bea raises her face to the sun, twisting the new ring she bought herself with her finger and thumb. She has kept her wedding ring just in case either of the girls ever want it.

From over on Huddingevägen, she can hear the familiar roar of traffic. Bea isn't sure how or when it happened, but somehow this place has become home to her. Maybe it was after she smashed the kitchen and tore up the floor? That didn't end particularly well, though she sorted it out in the end, without having to ask Niklas or anyone else for help. She retiled, painted every room and put up paper on the feature walls. Built her own bookshelves.

Little by little, she has made this place her own. It isn't her dream home, and this isn't her dream location, but it is hers, and in a year or two, if she sells up, she could probably make a small profit. Assuming she wants to, of course. Little by little, her new life seems to have crept up on her and become a source of comfort.

These days, when she gets home after the stresses of work and the metro ride, she always feels her shoulders relax. No busy shops, no hustle and bustle. No crowds of people rushing to get somewhere else. Just a sleepy little neighbourhood full of sleepy little buildings. Like a small town, almost. And whenever she feels a longing for Gärdet or Gustav Adolfsparken, she reminds herself that they are just like the sand dunes in Grynge: they're still there, and she can go over there whenever she likes. Soon, she'll even be able to *drive* over.

Bea leans back in her chair and opens her book. *Driving Essentials – Your Highway to a Driving Licence.*

Thank you to:
Jennifer Lindström
Mikaela Haglund
Emma Graves
Katarina Lindell
Unn Knape
Marie-Ann Knutas
Per Flink
Kajsa Leander
Ditta Bongenhielm
Kajsa Herngren
Clara Herngren
Tomas Westlund
Otis Rönn